BLITZ SPIRIT AT HARBOUR HOUSE

FENELLA J. MILLER

Boldwood

First published in Great Britain in 2025 by Boldwood Books Ltd.

Copyright © Fenella J. Miller, 2025

Cover Design by Colin Thomas

Cover Images: Colin Thomas

A CIP catalogue record for this book is available from the British Library.

Paperback ISBN 978-1-80549-320-4

Large Print ISBN 978-1-80549-321-1

Hardback ISBN 978-1-80549-319-8

Trade Paperback ISBN 978-1-80656-018-9

Ebook ISBN 978-1-80549-322-8

Kindle ISBN 978-1-80549-323-5

Audio CD ISBN 978-1-80549-314-3

MP3 CD ISBN 978-1-80549-315-0

Digital audio download ISBN 978-1-80549-316-7

This book is printed on certified sustainable paper. Boldwood Books is dedicated to putting sustainability at the heart of our business. For more information please visit https://www.boldwoodbooks.com/about-us/sustainability/

Boldwood Books Ltd, 23 Bowerdean Street, London, SW6 3TN

www.boldwoodbooks.com

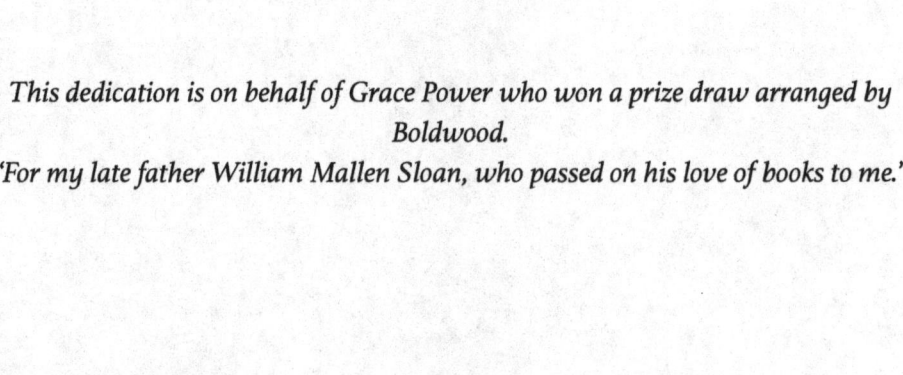

This dedication is on behalf of Grace Power who won a prize draw arranged by Boldwood.
'For my late father William Mallen Sloan, who passed on his love of books to me.'

1

WIVENHOE, SEPTEMBER 1940

Lily Turner had heard the German bombers, but the air-raid siren hadn't sounded so she and her daughter Daphne had remained in bed. Everybody who lived in Clifton Terrace was so used to the trains going past the bottom of their gardens and shaking the houses that they scarcely noticed the planes overhead.

'Daph, you need to get a move on or your train will be going without you this morning,' she yelled up the stairs.

'I'm coming, Mum, but I've no time for breakfast.'

Her daughter, who had just turned sixteen, worked at the Red Lion in the High Street in Colchester. She was doing ever so well in the kitchen and reckoned she was going to be a chef when she was older.

At least Lily didn't have to worry about Daphne missing her breakfast as she'd get plenty to eat in the kitchen, they weren't stingy with their staff. She held out Daph's cardi, handbag and gas mask and they were grabbed from her as her daughter ran out.

The back of the terraced cottage opened onto a path that led down to the station – it was the wrong side of the line for going to Colchester but there was a bridge across so that wasn't a problem. The front door was really at the back but nobody used it. The garden was steep, but the previous owners had terraced it so there were three levels, all useable with steps going down to each one.

Ten minutes later, Lily was going in the other direction, across the High Street and around to the back of Harbour House where she worked as cook and housekeeper. She didn't mind starting at seven every day except for Sunday because she always got up to see her daughter off.

Ginger, the huge tomcat who lived at Harbour House, was waiting outside the door to greet her. 'Good morning, sir, have you left me any nasty surprises?'

The cat purred and, stiff-tailed, walked in and out of her legs as she unlocked the back door and went in. She checked in the scullery and sure enough there were two dead rats but also a nice plump rabbit. Ginger had been busy last night.

After disposing of the rodents, she quickly skinned the rabbit, jointed the carcass and put it on a tin plate in the meat safe in the pantry. It would make a tasty pie for dinner tonight.

'Good morning, Lily, I've done the range and the kettle's singing.'

'Good morning, Mr Roby, thank you so much. Couldn't you sleep last night?'

The old man had arrived to live at Harbour House a few weeks ago. Mostly he seemed bright and alert, but some days he was confused and thought he was still fighting in the first war. He also tended to wander off during these episodes and had been found at the far end of the river path right up at Alresford Creek just the other day.

'The boys are still snoring, Emily's doing some homework she missed last night. I heard my son moving about so I think he'll be down soon.'

'Mr Roby junior works too hard, sir, he's gone by half past seven and doesn't get home until after I've finished.'

'There's a war on, my dear, in case you haven't noticed. The nights will be drawing in soon and then he'll have to come home earlier – can't build ships at night as the Huns would see the light and drop bombs on them.'

'Gregory, you're up early, I hope you're not getting in Lily's way,' Mrs Roby senior said as she hurried in.

Lily smiled and shook her head, indicating that he wasn't having a bad day today.

'It's those bombers, they keep me awake. I think I might sleep in the shelter in future, then I don't have to keep thinking I might have to get up in the dark and go down there.'

'Will you be ready for our outing, Mr Roby, in about an hour?'

He beamed and nodded. 'Can't wait, my dear, it's high time I had a look around the oldest city in the land.'

The two of them wandered off to the dining room, leaving Lily to make the first pot of tea of the day. There'd probably be half a dozen made before she left. The young Mr Roby preferred coffee but that was only for high days and holidays and certainly not for her.

* * *

The children rushed off before eight o'clock to catch their train to school. The older couple had eaten and were now in the sitting room. Mr Roby had left for work so only his wife and the baby, Grace, had still to come down for breakfast.

Lily loved this job, and she owed Annie Stoneleigh for recommending her. Previously she'd been working in the canning factory, ankle-deep in river water and fish guts. However much she'd washed herself and her clothes she could always smell the fish.

Now she could dress in her normal clothes, didn't have to do anything unpleasant, and got her breakfast and lunch provided. Having been married at sixteen, had Daphne at seventeen and been abandoned by her husband, Patrick, when she was nineteen, she was used to being independent.

The only good thing about Patrick going was that he'd transferred his house in Clifton Terrace to her name. His going had broken her heart; she'd believed they were a happy couple and she'd no idea why he'd gone so suddenly. And she'd heard not a word from him since. He wouldn't have been conscripted because he was deaf in one ear, so heaven knows what he was doing or where he was.

Her eyesight was poor and she'd been wearing the same thick, unattractive glasses since she was at school. She believed that was why Patrick and she had made a go of it when they were so young. They both had physical defects. They couldn't have got married if he hadn't been left the cottage she was living in now, as well as a few hundred pounds, when his gran had died. Like her he'd been orphaned at a young age, but she'd not been so lucky and had been reluctantly raised by an aunt.

When the evacuees had come to Wivenhoe last year she'd had a young mother with two small children living with her but they'd gone back home after a few weeks. Now she would be getting more lodgers. Not having to pay rent meant she could manage on her wages and her daughter helped out now she was working but the extra would be put aside for a rainy day.

She was listening out for Mrs Roby and the baby and had their breakfast ready as they went into the dining room.

'Good morning, Mrs Roby, I've got porridge for baby Grace and scrambled eggs on toast for you.'

'Thank you, Lily, exactly what we both need. Did I tell you that I'm going to be out until teatime today? My mother-in-law will be taking care of the baby.'

'Yes, you did say. Emily and the boys are going to visit Mrs Brooks for tea. Old Mr Roby is desperate to see the castle, I'm taking him as I'm not that busy today.'

'How kind of you, he'll love that. Are you going by train or on the bus?'

Lily smiled. 'He's not a fan of trains, I think hearing them puffing up and down beside this house has put him off. Definitely on the bus. He insists that we have a bite of lunch at the Red Lion. He's hoping that my Daphne will have cooked his meal.'

'Even better. We love having you here, Lily, and hope you're as happy working for us.'

'I am, Mrs Roby, thank you for asking. Mr Roby told me that there'll be shipyard workers coming to work here who are going to need lodgings. I've got a spare room so I'm taking a couple.'

She wasn't sure why she'd told her employer but she thought if neither of the Mrs Robys thought it wrong to have two men living with her who weren't related in any way then she'd ignore the looks and comments she was bound to get from some of the locals.

'I know that Jonathan appreciates your offer, Wivenhoe's already somewhat overcrowded, especially at this end of the town. The two that you'll be getting will be older men, married, perfectly respectable.'

'That's good, I'm not bothered about gossip but I don't want anyone saying anything nasty about my girl. She's not interested in walking out with a boy, thank goodness, but being so pretty I know people would have gossiped something rotten if it was young men coming to live with us.'

'It must be very difficult for you, Lily, not being able to move on because you don't know what happened to your husband.'

'My Daphne thinks her dad died; she's often asked me why I don't find somebody else.' She shrugged. 'Even if I wanted to, no man would look at me.'

Mrs Roby smiled. 'Why ever not? I know you wear glasses but you're still a lovely young woman and could be mistaken for Daphne's sister.'

Lily was stunned. Patrick had called her beautiful but she'd always thought that was because he loved her – after he'd gone she'd kept herself to herself.

'Me? With these glasses?'

'Forgive me for asking, Lily, but when did you purchase those glasses? Have you had your eyes tested since then?'

'No, my aunt paid for them when I was about ten years old. Not been back to an optician since as I can see all right with them.'

'Why don't you speak to an optician?'

'I've got a bit put by so maybe one day I'll do that, but doubt there's anything available at the moment even if I could afford it. Not that I'm interested in finding someone else, but it would be nice to have a different pair of spectacles.'

* * *

Emily Roby was enjoying being in the upper fourth, her second year at the grammar school in Greyfriars House. Knowing where everything was, the way the school worked, how to get to the air-raid shelter in the garden without panicking, made her feel safe and comfortable in her surroundings. School had reopened last week but things didn't seem quite the same – there certainly weren't as many new girls as there had been when she'd started last year. Was she imagining the fact that the teachers seemed somewhat distracted and that lessons weren't as interesting as they should be?

She'd be twelve at the weekend, really someone in the upper fourth should be thirteen during this academic year but she was a year ahead. Daddy had said that he wouldn't have let her go if she'd been a summer birthday – as it was she was only a bit younger than the girls born in June and July.

'Emily, are you coming to the art room this lunchtime?'

'Yes, where else would I go?'

The girl who'd asked the question wasn't a particular friend, more an acquaintance really, but she was pleasant enough. Her particular friend had been removed from the school for some reason and she missed having someone she really liked to talk to at break and lunchtime.

Nobody at school knew that it would be her birthday and she was pretty sure they didn't know she was a year ahead either. Nobody had birthday parties any more, which was a good thing as she didn't have anyone to invite.

She was halfway up the stairs to the art rooms when the siren began to wail. It had happened several times before but thank goodness no bombs had been dropped in Colchester so far – in fact, she didn't think bombs had been dropped on anywhere much apart from the RAF bases.

Everybody walked briskly to the doors that led into the playground at the back of the building. The first few times the siren had gone off they'd been told to collect their gas masks from their coat pegs before going outside but that had caused absolute chaos. The headmistress had since decided that it was unlikely they'd be gassed during the short walk from the school to the air-raid shelters.

They shuffled into the shelter, everybody silent, in no particular order. The place smelt of damp, and something a bit worse, but nobody mentioned this. There was a primitive WC installed at the far end behind the curtain – it was a chemical contraption called an Elsan – but you'd have to be absolutely desperate to walk the length of the shelter in order to use it in front of all the other girls.

They were allowed to talk once the heavy outside door was closed and as always they played 'I packed my bag'. The challenge was for every girl in the shelter – about sixty of them – to repeat all the things that had been packed without a mistake.

This was of course impossible, but it caused great hilarity and helped to pass the time. They weren't down there very long today and soon they all trooped out – again in silence – and back into school. The all-clear was still sounding. The entire school gathered in the hall to be told which lessons had been cancelled and which were to continue.

The senior girls had their own school at the top of North Hill so next year when Emily was in the lower fifth it would be her last year in this building.

As they took their places in the hall, she noticed that all the staff were standing on the dais, which hadn't happened before.

Miss King, the headmistress, was looking particularly grim. There was no need for her to raise her hand for silence as every girl was staring at her, sensing something momentous was about to happen.

'Girls, I've the most upsetting news to give you. All school-age children and mothers with children under five are to be evacuated from Colchester. They will be leaving at the weekend by train. Teachers will be accompanying them.'

There was a ripple of unease around the hall. Emily found her hand was up without knowing she'd done it.

'Yes, Emily, I hope your question is important,' Miss King snapped.

Emily stood up. Every eye was on her. 'I don't live in Colchester, I don't think many of us do. Does that mean that we can stay at home and the school will still be open for us?'

'That is in fact an excellent question. Thank you for asking it.' The head-mistress turned and spoke quietly to the deputy head then turned back. 'Evacuation is voluntary, even those who do reside within Colchester's boundary are free to remain. Our school will be staying open but it's possible that could change.'

As Emily was already on her feet she asked another question. 'Excuse me, Miss King, but does that work in reverse? Can children that attend school in Colchester but live elsewhere be evacuated with the school if their parents want them to go?'

Hastily she sat down before she could be reprimanded for speaking without permission. Miss King looked directly at her.

'Another excellent question, Emily. The answer to it is yes, if any parent wishes their daughter to be evacuated with the school then that too is allowed.'

* * *

Emily found it hard to concentrate on her lessons as she'd made a momentous decision. Since she'd stopped going to the Peterson farm to look after the children she'd had to spend all her free time at Harbour House.

This usually meant doing something domestic or taking care of her baby sister.

Grandpa had come to live with them a few weeks ago and she loved him, but now Grandma didn't have time to spend with her as she had to look after him. Her brothers – George, her actual brother and Sammy, her adopted one – were inseparable and she'd begun to feel like an outsider in her own home.

So she'd decided she'd ask Mummy and Daddy if she could go with the school – being evacuated would be an adventure and if she wasn't happy she was in the fortunate position to be able to come home. The more she thought about it, the more eager she was to become part of this evacuation. It would mostly be younger children and her experience with the Petersons would mean she'd be really useful.

She'd tell Nancy and Annie about her idea when she went there after school for tea – if they weren't horrified, then she'd ask her parents when she got home. The trains would be leaving from Colchester station at the weekend so if she was going the decision had to be made immediately.

'Emily Roby, have you finished translating that passage of French?' Madame asked.

'Almost, Madame, I was just thinking what to put next.'

After that she pushed her exciting ideas out of her head and concentrated on her work as she didn't want to get an order mark for inattention.

* * *

Lily went in search of old Mr Roby once the house was clear, and the soup was in the saucepan ready to be put on to heat for old Mrs Roby's lunch, but she couldn't find him.

'Excuse me, Mrs Roby, I can't find him anywhere. He was so excited about going on the bus and I don't think he's having one of his funny days.'

'Don't look so worried, my dear, I know exactly where he is. He's in the air-raid shelter.'

'He did say something about wanting to sleep there so he didn't have to worry about getting up in the night. Ta, I'll go and fetch him. We're going to miss the next bus if we don't get a move on.'

'Just a minute, Lily, are you quite sure you want to do this? If he becomes confused whilst you're out he might refuse to go with you and then what will you do?'

'I'll go where he wants, Mrs Roby, I'm not daft. I wouldn't let him wander off on his own. He's a lovely old gent, I'll not let anything bad happen to him.'

'Good girl. You need to take this, I don't expect you to pay for his lunch or your own. He does have money in his wallet, but he might forget that he said he was going to pay.'

Lily took the pound note gladly as she couldn't afford to buy lunch at the Red Lion for both of them. 'Ta, I'll give it back if I don't need it.'

Old Mr Roby was just emerging from the air-raid shelter as she stepped out the back door. It had been a vegetable cellar but had been converted when the war started. It was lovely and comfortable down there, not like the public shelters which were smelly, but she didn't think it had been used yet. The folk in Wivenhoe were convinced that the Germans were too busy taking their bombs to London to drop any on them.

'Have I kept you waiting, my dear girl? I do apologise, I'm ready to leave now. I hope we haven't missed the bus,' the old man said.

'No, sir, we've got five minutes to get to the bus stop and it's just at the top of Station Road. No distance at all from here.'

2

Lily enjoyed the bus ride into Colchester but not as much as her companion. He was in the window seat and constantly pointing out things that he thought were interesting. They stopped opposite the school that Emily attended.

'Come along, sir, this is where we get out. It's the closest one to the castle and I know you want to look at that.'

'I do indeed, my dear girl, it's such a pity we can't go inside. Did you know that the Romans settled here before they went to London?'

'I did know that, but the castle's Norman, I was told it was built by the same man who did the Tower of London. There's some Roman remains in front of the castle we can see, and a large bit of the wall we can go and have a look at if you want.'

* * *

By the time Mr Roby senior had seen everything he wanted to, the market stalls were beginning to close up, but this didn't bother Lily as you got the best bargains then as none of the stallholders wanted to take anything home.

At least the cattle were no longer sold in the High Street as they had been in Victorian times but it was still noisy and Lily was concerned that old Mr Roby would find it too much.

'My word, isn't this splendid fun? I really didn't expect to see so much produce on sale.'

'Farmers and market gardeners sell it directly to the public, I think some of the stalls are just ordinary folk with big gardens and spare veg. I know exactly what I want to buy, sir, I'd be grateful if you would hold my basket for me whilst I do it,' Lily said, hoping this would keep the old gentleman at her side. She was a bit worried that he was becoming confused by the noise, by having overexerted himself.

'I'd be happy to, my dear, but I need to find a bathroom rather urgently.'

They were close to the Red Lion so she quickly escorted him inside. 'It's there, Mr Roby, I'll make sure they have a table for us. I'll be waiting just over there.' She pointed to the door to the public bar.

He nodded and hurried off. He'd probably be gone a few minutes so she'd got time to reserve a table for midday. As she'd been in a couple of times the waiter on duty recognised her and immediately put a reserved sign on a table for two.

She took up her position opposite the door that led outside to the gentleman's WC and had been waiting for ten minutes with no sign of him. She could hardly go through the door herself and to ask anybody using it would be embarrassing.

The dining room wasn't busy yet and the waiter saw her and came over. She quickly explained why she was so concerned and he offered to look for Mr Roby. He was back moments later.

'He's not there, he must have gone out through the yard. He could be anywhere by now. I'd offer to help you, Mrs Turner, but I'd get the sack if I did.'

'I'll start looking, he's a tall, distinguished gentleman, so I'm hoping someone will remember him.'

Lily ran out into Crouch Street, the road behind the Red Lion, but he was nowhere in sight. He'd seemed a bit tired but apart from that not the way he was when he was having one of his funny turns.

There were no stalls in this road but there were plenty of housewives in headscarves going home with bulging baskets. Mr Roby hadn't been into Colchester before – maybe when he'd emerged somewhere unexpected he'd become even more confused and disorientated.

She asked a few passers-by, but nobody had seen him. Would he try to find his way back to the inn? She nipped down an alleyway between two houses and back into the High Street. Her heart was hammering, her hands clammy, terrified the old man had been enticed away by someone unscrupulous who was right now stealing his money and his expensive gold pocket watch.

Then, to her immense relief, she saw him standing at the fruit and veg stall she'd been going to visit herself. She unclenched her hands and smiled at the old man. 'Mr Roby, you've given me a real fright. I thought you'd got lost.'

He looked round and smiled. 'I was a bit disorientated when I came out in a different street but a kind pedestrian directed me back here. I hoped you'd think to come out here when you couldn't see me anywhere else.'

'Right, I'll just get the things I wanted. Then we can go in and have a nice bit of lunch.'

As she'd hoped, everything was half price, not all of it perfect, but all edible and fresh.

* * *

The waiter, she thought Daphne had said his name was Cyril, looked as happy to see them as she'd been when she found Mr Roby.

'Your Daphne was that worried you'd lost Mr Roby, I'm glad to see you both. I'll just show you to your table and tell you what's available today then let your Daphne know.'

From the way the young man used her daughter's name, Lily suspected he was interested in her – she didn't want Daphne to follow in her footsteps and be married with a baby by the time she was seventeen. She'd have a word with her tonight, warn her not to be alone with Cyril as he might take liberties.

'We know what we want, Cyril, we both want whatever pie is on today. We'll have a nice pot of tea to go with them, ta.'

Mr Roby was frowning at her and she realised she should have asked him what he wanted and not chosen for him.

'Daphne has told me she's making the pies today and you wanted to have whatever she'd made. I should have asked you, sorry about that.'

'It's not the pie, Lily, it's the drink or rather the lack of it. I'd like half a pint of bitter, you can have the tea.'

'Righto, I'll just go and tell him to add that to the order,' Lily said.

* * *

They chatted over the tasty lunch and she learnt a lot more about her companion.

'I was too old for active service but worked in logistics in the first war, Lily, a bloody horrible business that was. It was supposed to be the war to end all wars and look where we are now. I'm far too old to be of any use to the army – I left as Major Roby – but felt useful running the Home Guard.'

'Mrs Roby told me all about that. Seems like a lot of older men and boys are having a bit of a lark. Absolutely no use at all if there was an invasion.'

He nodded and then leaned forward. 'You're absolutely right, my dear, a lot of old buffers and young boys would have difficulty stopping a girl guide parade. However, the best of them are being secretly trained as resistance. Now they'll be able to do some damage if the blighters set foot on English soil.'

'Goodness me, how exciting. Do you want any afters?'

'I don't think so, this is only luncheon, after all, we have a main meal in the evening.'

Lily had quickly changed the subject as she was quite certain he shouldn't have told her about the secret resistance soldiers. He did look a bit distracted and she thought that maybe he was about to have one of his episodes.

'I'll just settle the bill, your Mrs Roby gave me enough to do that, and then we better go across and catch the bus. As you said, sir, I have to prepare the evening meal and can't be out all day.'

He didn't quibble about her paying and she kept her eye on him whilst she handed over what was owed plus sixpence for the tip. By the time she'd done this, Mr Roby was on his feet and she just managed to prevent him from going off on his own – in the wrong direction again.

'Here you are, Mr Roby, you promised to carry the heaviest basket for me. I can manage this one.'

'I can certainly do that. Hand it over, my dear.'

Lily shepherded him across the busy High Street, narrowly avoiding the stallholders as they packed up ready to leave. The street was strewn with bits of vegetable, piles of rubbish, but she knew it would all be gone by morning.

'Look, the bus coming has Wivenhoe written on the front. We've arrived just in time and won't have to wait at all.'

There was a queue of housewives all carrying baskets and bags full of fresh produce, but the bus wasn't full and she was able to negotiate the narrow gap between the seats and find two empty ones.

'There you are, Mr Roby, you can sit by the window and you'll see the other side of the road on the way home.'

They were approaching the Flag Hotel on the outskirts of the village when he became agitated. 'I don't know this place, where are you taking me? I don't live here. Who are you? Where's my wife?'

'She's at Harbour House, Mr Roby. The both of you are staying with your son, Jonathan, for a few weeks. I expect you'll be going home to Kent very soon. That's why you don't recognise it.'

Lily had spoken quietly, calmly, and hoped that would be enough to keep him in his seat. If he tried to get up, the basket on his lap would empty its contents and cause chaos on the bus.

Someone tapped her on the shoulder and she glanced round. A woman she recognised as a friend of young Mrs Roby was sitting behind her.

'Keep reassuring him, Mrs Turner, it's all you can do. So sad when the mind starts to go before the body's ready.'

'He was all right on the way in. I just hope I can get him home safely. If he wants to go in a different direction there's nothing I can do to stop him as he's a big man.'

'Well, he can't go anywhere at the moment. Why don't you hand me your basket and I'll hold that for you then you can take his. That way if he does try and stand up you won't lose your precious vegetables.'

The woman stood up and leaned over the back of the seat. Lily passed the basket to her. Then she carefully removed the second one from his lap.

'Thank you, I don't know why I'm holding your shopping. Is it much further to go? I want to get off the bus now.'

'Just a few more stops, Major Roby, and then we'll be there,' Lily said with a forced smile, hoping her voice didn't betray her nervousness.

Addressing him as Major would make things a lot easier, as having two Mr Robys was very confusing.

It seemed to help. His eyes became more focused and he nodded. 'I've got my uniform in my wardrobe; I think I'd be more comfortable wearing that. I'm Major Roby, people need to know that I'm not just a silly old man.'

* * *

Emily enjoyed their fortnightly visit to Nancy at her haberdasher's shop in Head Street but didn't mention her plan to join the evacuation the next day. Both George and Sammy had arrived first and were busy telling Nancy and Annie about the proposed evacuation.

'We don't have to go because we don't live in Colchester, in fact, Nancy, it doesn't seem as if more than half a dozen boys in our class qualify for evacuation,' George said.

'Actually, George, any family can send their child if they want to as long as they go to school in Colchester,' Emily told him.

'Well, I'm not going,' Sammy said firmly. 'I love it at Harbour House, you could end up anywhere, nobody seems to know, not even the teachers, where they're going to be sent on that train.'

Emily kept quiet, now wasn't the time to mention her decision to ask if she could go. Nancy thought that children should stay with their parents, that they were safe enough in Colchester and certainly safe in Wivenhoe.

On the way home on the train the boys were craning out of the window which they'd let down by the leather strap against her wishes.

'That was a squadron of Spitfires that just flew over us, Emily. I'm going to fly one of those when I'm old enough. I really hope the war doesn't finish before I can do that,' George said.

She was tempted to tip him out of the window for his stupidity. Instead, she grabbed him by the scruff of his neck and lifted him bodily back onto the seat then pulled the window up.

'Sometimes I think you've got feathers in your head instead of brains. Why don't you think before you open your mouth and say such stupid things? The longer the war goes on, the more people will die.'

George often argued with her but this time he didn't. 'I'm sorry, I shouldn't have said that. Do you think they'll still have Spitfires flying when I'm old enough to join the RAF?'

'I shouldn't think so, they're fighter planes, so if there's nothing to fight then there'll be no Spitfires or Hurricanes.'

He pulled a face and didn't answer. Emily felt a bit mean because if she had her way she might not see him or Sammy for ages when she went away.

'I'm sorry, George, I know you love the idea. There won't be many fighter planes but they'll still have aircraft of some sort. You could always become a commercial pilot. I think that flying all over the world in one of the passenger planes would be even better.'

Sammy stepped in before George could make things worse. 'I think it's going to be good fun when the classes are smaller, don't you, George?'

The conversation turned to the evacuation and Emily was dreading being asked her opinion. Fortunately, they arrived at Wivenhoe station before that happened. As always, the boys ran off ahead, their satchels and gas masks banging behind their backs as they went.

This gave her a precious few minutes to marshal her thoughts, work out exactly how she was going to introduce the subject without upsetting her parents. She wanted to present her request as an adventure for her, instead of because she was unhappy at home.

* * *

Grandpa was dressed in his uniform and was marching up and down the passageway talking to himself. The boys took one look at him and shot upstairs. Emily was tempted to do the same but her grandfather couldn't help being confused, Daddy had told her this sometimes happened to old people and they just needed love and support from their family.

'Grandpa, you look very smart. Should I call you Major Roby from now on?'

He stopped and looked down at her as if he didn't know who she was. Then he smiled. 'Emily, you certainly won't call me anything but Grandpa. I like being your grandfather.'

'I like having you living here. I think calling you Major will make it a bit easier as we've already got my daddy with the same name as you.'

He nodded, then seemed to lose interest in the conversation and began muttering to himself and resumed his marching. This was another thing to consider – would her asking to leave tomorrow seem as if she was trying to get away from what was happening with her grandfather?

She and the boys ate tea in the kitchen and then went upstairs to do their homework. Lily went home as soon as she'd served dinner to the grown-ups and Emily thought that when everybody was full, and Grandma had taken Grandpa upstairs, would be the best time to speak to Mummy and Daddy.

In fact, things didn't work out as she'd hoped because her baby sister was getting more teeth and wouldn't settle so her mummy had to stay upstairs. Grace was now a few months old and she'd heard her parents saying it would be better if the baby had her own room. If her grandparents were sharing the same bedroom then Grace could have one of those but if her attic room was empty this might help things even more.

She joined her father in the sitting room. 'Daddy, I need to talk to you about something very serious. I wanted to speak to both of you, but it won't wait until tomorrow.'

He nodded, got up and turned off the wireless. 'Right, sweetheart, fire away. Is it about your grandfather?'

'Not really, but what I'm going to suggest might help with that. I'm sure you've heard that there's a mass evacuation of Colchester children and their teachers on Saturday. I'd like to go with them.'

She was watching him closely, trying to gauge his reaction before she continued. He didn't look cross, not even sad, just his usual lovely self.

'Go on, sweetheart, I'm listening. Why do you want to go?'

She took a deep breath. 'I'm not unhappy, I love all of you, but sometimes I feel lonely, I've got no friends of my own, Grandma now has to take care of Grandpa, this is the first night you've been home in time for dinner for weeks.'

'Why do you think that leaving your family to go and live with strangers God knows where is going to be an improvement?'

His tone was friendly but he clearly wasn't happy about this suggestion.

'It will be an adventure for me, if I don't like it then I can come home, can't I? If you want me back for any reason, then there's nothing to stop me coming. If I'm not here, then the boys can move up into the attic and Grace can have their room. I know you and Mummy have been talking about that.'

He ran his hand through his hair and held out his arms. She jumped up and threw herself into them. He held her tight and she knew he was going to say she could go because he loved her so much and wanted her to be happy even if it meant it would make everyone else sad.

3

Lily arrived home after Daphne, who finished work when lunch was cleared at the Red Lion. Her daughter had her own key and if she was old enough to work she was certainly old enough to be at home on her own.

The front door was unlocked and Lily stepped in, about to call out that she was home, when she realised there was someone else in the house. She dropped her handbag and gas mask on the stairs and marched through to the kitchen, bristling with annoyance.

Her daughter knew better than to invite men friends in without getting permission first. The man who'd been talking to Daphne jumped to his feet and smiled.

'Mrs Turner, from your expression you didn't know I was coming today. I'm Frank Burton, I'm to lodge here whilst I'm working at the shipyard.'

'Good heavens, you're right, I wasn't told. I thought you weren't coming until Saturday.'

'It's all right, Mum, I've made Mr Burton a cup of tea and showed him where he'll be sleeping,' Daphne said.

'Good girl, it's cottage pie tonight and that'll do three easily.' She walked across and held out her hand. 'Pleased to meet you, Mr Burton.'

He shook her hand, his was gnarled and rough, most likely from being a carpenter and being in his forties.

'Call me Frank, why don't you? And I'm pleased to meet you.'

Lily wasn't sure she wanted to be on first-name terms right away but he seemed a nice enough sort of bloke so she nodded. 'I'm Lily, welcome to our home.'

* * *

The cottage pie and apple crumble for afters went down a treat. She now knew Frank had three grown-up children, two girls and a boy. His daughters were married with nippers of their own and his son was in the navy. He didn't mention his wife and she didn't like to ask.

'I don't have alcohol in the house, Frank, but you can get a drink at the Greyhound, unless they've run out they usually have beer on tap. It's a few doors down. I won't be giving you a key, I've only got the two, but you'll be working longer hours than my Daphne so she'll be here to let you in.

'Another thing, the privy's outside the back, there's a you-know-what under your bed but if you use it you have to empty it yourself. There's a tin bath hanging in the shed and there will be hot water to fill it once a week.'

She wasn't going to apologise for the lack of facilities; he was going to get good food and his laundry done, and not many people had indoor plumbing.

'Okay, I'll nip out for a pint. What time do you lock up?'

'Ten o'clock, I have to be at work by seven.'

He nodded and headed for the pub. Daphne followed him out as the front door was sometimes tricky to shut until you got the hang of it. Lily began to clear the table and take everything into the kitchen.

'Mum, he never took his gas mask, it's still on the peg in the hall.'

'Then he'll get fined if he's caught by an ARP warden. Silly beggar, he's probably forgotten and it isn't deliberate.'

'I'll take it to him, I can go in the saloon bar and hand it over.'

'Go on then, always a reason to avoid the washing up,' Lily said, laughing.

Daphne left the door ajar, as she'd only be a tick. If the other lodger turned up as well he'd have to make do with soup and toast.

A train steamed past at the bottom of the garden and a few minutes later someone knocked on the door. The second man had arrived – why hadn't Mr Roby warned her they were both coming today?

'Come in,' she called down the passageway, 'I'm in the dining room.'

She had the last few bits from the table in her hands and looked towards the door, expecting to see Daphne. But when she saw the man standing there, her mouth dropped open and the crockery smashed on the floor.

Patrick Turner, the husband who'd abandoned her and Daphne fourteen years ago, was standing there bold as brass, as if he had every right to be there. He was taller, broader and looked different but she'd recognised him immediately.

He put down his belongings as if he intended to stay.

Finally, she found her voice. 'I don't want you here. You'll have to find somewhere else to go. You can't just walk in here after all these years and expect me to be pleased to see you.'

Before he could answer, the door banged a second time. Daphne rushed in.

'Oh, you must be the other man come to lodge here. You missed a lovely cottage pie, but I reckon there's soup you can have.' Then her daughter saw the broken plates. 'Crikey, that's a pity, you can't get new plates for love or money. I'll get the dustpan and brush, Mum.'

She dashed past her father without giving him another glance. Lily had a few seconds to stop Patrick from revealing who he was.

'Please, she thinks you're dead, don't tell her who you are.'

He seemed incapable of speech. Then he nodded. 'Fair enough, I'm your new lodger, nothing else.'

Lily shook her head. 'Daphne love, I'll take Mr Brown up to his room. Will you get the kettle on and the soup heated up?'

Patrick backed out, picking up his case and other things as he went. 'You and Frank Burton are sharing the front bedroom. Twin beds in there now.'

He spoke from behind her. 'I'm not here to cause any trouble, Lily. I didn't know until this morning that I'd be boarding with you, I'd have not come if I'd had any choice.'

She didn't answer until they were safely inside the front bedroom, it over-looked the place where the children played football and cricket.

'I work for your boss, Mr Roby. I'll speak to him tomorrow and get you moved somewhere else. You can stay tonight, but don't unpack your case, I'm not having you here more than that.'

'You've not changed, Lily, not really. You don't look a day over twenty. Our girl's the image of you, I don't blame you for telling her I'd died.'

'I don't care what you think. I got divorce papers drawn up, I've been waiting all these years to be able to give them to you. I'm glad you've come as now I can finally be free from you.'

'Give them to me now, I'll sign them, if that's what you want.'

Light dawned. 'You want a divorce too, that's why you've come. It makes sense to me now. Good, Daphne doesn't need to know who you are, doesn't need to know that you walked out on us without a word when she was not even two years old.'

'Can I have something to eat if I promise that I won't rock any boats?'

'Yes, as long as you've given me your word you'll say nothing about who you really are to anyone.'

'That cat's already out of the bag, Lily. I've not changed that much either and the guard at the station recognised me.'

'Daphne goes in to work on the train every day. Even after all these years you're going to cause us heartbreak. You could have written to me to warn me you were coming. I'm not the one who ran away, I've lived here since you left.'

'You could have sold the property and moved away, that's what I thought you'd do. It's what I'd have done. Honestly, if I'd thought there was the slightest chance of—'

'Don't say any more, it's all lies. You told me you knew you were coming here this morning, you're despicable. If you think you can blackmail me out of this house, then you can think again. I don't want you downstairs, not now, you can go hungry tonight.'

* * *

Emily thought she'd made an excellent case to join the evacuation and waited for her daddy to agree that she could go on Saturday.

'I'm disappointed that you'd make such a suggestion. Children and adults who are evacuated are not doing it for an adventure, for excitement, but because they have no option, because they believe that by doing so their children won't be killed by the bombs that are about to drop.'

Emily blinked, scarcely able to believe what she was hearing. She was about to interrupt but he gave her one of those looks and she held her tongue.

'What makes you think that you can tag along and then just come home again? Evacuees don't have that choice, they have to live where they're put, endure or enjoy whatever circumstances they find themselves in. Good God, Emily, have you learned nothing? I'm tempted to send you to boarding school, you certainly couldn't come home from there, as you seem so keen to abandon your family.'

Daddy looked at her as if she was someone he didn't know, someone he no longer loved, and tears trickled down her cheeks. She was ashamed that she'd suggested she be evacuated.

'I think it would better if you spend the rest of the evening in your room,' he said.

She fled, didn't even stop to apologise, now wasn't the time. She was a horrible, selfish girl, putting herself first. After the dreadful things she'd said to Mummy a few weeks ago she'd promised her parents and herself that she'd not let them down again.

She closed the door of her attic room but didn't fling herself face down on her bed to sob as she'd done the last time. She wasn't that girl any more but she didn't know what sort of girl she was.

Then she remembered that it was her birthday on Saturday, the day she'd said she wanted to leave Harbour House and pretend to be an evacuee. Twelve wasn't grown up, not even a bit, but she was certainly old enough to know better.

Why wasn't she satisfied with her life? She had a loving family, went to an excellent school, lived in a lovely old house – all she didn't have were friends of her own. She pulled out the chair that she used when she was doing her homework at the table and sat down.

There was only a small window in the roof so it was always dark up here. She needed to light the oil lamps now as soon it would be too dark to see to trim the wick.

There was no electricity, no fireplace, no plumbing, but the room was large and it was entirely hers. She'd offered to move to the attic so that her grandma could have her room. She didn't regret this, didn't resent that her brothers were still on the main floor, so why had she thought it a good idea to run away?

Technically it wouldn't have been running away, but she understood now that's what she'd have been doing. There weren't other girls in Wivenhoe like her who maybe went to boarding school as she'd tried to look for them.

Neither were there any in her year at school who lived in Wivenhoe, if there had been then she'd have seen them either getting off the bus opposite the school or they'd have travelled in with her on the same train.

Having no friends wasn't a good enough reason to want to leave home. Instead of being selfish, in future she'd put everybody else first. Grandpa needed a friend; she could spend more time with him and then Grandma wouldn't look so tired and worried all the time.

She could help the boys with their homework, go and watch them play football, take more of an interest in their lives, then she wouldn't be bored. Maybe her parents would consider her old enough to babysit for Mrs Cousins, the doctor's wife, and then she'd be able to earn a bit of pocket money.

She'd been told to stay in her room but going down to use the WC wouldn't count as being disobedient. Thinking about that had made her actually want to go. She checked there were no tear streaks on her face – there weren't – and then ran a brush through her hair. It was growing nicely but still not long enough to plait. She pinned it back from her face with the two tortoiseshell slides that Grandma had given her.

Satisfied she looked composed, not defiant or upset, just in case her father happened to see her, Emily opened the bedroom door.

She could hear the boys playing with their toy soldiers – their favourite game – you'd think they had enough of war without playing it as well. Mummy was still trying to settle Grace, Grandma was talking with Grandpa and she paused to listen. From what she could overhear it was a perfectly sensible conversation.

Downstairs the soft sound of the evening concert drifted up the stairs. Daddy would be listening to that so there was no chance of him coming out and ticking her off for having left her room.

She wasn't going to creep down like a thief, she'd a perfectly legitimate reason for being downstairs. The sitting-room door opened as she reached the bottom step.

'I thought I heard you coming, hurry up and do what you have to do, then I need to talk to you.'

She nodded and flew past. She couldn't tell from his expression whether he was still furious, disappointed or had decided to send her away to school.

When she emerged from the WC she could hear him banging about in the kitchen. 'Join me in here, sweetheart, I think we both need a reviving cup of cocoa. There's also cake in the tin – shall we steal a couple of slices and hope nobody notices?'

'I'm coming, Daddy, if you make enough I'll take some up to those in their bedrooms.'

The milk was already hot and he'd put out seven mugs – one for each of them.

'If you get the cake tin from the pantry, I'll finish making this. I wonder if the baby would like a bit of cake?'

'She certainly wouldn't, but I would,' Mummy said as she came into the kitchen.

'Is my sister asleep? I'll take my cocoa up and sit with her if not so you can have yours in peace.'

'No, darling girl. Why don't you take up cocoa and cake to your grandparents and then ask the boys to come down and collect theirs?'

'I'll do that, Mummy, I'm just going to fetch the cake and cut it.'

Emily wanted to let her parents talk about what she'd said, how badly she'd behaved, as it would be easier for her to apologise to them together. Thank goodness the boys and grandparents didn't know.

A year ago she wouldn't have been trusted to carry a tray upstairs without dropping it, certainly some things had changed for the better. She balanced it on one arm whilst she knocked on her grandfather's bedroom door – they were both in there.

'I've got cocoa and cake, shall bring it in?' Emily spoke quietly, nobody raised their voice up here once Grace was asleep.

The door opened and she was delighted and surprised to see it was her grandfather and he seemed his usual jolly self. He was in his pyjamas and dressing gown but didn't seem at all put out that she'd seen him like this.

'Good girl, just the ticket. Here, let me take the tray.'

She handed it over and knocked on the adjacent door. She opened it before they answered. 'Cocoa and cake downstairs if you want it, boys. Mummy said you can bring it upstairs if you want.'

'We'll be down in a minute, need to finish this battle,' George said without looking up.

She left them to it. Whilst she'd been talking she'd heard her parents go into the sitting room so that's where she had to go now. She wasn't looking forward to this uncomfortable conversation, but it had to be done.

'Everything all right upstairs, sweetheart?' Daddy asked.

'Yes, no problems at all,' Emily answered.

She didn't sit down – this would be easier to say if she was standing up. 'I'm very, very sorry, Daddy, for suggesting something so stupid. I love my home; I realise now that I'm only bored because I don't do anything interesting with my time. From now on I intend to appreciate what I have, which is a lot, and stop complaining about the fact that I've got no friends of my age.'

'Good, then the subject's closed. Exactly what have you in mind to make your life more exciting?' Daddy asked as she sat down.

'Am I old enough to offer to babysit for Mrs Cousins?'

'Yes, especially if they're only coming here for dinner, or you're just taking them for a walk round the village,' Mummy said.

'In that case, do you think it would be all right to expect to be paid? Not a lot, but perhaps a few pennies for an evening?'

'I don't see why not. Do you want me to mention it next time I see Mrs Cousins?'

'No, thank you, Mummy, if I'm old enough to look after children then I'm old enough to make the request myself. I also want to do more with my brothers, they might be three years younger than me but I do enjoy their company.'

'Drink your cocoa, sweetheart, and eat your cake. I can't tell you how relieved we are that you're not running away as a certain someone has a birthday on Saturday and there might be a certain something being planned for that certain person.'

Emily giggled. Daddy was very funny sometimes. 'I'm certainly not going anywhere, and neither is that certain person. Are you quite certain you can't tell me anything else?'

4

Patrick was buggered if he was going to miss out on a pint of beer at the pub that had always been his local just because Lily didn't want him downstairs. The War Office gave men not conscripted no choice in where they were wanted. He'd been pleased to discover he was going to be sent to Wivenhoe but horrified he was to be billeted in his old marital home.

He hadn't expected to find that Lily had changed from the quiet, softly spoken girl he'd once loved. He'd had this picture of her in his head, it had carried him through the bleak times, the days and months that he'd regretted having walked out and wished that he was back in Wivenhoe. He'd never met anyone he wanted to be with more than her. He'd been too young to deal with the responsibilities of being a husband and father – not that that was any excuse for what he'd done. The only thing he was proud of was that he'd signed the house over to her as he'd not given her a pennyworth of help since then.

He shrugged. Lily had had no choice in the matter; she'd had to get on with it. Too late to worry about that now, he was here, he'd met her and seen Daphne again and was pretty sure his bridges were well and truly burnt. Probably better that Lily got him moved somewhere else – when his daughter discovered who he really was, things would really kick off.

He listened at the top of the stairs and could hear them talking at the back of the house. They must have closed the door, which meant he could sneak out without Lily knowing he'd gone.

He walked into the public bar at the Greyhound and the place went quiet. Even though he was deaf in one ear, his other one worked all right. He guessed word had already spread around the village that he was back – he'd not changed that much either. A bit taller perhaps, certainly broader, but he still had his shock of dirty blond hair.

'Well, bugger me, the wanderer returns,' the landlord said. 'What'll it be? A pint of my best?'

'Yes, that'll do me a treat,' Patrick replied. The other blokes in there resumed their conversations and the awkward moment was over. He'd expected his reception to be less friendly and was grateful to be allowed to drink in a place he was familiar with.

He took his brimming glass to a corner of the room where there were a couple of empty chairs. The other customers weren't bothered about him being there, but they certainly weren't including him in their conversations.

Then a stocky bloke, a lot older than him, joined him.

'I'm Frank Burton. I reckon you must be the bloke I'm sharing with. We're the only two being ignored.'

Patrick didn't offer his hand, he wasn't that sort of bloke, left all the fancy handshaking to the posh blokes, the ones in charge.

'I'm Patrick Turner, but I don't think I'll be staying long in Clifton Terrace. I'm being ignored because I'm a black sheep around here.'

'Turner? Any relation to our landlady?'

He nodded and took another mouthful of beer. 'Lily introduced me to my daughter as Mr Brown, so I reckon I'd be grateful if you stuck to that. Daphne thinks I'm dead.'

'Bleeding hell, that's not good. Probably best if you do move somewhere else. You been gone long?'

Patrick told him, didn't make any excuses for his behaviour, and explained why he'd had to come now.

'I regretted leaving almost as soon as I'd gone, but couldn't go back, stupid male pride or something. I decided to make something of myself, return when I was a man of means, grovel and apologise and put things right.'

'Why didn't you?'

'Things didn't work out too well, the only skill I had was carpentry, but with the depression and that nobody wanted anything made. The years passed, but I never stopped thinking about my family, didn't get involved with anyone else, and then the war started and skilled carpenters are now in demand.'

Frank nodded as if he understood and then the siren started to howl. They jumped up, expecting everybody to leave the pub and go to the nearest shelter, but everybody ignored the warning.

Feeling a bit foolish, they grinned at each other and sat down sharpish, hoping nobody had noticed. 'Do they know something we don't? Surely with three shipyards so close together on the Colne, Wivenhoe must be a prime target,' Patrick said.

'Clear as mud, Patrick, but if the locals aren't bothered then neither am I. Listen, that's our boys going out to meet the bombers. The RAF will keep us safe.'

'To be honest I was glad to get out of London, the poor sods there are getting bombed every day. I didn't bring all my stuff, so I'll have to go back and get the rest of my things from the digs I had in the East End,' Patrick said.

'Rather you than me, mate, I'd not go back to London for love nor money. My wife and the grandnippers have moved to Devon to be with an old aunt of hers, I'll be surprised if our house is still there at the end of this lot,' Frank said as he slurped his beer.

Several of the blokes had wandered outside with their drinks to watch the German bombers fly overhead. They were like black specks in the sky but the noise they made even from so far away was distinctive.

'They don't sound like our RAF bombers, do they? I reckon they need to tune their engines,' one of the men said and there was a chorus of agreement.

Patrick drained his glass and put it back on the bar. 'I'm going to speak to the boss, Mr Roby, I know he lives at somewhere called Harbour House. I'm hoping I can arrange different digs, not have to spend the night where I'm not wanted.'

* * *

The all-clear had yet to sound and an ARP warden waved his arm and blew his whistle when he saw Patrick strolling down the street. He ignored the bloke and as he passed the house on the corner he was pleased to see it was the very place he was looking for. That was a bit of luck, maybe it was a sign that being sent to Wivenhoe was a good thing despite the frosty reception from Lily.

He hoped he wouldn't disturb the family eating their supper as it was only just after seven o'clock. Someone must have seen him as the front door opened before he got there.

It was an old gent in his pyjamas and dressing gown. 'What are you doing here? No strangers allowed,' the old bloke said. 'I'm going to check on my men, out of my way.'

Whoever he was he wasn't quite right in the head and shouldn't be walking about in his nightclothes. Patrick stood in front of him, nodding and smiling, hoping that someone had heard and would stop the old bloke escaping.

'Are you Mr Roby? I've come to see someone called Mr Roby. I'm going to be working in the shipyard from tomorrow.'

He deliberately raised his voice and it did the trick. The other Mr Roby, the one he'd come to see, appeared behind his father.

'Come along, Dad, it's time for cocoa. Mum's just taken it upstairs for you.'

Patrick remained firmly in the doorway, blocking any possible escape. Old Mr Roby pushed him violently in the chest but Patrick had braced himself and didn't budge.

Then the old man's face changed and he smiled. 'It's a lovely night, have you come to see my son, young man? I'm just going to have my cocoa, you know. One of life's remaining luxuries in this beastly war.'

A smart but harassed-looking lady in her sixties, presumably the wife, took over and guided her husband back into the house, leaving Patrick standing with his boss on the front doorstep.

'I'm sorry about that, did he hurt you?'

'No, sir, I'm fine. If you can spare me a few minutes, I'm Patrick Turner, unfortunately the lodgings I've been allocated are with my wife, Lily. Is there anywhere else I can go? As you can imagine, I wasn't made welcome and I don't blame her.'

'Good God, that's all I need, more confusion. We thought you were dead, but obviously that's incorrect. It didn't occur to me that you were related to Lily – Turner's a fairly common name.'

Patrick wasn't invited in but that was okay, he didn't expect to be treated like one of the boss's friends. 'I was happy to be able to leave London, as you can imagine, but I was told to come to Wivenhoe to work in your shipyard and I wasn't given a choice. I can't serve in the forces because I'm deaf in one ear, in case you're wondering.'

'Look, Turner, I can't do anything at the moment. There are a dozen men arriving over the next few days, I'm sure I can juggle things and have you moved tomorrow.' With that, Mr Roby bid him good night.

Patrick decided to try his luck at the Grosvenor Hotel, which was opposite where he was standing. If they had a room free then he'd take that. He didn't want to make matters worse in his old home.

* * *

Lily heard Frank return and was relieved that Patrick hadn't appeared in the kitchen. The two lodgers would have the use of the front room if they wanted somewhere to sit as she didn't want them in with her and Daphne. She locked the front door and made her way upstairs. Her daughter was already asleep and there was no sound coming from the spare room so the men must be dead to the world as well.

She wondered if Frank snored – if he did, she'd probably hear him – but Patrick didn't, she remembered that much about him.

The information she'd been given about her lodgers was that they required a cooked breakfast at seven o'clock and a cooked evening meal whenever they returned. This was going to present problems as it was impossible to have a hot meal ready and then keep it warm for more than half an hour.

The money for the board and lodging was generous, which made up for the inconvenience. She could hardly refuse to feed Patrick a second time so with considerable reluctance she decided to cook for him just this once and try not to stir things up again.

Lily was up just after five o'clock to put the laundry in to soak. Monday was supposed to be washing day, Tuesday drying, Wednesday ironing, but she'd no time for that nonsense. There was a war on, she was now doing two jobs, and she was blowed if she was going to be doing washing on days that weren't convenient for her.

Frank had given her his ration book and she'd register him at Mr Moore's shop sometime today. Daphne didn't need calling this morning as she was down early.

'I thought you might need a bit of a hand, Mum, what with two extra to feed,' she said.

'Ta, love, I hope they think that porridge is a cooked breakfast as I haven't got anything else. I've almost forgotten what it's like being able to have a lovely plate of egg and bacon of a morning. Rationing is supposed to be fair but those with the money can get what they want whilst folks like us have to stick to the rations.'

'Don't go all political on me, Mum, it's too early in the morning.'

Lily laughed. 'Sorry, me and my soapbox. I reckon things will be different for women after the war, we won't be expected to stop home and bring up the children and not have a job of our own.'

Frank walked in and interrupted the conversation. 'Mrs Turner, Mr Brown didn't come home last night. I think he must have found a bed at a hotel, there are certainly plenty of them in Wivenhoe.'

Before Lily could say anything, Daphne spoke up. 'Why would he do that? It doesn't make any sense. What's going on, Mum?'

'Come into the kitchen, love, and I'll tell you.' She turned to the lodger. 'The porridge is lovely and hot, there's sugar or salt, or top of the milk. The tea's just been made and I'll bring through your toast in a minute.'

Lily closed the door and put two pieces of bread on the end of the toasting forks and held them in front of the range. This gave her a few moments to try and think of a way to tell her daughter that her father was Mr Brown, and that Lily had lied to her.

Daphne listened and instead of shouting at Lily for lying she rushed forward and hugged her.

'I don't blame you, it's better that I grew up thinking he was dead or I'd have been looking at the door every day wondering when he was coming back. Why has he? Did he tell you?'

'He said he wanted to see us but that doesn't make sense. I've not gone anywhere, he could have written to me, come down for the day any time in the past fourteen years.' Lily frowned. 'Maybe he wants a divorce, I've got the papers ready, I had them drawn up years ago and they cost me a pretty penny too.'

'Then I can't see there's a problem, Mum, I don't want anything to do with him. I don't know him, I don't need him, and the sooner you're divorced the sooner you can find someone who won't walk out on you like he did.'

'I'm not sure I ever want to get married again, love, I've been happy on my own. Anyway, even if I did want to, nobody would look at me and most of the men are in the services.'

A strong smell of burning jerked Lily back to the present. 'Look at that! I've burnt the toast; I'll have to do some more.'

'I'll scrape it and we can eat this, but we can't give it to Mr Burton,' Daphne said as she removed the blackened bread and took it to the sink.

When Lily went in with the freshly made toast a few minutes later, Frank had finished his porridge.

He smiled at her. 'I don't mind it burnt, "waste not, want not", we'd be for the high jump if we put even a crust out for the birds nowadays.'

'Daphne and I are happy to eat it a bit singed, but ta for offering. Did Patrick tell you who he was?'

'He did. I'll take his things with me, shall I? Make it easier for both of you.'

Lily was going to thank him and agree but something stopped her. 'No, but thank you again for offering to help. I need to talk to him, there are things that have to be sorted out between us.'

* * *

Harbour House was quiet, just how it should be so early in the morning. Lily let herself in, checked there were no surprises from the cat waiting in the scullery, and got on with her early-morning duties. The range had to be riddled and the ash cleared out from the bottom. There was a lovely new gas stove in the kitchen but the old-fashioned range, like hers but bigger, was on all the time and ever so useful. It also heated the hot water for the laundry and filled the big tin bath when it was needed.

Gladys, who came in to do the laundry and heavy work twice a week, would want to talk about Patrick's unexpected arrival. Gladys was a gossip and anything she was told would be all around the village by teatime. This meant Lily would only have to explain what was going on once – but first she needed to speak to Mr Roby and she'd just heard him coming down for his breakfast.

'Good morning, Lily, I'm so sorry about sending Patrick to lodge with you. I promise you I wouldn't have done so if I'd realised who he actually was.'

'Not to worry, it was just a bit of a shock – especially for my Daphne, who thought he was dead.'

'He came here last night and I promised to find him somewhere else to stay. He'll have new digs before tonight, I give you my word.'

Mr Roby was a nice man, he'd sort things out for her. She took his breakfast through a few minutes later and he was reading yesterday's paper.

'There was an incident with my father last night and he seems to be getting worse. Patrick was able to prevent him from wandering off in his pyjamas,' Mr Roby told her as she poured out his tea.

'Such a shame, and so difficult for all of you.'

'Another thing, he now wants to be addressed as Major Roby and is going to wear his uniform. My mother's said she's going to be Grandma Roby, I hope that will make things easier for you and everyone else. Having two of each of us must be confusing for my dad as well.'

'That's a good idea, Mr Roby. I hope you don't mind me asking, but did Patrick say why he took this job?'

'He didn't have a choice, Lily. Men not in uniform are still controlled by the War Office. We needed competent carpenters urgently at the shipyard and he and the other eight men had no option but to come. That's why it's down to me to find them somewhere to live.'

'Thank you, that makes things a bit clearer.'

Breakfast was served in relays and the last to come was always Mrs Roby and the baby. Today there'd been no sign of the old couple, which was a bit of a worry.

'Good morning, Mrs Roby, your in-laws haven't come down. Do you want me to take a tray up or shall I wait for them?'

'A tray, if you don't mind, Lily. Dr Cousins will be coming to see Major Roby sometime this morning. We thought it best to keep him in his room until then.'

'Righto, I'll just fetch in your toast and then take it up,' Lily said.

Lily might be called the cook-housekeeper but she also had to do house-work – not something the previous person had had to do. Gladys washed the floors, cleaned the windows and that, but the daily tidying and dusting was down to Lily.

The doctor had been and gone – he'd spent an hour upstairs – and she wasn't sure if it would mean another tray for lunch or if the two old folk would come down and eat with Mrs Roby.

She left Gladys doing the ironing and nipped out to the shops. She needed to register Frank so she could get the extra rations. Today being Friday it would be fish for everyone. She ran home to Clifton Terrace with the lovely fresh mackerel she'd been able to buy from outside the cannery and found Patrick sitting on the doorstep.

5

Emily and the other girls were directed by a prefect straight to the assembly hall that Friday morning. There were no chairs put out even for the older girls – everybody had to sit cross-legged on the floor. Obviously, the staff had chairs.

One didn't talk in the hall, it was absolutely forbidden, but today girls were whispering to each other and staff weren't reacting and giving out order marks. Something was definitely going on and Emily thought it had to be to do with the evacuation.

Every class had its own place in the hall and it was immediately obvious from the gaps in the rows that a lot of girls were missing – there were at least ten girls missing from her form.

The headmistress came in but waved them down as they were about to jump to their feet. 'No, girls, stay where you are. Today's a very difficult day as you can see that almost half the junior school's missing.'

Heads turned this way and that, confirming what they already knew.

'Tonight you will take a letter home to your parents informing them that the school will continue to run for the moment. Classes are going to be combined and lessons will be curtailed or cancelled without notice depending on which member of staff is available.'

She nodded and marched out, leaving a deathly silence in her wake. This lasted only a few seconds and then even the senior girls, the prefects, turned to each other to talk about this worrying announcement.

'There's more of us than in the other class,' one of the girls said to Emily. 'I think that will mean they join us rather than the other way round.'

'Our form teacher's not here, that must mean she's going on the train tomorrow.' Emily swivelled and did a rapid headcount. 'There are more of the senior girls here than there are of the lower fourth and upper fourth. I hope they don't put all of us together,' Emily said.

'Golly, if they did that there'd be more than forty,' the girl on the other side said. She was now on her knees and counting properly.

The staff at the front on the dais had allowed them to chat for a few moments but now one of them stood up and clapped her hands for attention.

'Right, girls, this is how things are going to be.'

* * *

Emily was relieved to escape from Greyfriars when the bell went at the end of the day. There were now twenty-six in her class, there had been only twenty before, but it could have been worse. The main problem, in her opinion, was that even the teachers didn't know what was going on.

Today she'd had to remain in her form room all day, had only been allowed out at break and lunchtime. All she'd done was read silently – a dreadful book called *Silas Marner* by an author called Eliot. Then they'd been asked to write a story about food rationing – how boring was that! The only other thing they'd done was to work on a page of equally tedious maths problems. There'd been absolutely no teaching at all and for some of the day they'd been overseen by the school secretary.

Emily thought that being evacuated would have been much more fun but probably even less education. In her satchel she had the sealed envelope addressed to Daddy and she hoped that he'd share the contents with her.

Whatever the letter said, for the first time since the war started a year ago Emily knew her life was going to change. People in London were having bombs dropped on them but so far her family hadn't even gone down into the shelter when the sirens had gone off. People mostly still carried gas masks, but she thought that might stop soon too.

It was horrible to think people were dying every day, either killed by bombs, bullets or buildings falling on them. Wivenhoe seemed to be carrying on more or less as usual but there must be some families – even if she didn't know who they were – who'd already lost loved ones.

Tomorrow was her birthday and although there wouldn't be much of a fuss, Daddy had told her there was a little something planned.

* * *

Patrick had been given an hour off to sort out his accommodation. He was moving to a house in Queen's Road and needed to collect his belongings and give his ration book to his new landlady. He'd just been contemplating breaking in when Lily appeared and he jumped to his feet.

'I can't stop, Patrick, I'm just dropping off the fish for supper. I didn't expect you to come until this evening. I need to speak to you, but your stuff's waiting just in front of the front door.'

'I'll get it then. It's a bit of luck you coming round, I was given an hour off to move my belongings and no amount of explaining made any difference to the secretary. I told her you wouldn't be home but she wouldn't believe me.'

In order to open the door, Lily had to put her shoulder to it. Patrick decided that when he came round he'd bring his tools and sort that out for her.

She pointed to his suitcase, gas mask and tool bag. 'Can you come around at eight o'clock? I've spoken to Daphne and she knows who you are now. I expect you want to speak to her, although I don't think she's too keen.'

Patrick nodded and picked up his things. 'Ta, I'm only moving to Queen's Road, I'll see you tonight.'

Mrs Hatch was an elderly lady, her husband an invalid, and Patrick wasn't sure if she was taking him in to help out, for the company or the extra money. It didn't make any difference to him – he had a room to himself, preferable to sharing even with a nice bloke like Frank.

After dumping his stuff, he headed back to the shipyard in West Street. Minesweepers were made of wood so the magnetic mines they were looking for didn't cling to their hulls. This was why this particular shipyard needed so many experienced chippies. Patrick called in at the office to let the secretary know he was back and then returned to the work he'd temporarily abandoned.

The foreman, a decent enough bloke, checked on him a couple of times but then patted him on the shoulder. 'You'll do, Paddy, no need to keep an eye on you. Wish I could say the same about all the new blokes.'

There were no tea breaks or official lunchtime, you just had to nip off to the bog or for a cup of char when you could. Most of the men had bought a sandwich or two and ate them on the go.

Frank was working with him and they both paused during the afternoon for a breather and a fag. You couldn't smoke anywhere near the sheds; you had to stand outside in the road or by the river edge.

'What did you do at midday for grub?' Patrick asked. 'There used to be a decent bakers a couple of minutes from here – do you know if that's still open?'

'It is, they've sandwiches made up and ready for us. Spam and piccalilli or corned beef and mustard, tasty enough though,' Frank said.

'We need to get one of the lads to take the order for us lot, I reckon there's ten or more down from London and they'll be wanting a buttie too.'

'Good idea, why don't you ask the foreman? You seem to get on better with him than I do.'

* * *

The only good thing about the nights lengthening was that it meant they finished earlier. Working over twelve-hour shifts doing such physical work was exhausting even for someone as fit as Patrick was.

He hadn't eaten since breakfast at the hotel, and although he'd drunk several mugs of tea he was starving and hoped his new landlady was a decent cook and provided large portions of whatever she was making.

On the way past the foreman, Jimmy, he asked about sending an apprentice with a lunch order to save time.

'I should have thought of that, you can't work like you do without something to keep you going. I'll speak to the baker myself, make it a regular order, and you should get a bit of a discount.'

'Would be easier, Jimmy, if we settle the account at the end of each week. Do you think he'll go for that?'

'Reckon so, leave it to me, Paddy. You won't go hungry tomorrow.'

Most of the men headed for one pub or another to down a couple of pints before they headed home. What Patrick really wanted was a strip wash – there was no indoor plumbing at his new lodging but a standpipe in the garden that was used by four of the terraced cottages.

There was an arched passageway between the house he'd be living in and the one next door and he hurried down this. Mrs Hatch saw him from the kitchen window and came out with a bar of soap and a towel.

'Here you are, love, there's a jug and basin in the shed. You have a good wash and by the time you're done I'll have your tea ready.'

'Ta, Mrs Hatch, just what the doctor ordered.'

He filled the basin and the jug at the tap and took it into the shed. He stripped off to his underpants and twenty minutes later was more or less clean and certainly smelling a lot better. He scowled at his dirty clothes, not wanting to put them on, but had no option as he could hardly go in as he was.

Then he saw his landlady had put out clean things for him. He grinned as he dressed. He wouldn't have got that sort of service at Clifton Terrace, that's for sure.

Mr Hatch lived in the front room as the old bloke couldn't manage stairs any more. It was well after eight o'clock and more than twelve hours since Patrick had last eaten. It didn't matter what he was given, as long as there was lots of it.

'Here you are, love, rabbit stew and dumplings, carrots and cabbage to go with it. I've made a lovely apple crumble for afters. You help yourself; we've eaten and it's all for you. There's a freshly made pot of tea to wash it down.'

'Crikey, it smells good. I appreciate you feeding me so late. I'd be happy to heat up a pot of soup for myself some nights as long as there's plenty of bread to go with it.'

'Not in my house, young man, you'll get a decent meal whatever time you come. I knew you'd want a good wash so that gives me plenty of time to get it on the table.'

'About that, Mrs Hatch, I appreciate you putting out clean clothes. I'll just have clean vest and shirt of an evening in future, not change the lot,' Patrick said.

'Don't you worry, son, I'll have everything clean and ready when you need it. I'm a dab hand with the mangle and that gets trousers and that lovely and dry.'

He devoured everything on the table and Mrs Hatch came in from the kitchen to admire his empty plates.

'I like a man with a healthy appetite. My neighbour brings me rabbits, we've got a share of a pig which is in Mabel's garden down the bottom of the road. It'll mean we'll have a lovely bit of ham for Christmas.'

The house shook as a squadron of fighters screamed overhead. 'Do you have a shelter or don't you bother?'

'I'm not going in no shelter because my old man has to stay where he is. They might drop bombs on Colchester but I don't reckon we'll get any here.' She pointed down the garden. 'There's an Anderson down there, it's for all of us. Nobody's used it yet, you go ahead if you want to, son.'

'I'll stay in my bed like everybody else. I reckon if a bomb does drop in Wivenhoe things will change but until then we can pretend the East End isn't getting hammered every night.'

'Good for you, it's damp and cold down there.'

'I've got to see someone after supper, I don't think I'll be that long. Is there a curfew?'

'Go along with you, love, you come and go as you please. Nobody along this row locks the door.'

'Right, thank you. I'm already late so I'd better get off. That was the best meal I've had in years. I reckon I've fallen on my feet coming here and no mistake.'

* * *

Lily had asked him to go round at eight o'clock and it was already twenty past. She must know that they didn't finish work until seven thirty so getting to Clifton Terrace any earlier would have been a miracle.

He swore under his breath as he approached the front door – he'd forgotten to bring his tools and he'd wanted to fix the door. It was slightly ajar and he pushed it wider and called down the passage. Daphne was waiting for him in hall. It told him at once that he was to remain a stranger to them both.

'You're late, Mum said you were coming at eight,' the girl said belligerently.

'I'm sorry, I don't finish work until after seven thirty, so it just wasn't possible. You wouldn't have wanted to see me until I'd had a cleanup.'

'Well, you'd better come into the front room. Frank's still eating his supper. I'm going to talk to you until Mum's finished in there.'

He followed her into the room. 'Bloody hell, there's nothing changed in here since I left. Same ornaments, same antimacassars on the arms of the chairs, same rag rug in front of the fire. Has anybody ever sat in here?'

His daughter snorted. She was trying not to laugh. 'I keep telling her it's a waste of a room, but she says nobody uses the front room and it's only for funerals and vicars.'

'This furniture's almost as old as the house; it wasn't great when we got it and that must be eighteen years ago at least.'

* * *

Lily heard Patrick and Daphne laughing and something twisted inside her. That man wasn't going to make friends with her daughter, push his way into their lives and try and be a father to her, not after all this time. She'd been the one to take care of Daphne all these years, he'd no right to turn up now when things were easier and want to be part of her life.

'Excuse me, Mr Burton, I'll leave you to your dinner,' she said and headed for the front room, closing the living-room door firmly behind her.

She stood outside the front room for a few seconds, not wanting to burst in and say something she'd regret. If she was going to get rid of him then she'd have to be more subtle than that. Pinning on a smile was hard, but she managed it, she'd had years of practice pretending she was fine when she wasn't.

'Lily, sorry I'm late,' Patrick said.

'Don't worry about it, Mr Burton's only just eating his dinner. I forgot that you work such long hours.'

Daphne had plonked herself down on the uncomfortable Rexine sofa and obviously had every intention of remaining in the room whilst she and Patrick talked. This was going to make it more difficult to get rid of him. Lily didn't want to look bad in front of her daughter.

'I meant to bring my tools and sort out that door for you both.'

'There's no need, Mr Burton's going to do it for me. Are you intending to stay in Wivenhoe for long?'

'I have to go where the War Office sends me, I didn't have a choice about coming here and I don't have a choice about leaving.'

'Oh, well, I suppose it can't be helped.'

Lily had found the divorce papers in the back of a drawer and they were now waiting to be signed. She'd left them prominently on the small oval table under the window but if he'd noticed he certainly wasn't saying anything.

She picked them up and pushed them into his hands. They'd both remained on their feet and she thought it odd that her daughter was the only person seated.

'I wanted you to sign these. Because you've been gone more than seven years I can divorce you for desertion. You just have to sign it and then I'll take it in to my solicitors in Colchester.'

He looked puzzled, as if he didn't understand what she'd said. He looked at the papers, looked at her and then shook his head.

'This is a bit of a shock—'

'A shock? Did you expect me to be sitting here pining for you? Did you think you could walk back in here and I'd fall into your arms, thrilled that you deigned to return?'

He stepped back, still clutching the papers in one hand. 'That's not what I meant. Don't jump to conclusions or put words in my mouth. I didn't come here expecting anything so I'm not disappointed. Do you have a pen? I'll sign them willingly, then we can all move on.'

Lily had forgotten to bring her precious fountain pen in from the living room. 'I'll get mine. I won't be a tick.'

Then Daphne was blocking the door. 'No, Mum, I've only just found my dad, I've changed my mind, I reckon I'd like to know him a bit better. Please, let's give him a chance.'

'This is not your business, Daphne. You told me you didn't want anything to do with him – what's made you change your tune so fast?'

'He seems like a nice bloke. Until yesterday I thought he was dead, it's different now. I've always wanted my own dad like all my mates.'

Patrick was silent, listening and watching. If he'd joined in, said he wanted to make things up to them, wanted to get to know his daughter, then it would have been easier to throw him out. But he didn't and that made her reconsider. Lily seemed okay with the suggestion but he didn't really know her any more so wasn't sure if she was actually upset and angry at Daphne. Then he spoke.

'Lily, I'll do whatever you want me to. I'll sign the papers and you can be rid of me or I'll call in occasionally for a chat whilst I'm in Wivenhoe.'

'See, Mum, he does want to get to know me,' Daphne said.

'Very well, but it has to be on my terms.' Lily looked at him and he nodded. 'You can't come round whenever you like, I'll send word to your lodging when it's convenient.'

'Don't be daft, Mum, he doesn't get days off like we do. The only time he can come is in the evening like he did today.'

'Actually, Daphne love,' Patrick said, 'we do get the occasional afternoon free, sometimes a whole day, but we don't know when as it varies according to what's on. How about I let you know when I can come and you can decide if it's convenient?'

'All right, I have a Saturday afternoon and Sunday free,' Lily said. 'We'll wait until you get time off at a weekend.'

She couldn't believe they were talking about meeting as if this was the most normal thing in the world. She didn't want to see him at all – he'd abandoned both of them and didn't deserve a second chance.

'Right, I'll be getting along then. Thank you for seeing me. It's been a pleasure to meet you, Daphne.'

Then he was gone and only after the front door was yanked shut did Lily notice that he'd put the divorce papers back on the table.

Emily woke to find several handmade cards for her birthday. No gifts, but there was a war on. She now knew there was going to be a tea party for her and that Daddy was taking an hour away from work to be there.

She had no homework to do over the weekend which was unheard of and a really good thing on her birthday. She wasn't going to complain, it meant she'd got two whole days to herself. The boys weren't at breakfast as they were playing in a football match. This meant that if she was going to put her plan into action it would have to be her grandfather she spent time with.

Her good intentions were thwarted a second time as Grandpa didn't need anybody to entertain him as he was as normal as everybody else. It was lovely hearing him laughing and talking with her grandma and she wasn't surprised when the two of them went off somewhere together. Daddy, as always, was working and she wasn't exactly sure where Mummy and Grace had gone, but they weren't indoors either. Usually, the weekend flashed past but this time it was the reverse. She was even looking forward to going to church in the morning.

Her little afternoon party was lovely and made the day special. There was even a Victoria sandwich, made with dried eggs, but it tasted nice. She loved having everyone there, even her daddy, and wondered if this would ever happen again.

* * *

On Monday morning over breakfast the mood in the house was sad. There'd been an absolutely dreadful raid on London over the weekend and Emily hated to think about those poor people who had been killed by the bombs or were now homeless.

There'd been no chance to talk to her parents about what was happening at school and they hadn't noticed that she'd had no homework either. Emily wasn't exactly sure what would happen to her if the school did close down because there weren't enough girls or teachers left to run it properly. The letter Daddy had got was just about evacuation as she'd thought.

She was a scholarship girl so they didn't get any money from her, but three quarters of the pupils were fee paying and if they were the ones that had left there wouldn't be enough money to keep it open. Maybe she'd got this wrong, these were only her ideas, after all.

As she and the boys walked down to the train, she voiced her fears. 'I don't know how many boys have left your school but more than half of my year and the year below are gone. I'm worried the school will close, what about you two?'

'I don't know how many of the seniors have gone as we don't mix with them. I don't think more than half a dozen boys were missing in our prep school,' George said.

'Then it's unlikely that your school will close down. I think mine might though – do you think that I'll be sent away to a boarding school if I can't be educated here?'

'Of course not,' Sammy said. 'We couldn't manage without you. You're so clever you could teach yourself what you need to know.'

'Thank you, that's a lovely thing to say. I don't want to go away, that would be absolutely beastly, but I do need to do more than write a few stories and read a few books if I want to be a lawyer, a doctor or an architect one day.'

'I bet there're retired teachers and professors who'd be happy to tutor you. I bet the doctor would know.'

'Which reminds me, Claire will be returning to school tomorrow. She's had chickenpox so couldn't start back last week.'

'She's a funny little girl,' Sammy said, 'I like her. She reminds me of the sisters I used to have.'

Emily hugged him. 'It must be hard for you not seeing them any more. But you're Sammy Roby now, you've got a big sister, a baby sister and a sort of twin brother to make up for what you've lost.'

'I never want to go back. Best thing ever happened to me being evacuated down here last year. I'm not as clever as you and George but I'm going to work hard and make something of myself, don't you worry.'

Emily dawdled on the way to school, usually she was eager to get there, but today she was dreading what she might discover. She waited to cross the busy road, watching the door of Greyfriars, and she was sure there was only a trickle of girls when there was usually a flood going in at this time.

Her stomach was churning as she dashed across, narrowly avoiding being hit by a milk cart drawn by a huge hairy horse.

* * *

Patrick slotted easily into the team, his years of working with wood made him a stand-out carpenter. He'd only worked on ships in the past couple of years but that gave him more experience than some of the new blokes.

His foreman told him that he'd be getting the afternoon off – after working seven days on the trot the thought of having even a few hours free of the backbreaking work, the noise, the sawdust everywhere, made him smile.

'Ta, something to look forward to. Pity it isn't a weekend as I'd have some-where to go then.'

'There's a bigwig coming from London next weekend – my team's the best in the yard so we've got to be inspected, have photos taken with a news-paper. I'm telling all the blokes to make sure they have a shave that morning.'

'Righto, that'll be a laugh. Do the others get the day off?'

'They get a couple of hours when they won't be actually working, but that's all. I'm giving you lot the Sunday off, you lucky buggers. It won't happen again so make the most of it,' he said and walked away chuckling.

At midday, Patrick left the yard along with a handful of others. He had his spam sandwiches in his pocket and was going to eat them in the park. He wasn't sure if he'd be welcome back at his digs in the middle of the day.

He bought himself a light ale at the Greyhound – promised to return the bottle – and took his picnic across the road.

'Hey, Mr Turner, shouldn't you be working? Did you get the sack already?'

Daphne was walking up the track from the station so she must have had the afternoon off too.

'No, got the afternoon off. I'm going to have a picnic in the park.'

She hurried over, looking heartbreakingly like her mum when they'd first met.

'Come in ours, I'll make you a cuppa.'

'No, best not, remember your mum said "by invitation only". I don't reckon she meant your invitation but hers. I'm not going to upset her.'

'Then I'll sit with you. I've been thinking about you all week. The other lodger turned up the other day – he's a young bloke, too full of himself if you ask me. Mum's not best pleased but doesn't like to complain after getting you thrown out.'

Patrick's lips tightened. He didn't like the sound of this bloke at all. 'What's his name?'

'Dave Benton, thinks he's the bee's knees.'

'I'll have a word.' As soon as he'd said that he regretted it. This was none of his business and interfering would just make things more difficult between him and Lily.

'Would you? Ta ever so, you'd think that Mr Burton would say something but he seems to think it's funny. I liked him before but I don't now – I reckon Mum will get rid of both of them by Christmas.'

He pointed to a spot under a large oak tree and he wished he'd got a blanket or at least a jacket he could put down for her to sit on but she dropped to the grass without a second thought.

'Here, I've got two rounds, made at the bakery down the road. Would you like to share with me?'

He opened his canvas haversack and pulled out the greaseproof paper parcel. 'I've got a beer to drink, so I can't offer to share that with you. Your mum would have my guts for garters if she heard you'd been drinking.'

She was back on her feet in one smooth graceful move. 'I'll get myself a cuppa. The kettle's always simmering on the range. I'll bring you a mug and I reckon there's something in the cake tin we can share to go with your sandwich.'

Whilst she was gone, he took a few swallows of his beer but didn't start on the sandwiches. Now his daughter had asked him to intervene he'd do so happily. Dave Benton had a nasty surprise coming tomorrow. He was puzzled by Frank's reaction as he thought him a decent sort of bloke and he'd have a word with him before he spoke to Benton.

'Here you are, all posh on a tray and all.'

Patrick was on his feet and took the tray from her hands whilst she spread out an old blanket. When she was seated, he handed down the tray and then joined her.

'Now this is just the ticket, better than tea at Buckingham Palace. You didn't have to bring me a glass, love, but as you have I'll tip the beer in. Blimey, this is the life, plates to eat off and everything.'

She tucked into his sandwiches with obvious enjoyment and then he returned the favour by eating a piece of Victoria sandwich. He smiled as he swallowed the last crumb.

'That was the best cake I've had in years. Your mum always used to make one at the weekend. You loved a bit of sponge cake back then, too.'

'Why did you leave? I don't understand how you could walk out on us. Did you have somebody else?'

Patrick wasn't sure it was fair to tell her the details but she was a young woman and was entitled to hear the unvarnished truth.

'We were married too young; we loved each other all right, never loved anyone else. But when you came along you didn't sleep at night, I had to be up and out to work at six thirty, so Lily moved into the spare room with you and she never moved back.'

He wasn't sure she understood the significance, but she nodded.

'That must have been hard, but it still doesn't seem a good enough reason to walk out like you did. You never even sent a birthday card to me over the years.'

'I should have done, but back then I thought you and your mum would be better off without me. I hadn't been gone more than a few weeks when I realised I'd done the wrong thing.'

She was listening closely but she didn't seem angry with him.

'I did come back then, came to the front door, but heard Lily talking to a neighbour out the back. She was saying that she was glad that I'd gone, that she was better off without me as I'd been a useless husband and father. I turned tail and returned to the station.'

'Blooming heck! That's no excuse – no wonder she didn't want you back. A real man would have had the courage to come in. I don't reckon she meant that, she was just upset. And what about me? Did it ever occur to you that I might have wanted a dad like most other children in the village?'

She was now on her feet and glaring down at him. She held out her hand and he handed up his mug. Without another word, she flounced off and he wished he'd not said so much.

She was right to tell him he'd behaved badly. She'd deserved a father and Lily a husband but he'd abandoned both of them and he'd not had the courage to come back and try to put things right.

He was still sitting on the blanket she'd brought out. In her hurry to go, she'd forgotten to take that with her. When he stood up, he shook it out to remove the crumbs and then carefully folded it. He left it on her doorstep and returned the empty bottle to the pub.

He had an afternoon off, a rare occurrence, but he wasn't sure what to do with the free time. Mrs Hatch saw him appear from the passageway and flung the back door open.

'Thank the good Lord that you've come, I'm that desperate.'

'What's wrong?'

'My old man's on the floor and I can't get him up. He's been there an hour already.'

Patrick lifted the old boy back into bed and checked he hadn't hurt himself. 'There, Mr Hatch, safely restored. Is there anything else I can do for you?'

'He doesn't talk, but he can understand. Ta, you're a godsend.'

'Is there anything else I can do? I like to keep busy,' Patrick said.

* * *

For the remainder of the afternoon he fetched water from the standpipe, rehung a door and cleaned out the chicken coop. He was pleasantly tired when he eventually sat down for supper.

'I'll be sleeping downstairs tonight, Mr Turner, just in case my old man has another funny turn.'

'If he does and you need me, just yell up the stairs and I'll be down. What you need is a wireless, then your Joe can listen to that.'

'Cor, chance would be a fine thing. If you could find us one of them we'd be ever so grateful.'

'There's a bloke at work who seems to have a finger in a lot of pies, if you know what I mean, if you don't care too much about where it comes from I reckon I might be able to find one for you.'

* * *

Lily wanted to get back and get herself and Daphne fed before the two lodgers returned. The new one was full of himself, and she'd had to tell him a couple of times to mind his language. If Mr Roby knew that she'd been given a young single bloke to replace Patrick then she was sure he'd get him moved. Having Johnny Smith under the same roof with her Daphne wasn't a good idea. She didn't trust him one bit.

She thought she'd have to give this new bloke a chance; he might have been nervous and that made him act like that. But if he was the same tonight then she'd definitely speak to Mr Roby tomorrow. The idea of him being just across the passageway from her daughter made her uneasy. She intended to tell Daphne to put a tilted chair against the door tonight just to be sure.

There was a folded blanket on the doorstep and she recognised it as being one of hers. What was going on? She picked it up and pushed the door open, immediately calling out to her daughter who was always in at this time.

'Daphne, love, I'm back.'

Her daughter called from the kitchen. 'I'm in here, Mum, tea will be ready in a minute. These mackerel are lovely and fresh, they're crisping up a treat in the frying pan.'

The table was laid for two, the teapot under its knitted cosy, bread and marge ready on the plate.

'Ta, love. I keep forgetting you're a dab hand in the kitchen now.' Lily held up the blanket. 'What's this doing outside?'

Daphne flushed. For a horrible moment, Lily thought her daughter had been up to no good with a boyfriend somewhere in the woods.

'Mr Turner and I had a picnic in the park. Don't look so peeved, Mum, you'll be pleased to know it didn't go well.'

'What happened? You can tell me, I won't be cross. It's only natural that you need to know a bit about your dad.'

'He said he did come back a few weeks after he left but heard you telling Aggie next door that you were glad he'd gone so he didn't bother to knock.'

Lily grabbed the back of a chair. It was as if she'd been punched in the chest. 'He came back? He should have come in; things could have been so different if he had.'

She pulled herself together, not wanting her daughter to know how much her casual comment had upset her. All these years she'd thought Patrick had walked away and forgotten her but it had been a dreadful misunderstanding. Then she reconsidered. He'd not come in when he could have done so it wasn't a misunderstanding, it was more that he'd been a coward and not wanted to face the music. If only he had spoken to her, things might have been so much better for her and Daphne.

'Do you need any help in there, love?'

'No, you pour the tea, Mum, I'll bring in the fish now.'

* * *

There was nothing like a fresh mackerel served with salt and pepper, eaten with bread and butter and washed down with mugs of tea.

'I enjoyed that, couldn't have cooked them better myself, love. I'm giving the lodgers the same but they'll get mash and carrots too. I've brought back the last of the apple pie I made for the family yesterday. There's enough for the two of them and with a bit of custard I don't reckon they'll notice the pie's not fresh.'

'I don't like that Johnny Smith, Mum. He looks at me a bit funny, makes me feel uncomfortable.'

'I know, love, and I was going to say you need to put a chair against your door tonight. I'll speak to Mr Roby tomorrow as they shouldn't have given us someone like him. It's not right to have him here, should only be older married men.'

'Good, as long as it's only for one more night I don't mind. I told Mr Turner, and you should have seen his face. He looked ever so fierce.'

'Patrick was never a violent man, but then he was scarcely a man when I knew him.' She smiled as she thought about this. 'I reckon he's grown several inches and put on a stone or more since he was here. I don't think I've changed as much.' Her lips curved. He was twice the man he'd been back then and despite her reservations she found him very appealing.

'You look smashing, Mum, folk think that you're my big sister. You've not got a grey hair nor a wrinkle.'

Lily laughed. 'I'm still as slim as I ever was and my boobs haven't changed either.'

'I reckon if you'd stayed married you'd have had half a dozen more kiddies and still look like you do now,' Daphne said, giggling.

'I'd have liked to have had a couple more children just so you weren't on your own,' Lily said.

'Plenty of time, Aggie next door had her last when she was in her forties—'

'That's quite enough of that talk, young lady, I've not looked at another man in all these years and I'm not going to start now.'

Daphne nodded and smiled. 'You're a married woman, what's to stop you getting back with my dad and having a couple more before it's too late?'

'I don't want to have any more children, not at my age and certainly not with him. Next time he comes I'm going to make sure he takes the divorce papers.'

Emily decided that she rather liked being at school with half the number of girls and teachers. The lunches were better, it was easier to get in and out of the cloakroom and after the first couple of days of chaos even the teaching was better – at least in most of the lessons.

Claire, the doctor's little daughter, was back at school too and informed Emily that none of her class had gone away. This meant that Emily was escorting her to school and bringing her home again afterwards – apart from the one afternoon when she and her brothers went to have tea with Nancy.

Her form now had nine scholarship girls, which meant Emily had more girls to mix with. However hard the teachers tried, the girls that paid just didn't want to mix with those that came on merit alone.

Halfway through the week, she was sitting in the sunshine on a bench in the garden with two new friends. Both of them lived in Rowhedge.

'It's only across the river and there's a ferry every fifteen minutes,' Emily said excitedly. 'That means I can come and see you and vice versa. I wish I'd known that I had friends so close.'

'It must be beastly being on your own all the time,' Amy Curtis said. 'Penny and I spend loads of time together. Shall we spend the day with you on Saturday or do you want to come to one of us?'

'Do you mind if I come to you the first time? I've not been on the ferry and I can't wait to do so.'

'I'll speak to my mum tonight and tell you tomorrow. I'm sure it'll be all right, she likes me to have friends over,' Amy said and Penny agreed.

'We'll meet you where the ferry stops, we both live about half a mile from the river, sort of next door to each other but not quite,' Amy explained.

'I rather like it being so much quieter with half the girls and teachers gone, don't you?' Penny said.

'I thought I might like to go with them but changed my mind. There haven't been any bombs dropped on Colchester, only that German bomber that crashed on a house and killed two people last week, but that doesn't really count,' Emily said.

'I expect it counts if you were the poor souls who died,' Penny said but she was smiling so wasn't cross.

'As Miss King said it wasn't an evacuation, more a relocation, do you think that they'll come back if no actual bombs are dropped here?' Emily had been thinking about this a lot.

'Well, last year the evacuees went home before Christmas so maybe our school and the boys' school will do the same,' Amy said as she jumped up.

The prefect with the bell had just appeared in front of the school and they started walking towards the door. Previously when the bell went everybody had to stand still until it was their turn to troop in. Now the remaining girls just walked in sensibly and went straight to their form room.

She couldn't wait to tell her parents about her new friends and ask their permission to take the ferry from Wivenhoe to Rowhedge across the River Colne. The boys had got into the most dreadful trouble a few months ago when they'd taken the other ferry that went to Fingringhoe and she didn't want to do anything to upset Mummy and Daddy as they had a lot to deal with at the moment.

Grandpa had only worn his Home Guard uniform for a couple of days and then gone back into civilian clothes but the staff continued to call him Major Roby as that was a bit less confusing for them.

Grandma was still called 'old Mrs Roby', which Emily thought was rather impolite but if her grandma didn't mind then it had to be all right. Having someone in the house who was fine one day and then didn't know who he was or where he was made things awkward for everyone.

* * *

On the way back, Claire skipped along beside her, chattering on about Peter Rabbit as her class had been reading the Beatrix Potter books. Then the little girl said something that made Emily listen more carefully.

'I heard my daddy say to my mummy that your grandpa has amentia. What's amentia?'

Emily's first thought was that the doctor shouldn't have been discussing his patients with his wife as that should be confidential. As everybody who lived or worked at Harbour House already knew that Grandpa wasn't well, she supposed Dr Cousins wasn't revealing anything he shouldn't, just using the correct term.

'My grandfather is just a bit confused, it's called dementia, but it just means being confused sometimes.'

'I don't see my grandparents, I don't know if I've got any really, I don't mind.'

'That's good, as there's nothing much you can do about it. I've got another set of grandparents who belong to my mother but they moved to America when the war started.'

'Is that a long way away?'

Emily laughed. 'It's the other side of the world, well, not as far as Australia or New Zealand but still thousands of miles from here.'

'Can we stop for cakes today, Emily? Mummy gave me some pennies just in case.'

So that was why the little girl hadn't been dawdling, gazing into shop windows and stopping to talk to people like she usually did.

'I've got threepence. How many pennies have you got?' Emily asked.

They were now outside the bakers who were happy to sell anything that might be left on the shelves at this time as nobody wanted stale cakes.

'I've got the same.' The little girl delved into her satchel and pulled out three large brown pennies triumphantly.

Emily had a threepenny bit, a small yellow coin with bumpy edges. She took hers out and showed Claire, who was a bit puzzled that her three big coins weren't worth more than her little one.

'We can't stand out here talking about this or we'll miss our train. Don't be disappointed if there isn't anything we can buy. They don't always have cakes left over at four o'clock,' Emily said.

Today they were lucky as the lady behind the counter had seen them outside and already had a large paper bag with several sticky treats in it.

'There's enough in here for the boys as well as you two,' the baker said as she handed over the bag.

'Goodness, thank you so much. Is sixpence enough? I'm afraid that's all we've got today.'

'Go on with you, love, it's more than enough. Enjoy your cakes.'

Emily insisted on putting the bulging bag in her satchel which had more room in it than the little leather one Claire had over her shoulder.

'Can I have one now? I paid for those as well, I should be able to have one now,' she whined.

'If you carry on like that, young lady, you'll not get anything. I'll just return your pennies to Mrs Cousins and tell her why.'

The little girl scowled, stamped her feet and Emily knew what was coming. Last year Claire had had a tantrum in the street but she'd promised never to do it again. Then the child's face lit up and she was smiling and waving.

'Look, look, it's George and Sammy. Come on, Emily, let's run. I want to tell them that we've got cakes to share on the train.'

Emily didn't need asking twice. Hand in hand they ran, gas masks and satchels bouncing, to join her brothers who'd seen them coming and were waiting.

'What's the hurry, girls? We've still got ten minutes,' George said as he leaned down and hugged the little girl.

'We've got cakes, we've got lots of cakes, and I paid three pennies and so did Emily.'

Sammy bent his knees and Claire hopped up for a piggyback. This always happened if they met the boys. Before Sammy had been adopted and become part of the Roby family he'd had twin sisters about the same age as Claire. Emily thought that was why he always made a fuss of the little girl.

* * *

Patrick made sure he was early to work the next day. He wanted a word with this new lodger, this Johnny Smith, and was prepared to back up his words with his fists if necessary. He wouldn't get the sack because he was needed –

if the coppers were involved then he might get arrested but he was prepared to risk that. Nobody was going to make his daughter or his wife feel uncomfortable in their own home.

He saw Frank first and the bloke took one look at his face and hurried over. 'Don't do nothing stupid, he's not worth it. Mrs Turner is getting him moved today. He shouldn't have been put with them in the first place.'

'He needs to know he can't behave like that; my Daphne and Lily aren't the only two women without their menfolk at home.'

'Fair enough, but keep it civil, don't smash him in the face even if you want to. He's just walked in, remember what I said.'

Patrick strode across and before Smith could react he grabbed his arm and bundled him behind a pile of timber where they couldn't be seen.

'I want a word with you. You upset my daughter and my wife. I'm not having that.'

For a second, Smith looked puzzled, then he understood. 'I never meant nothing, just a bit of fun, I'd not have done nothing I shouldn't.'

The tight band around Patrick's chest slackened. He'd made his point without having to hit the man. In fact, the bloke was trembling. This made him even angrier – only a coward would frighten women.

He grabbed the man by the collar, lifted him from his feet and threw him against the wood. Several pieces slipped and clouted Smith across the head, which saved Patrick from having to do it himself.

'You'll not go back to Clifton Terrace, if the boss doesn't find you somewhere you can sleep in the gutter. You've got off easy – I'll tear your head off if you go anywhere near them again.'

Smith was still slumped against the timber and hadn't dared move. Patrick gave him a last filthy look and then walked away smiling. He'd learnt to look after himself over the years, spent a lot of time boxing and that. He wasn't the skinny bloke he'd been when he'd run away from the best things in his life. Smith wasn't the only one who was a coward – that hat fitted him too.

Frank's look of relief was comical. 'That little bastard won't try that on again, not with any other girl. You scared the bejesus out of him. Word will get round, you'll not have any trouble from any of these blokes.'

Patrick shook his head. 'Trouble? Why should any of these blokes want to pick a fight with me?'

'Blimey, didn't you know? You're the foreman's favourite, nobody else got an afternoon off and on Saturday too.'

'I keep my head down and get on with my work, maybe if you did more of that you'd get an afternoon off too.'

Frank scowled, then his face relaxed and he nodded. 'Fair enough, I'll follow your example and maybe I'll get a few hours off next week.'

* * *

Patrick was aware that he was getting surreptitious looks, that some of the blokes looked the other way when he walked past, that hadn't been his intention. He just wanted to let Smith know that what he'd done was unacceptable.

The foreman brought round the sandwiches as usual at midday. 'Mr Roby wants a word, Paddy, I should take your lunch with you.'

With the greaseproof-paper-wrapped sandwiches in his hand, Patrick headed for the office. His arrival was spotted and the boss came out. If he was going to get a bollocking it would have been done inside.

'Patrick, I just wanted to offer my apologies for sending Smith to Clifton Terrace. My secretary should have known better than to send a single young man to that house. I hear that you sorted the matter out yourself. Do I need to speak to him as well?'

'No, ta, sir. Just make sure he's billeted where there's no young women or girls for him to take an interest in.'

'There's three of the new men staying in an annex at the Falcon Hotel, I've put him with them.'

'Right. Was there anything else, sir?'

'Yes, I know why you stepped in, but it won't happen again, will it? This is a place of work, important war work, I'm not having it disrupted by personal animosity between my men. I hope that's clear.'

'Yes, sir, I understand.'

Patrick didn't join his team as he usually did, where they sat together on a pile of pipes overlooking the river. Instead he found himself a corner and drank the stewed tea that his landlady had provided in her precious thermos. He was now being treated like one of the family and that suited him just fine.

He was happy to do whatever was needed for the old couple and would have done so willingly without expecting any favours in return.

Nobody asked him to go for a drink but that didn't bother him. He wasn't there to make friends; he was there to work. Mrs Hatch had left out a jug of hot water so he didn't have to wash in cold, which was a real treat.

He rinsed the flask out and handed it to his landlady as he walked into the kitchen. 'Ta, having a hot drink with my lunch was much appreciated.'

'Go on with you, son, you don't have to thank me for looking after you. My old man wants to know if you play chess.'

This question surprised Patrick as he didn't know someone who couldn't speak could still do something like play chess.

'I do, I reckon I'm not bad, I'd be happy to play a game with him after I've eaten.'

She looked a bit uncomfortable. 'Would you mind very much, son, doing it now? He's usually asleep by nine o'clock.'

'Happy to, I'll eat after.'

The chessboard was already set out and the old bloke nodded and smiled when he came in. Mr Hatch might be an invalid and unable to hold a conversation but he was a good chess player. Patrick didn't let him win, and it was touch and go a couple of times before he eventually achieved checkmate.

'I enjoyed that, Mr Hatch, I'd be happy to play again. It would suit me better to play before I go to work. Would you be awake then?'

The old man nodded vigorously and reached out and patted Patrick's hand. 'Right you are, I'll see you at six tomorrow morning. I can play for three quarters of an hour but then I need to have my breakfast and get to work. Is that all right with you?'

Mrs Hatch came in beaming. 'That'll be just fine, son, we're both awake early. It's really kind of you, we won't forget it.'

Patrick shook the old man's hand and then sat down to eat. He couldn't turn in after eating such a big meal.

'That was great, but I'm going to have to take a walk around the block before I can go to bed. Don't let me keep you up, Mrs Hatch.'

'I told you before, I don't lock the back door. I reckon you could still get a pint at the Greyhound – they don't close until after ten unless they run out of beer.'

'I'm not a big drinker. I'll walk down to the river, it'll be high tide and I like to see the lighters and the barges being towed up to Hythe. The fishing boats should be in too – why don't I bring back some fish for tomorrow night? I know it's not Friday, but I'll eat it any day of the week.'

'A nice bit of cod would go down a treat, but anything really. If you put it in the pantry on the slate shelf with a plate over the top it'll do lovely tomorrow night.'

Having a purpose for his walk suited Patrick, he wasn't one for wandering about just to get exercise. It was dusk now, not quite dark, no need to use a torch to get around. There wasn't any cod going spare but he got three nice dabs, not as good as plaice, but they'd still taste good fried up with a bit of butter or marge and served with a parsley sauce.

Lily didn't have the opportunity to speak to Mr Roby as his father was down early and ate breakfast with him and she left, as always, before he returned from work. Daphne was always home before her and was waiting for her outside Harbour House.

'Is something wrong, love? I can't remember the last time you came to see me at work.'

'No, you won't believe it, but that nasty Mr Smith turned up half an hour ago to collect his things. He never said a word out of place, didn't even look at me, just grabbed his things and vanished.'

'This has nothing to do with me, but I reckon I know who had him leave,' Lily said. 'It was Patrick, I can't think of any other reason.'

Daphne grinned. 'I'm sure it was, Mum, my dad looked that cross when I told him. I knew he'd sort it out for us. Do you think he punched him?'

'He couldn't have punched his way out of a wet paper bag when I knew him all those years ago.'

'I reckon he's almost six foot now and got loads of muscles and that. Doing the kind of work he does would make him tough, wouldn't it?'

'I expect so,' Lily replied, not wanting to continue the conversation.

'Will we get somebody else now?'

'I doubt it. I left a note for Mr Roby saying what had happened and that it might be better if we just stuck with Frank.'

'You don't have to cook nothing tonight, Mum. I was allowed to bring back three lovely pies that I'd made. We weren't that busy at lunchtime service and as I'm allowed to have breakfast and lunch and didn't have neither today, Chef said I could bring them home.'

'So, we just need to do some taters and a few veg. I was lucky too, I got a tin of peaches, like gold dust they are, and we'll have them for Sunday tea with a drop of evaporated milk.'

* * *

Frank enjoyed his meal and then rushed off to the pub. Had Patrick had words with him too for not intervening? Lily half-expected her ex to turn up but he didn't and she wasn't sure if she was relieved or disappointed.

Daphne was curled up on the battered sofa with a book she'd borrowed off someone at work. It was by Agatha Christie, a murder mystery, and not something Lily wanted to read.

'I'm just popping out for a bit, love, I'll not be gone more than half an hour,' she told her daughter and waited for the inquisition. Lily never went out – this would be the first time since she'd had the job at Harbour House.

'All right, I'll have some nice cocoa ready for when you get back and there's still some of those broken biscuits left.'

'Ta, that'll be lovely,' Lily said and dashed out before she could be asked any awkward questions.

She'd made discreet enquiries and knew Patrick was stopping with Mrs Hatch. It was number thirteen, easy to find. Mr Hatch, poor old soul, was more or less bedridden and their two sons had left Wivenhoe years ago and she wasn't exactly sure where they were now. They certainly didn't come back to visit their parents.

It was a little after nine, still light for another half hour, so she wouldn't be out in the blackout. Stumbling around in the dark with just a tiny beam from a torch wasn't any fun. She'd read somewhere that more people died in accidents in the dark than in the war the first few months.

She stepped into the arched passageway, paused for a few seconds to steady her hectic pulse, not exactly sure why she'd come and hoped that it wouldn't be misconstrued. She definitely wasn't interested in Patrick, but did want to thank him for getting that nasty bit of work to leave.

She could hear somebody hammering at the bottom of the garden and guessed at once it would be him. After all, wasn't he a carpenter? Who else would be banging with a hammer at this time of night?

There was no sign of Mrs Hatch at the kitchen window but as she hadn't come to see his landlady she didn't knock on the door to announce herself. Patrick had his back to her. He'd removed his thick flannel shirt and was in his vest. Her mouth dropped open. Daphne hadn't been wrong when she'd said that Patrick had changed. From the back she wouldn't have known it was her husband as he now had broad shoulders, equally muscled arms, and for a moment she regretted that she wasn't still his wife.

Then she laughed, forgetting he didn't know she was there. He hit his thumb with a hammer and his language was terrible.

'I'm sorry, I didn't mean to startle you. I hope you haven't broken it.'

He grinned as he sucked the injured thumb and shook his head. 'Just bruised, not even broken the skin. I didn't expect to see you here, Lily.'

He suddenly realised he wasn't wearing a shirt and looked around desperately, his cheeks pink. She picked it up from the tatty wooden chair he'd left it on and chucked it over.

'Don't worry on my account, Patrick, I've seen a lot more of you than that.' The words had just popped out of her mouth, and she wished she'd not said something so provocative as it would give him the wrong idea entirely.

He didn't answer as he was busy shoving his arms into the sleeves of his shirt and didn't turn back until he was decent – not that he wasn't before.

'Right, have you brought the papers for me to sign? Is that why you're here?'

Flustered by his question, she shook her head. 'No, I put them back in the drawer for now. I just wanted to thank you for getting that Smith moved. I hope you didn't get into trouble on our account.'

'A mild ticking off from the boss, and a lot of dirty looks from the other blokes. That nasty bit of work is living at the Falcon with three others. No chance of him doing the same anywhere else.'

Patrick hadn't confirmed or denied that he'd hit the man and she wasn't going to ask him. He was certainly big enough to intimidate most blokes, although for some reason he was still the same gentle, shy Patrick to her.

'I'm not having anyone else stay with us apart from Frank Burton, he could have said something but he didn't and that's put me off him. As long as he minds his manners he can stop but I wouldn't be sorry if he left.'

'He's harmless, a lazy sod, but no malice in him, not like the other one. I'm going to be here for several months so will have to go to London and collect my stuff. I don't suppose you and Daphne fancy a day out?'

Lily was about to say no but said the opposite. 'I can probably arrange to have Saturday morning off if I work on the Sunday morning instead. Can you get a whole day?'

His eyes lit up and his smile made him look ever so handsome. 'I'm not sure, but I'll speak to the foreman and tell him the reason and offer to work extra hours to make up for it. I doubt it'll be for a bit, probably next month, will that work for you?'

'That's perfect, it'll give Daphne time to arrange to have Saturday morning off as well. It'd help if we knew the date, but I don't expect you can tell us that.'

'I'll speak to Mr Roby, he's a good boss, if he knows I'm moving back here permanently I reckon he'll be prepared to help out. I thought we could have a bit of lunch, and go to the pictures after, what do you think?'

'I know things aren't the same up there what with all the paper on the windows, the blackout and that, but Daphne's never been to London and I've only been there the once when we went on our honeymoon.'

Whilst she'd been talking he was wiping down his tools, sweeping up the sawdust and making things tidy. Only then did she look to see what he'd been doing.

'Crikey, what's that when it's at home?' She was staring at a little wooden table with legs about eight inches long.

'It's so I can play chess with Mr Hatch of a morning. It was a bit tricky balancing it on a tray on his knees. He'll also be able to eat his meals off it. What do you think?'

'I think it's clever and very thoughtful of you. I'm sorry, but I told our Daphne I'd only be half an hour. You could come back with me for a cocoa and some biscuits if you felt like it, ask her yourself about going to London next month.'

She thought he was going to agree but then he shook his head. 'Ta for the invite, I want to take this in and explain how it works to Mrs Hatch. By then it'll be dark. I don't want to be jumped on by Smith and I wouldn't put it past him.'

'Another time then, good night, Patrick.'

* * *

Saturday couldn't come soon enough for Emily as she'd be going to Rowhedge to spend the day with her friends for the first time. It hadn't been possible to arrange it for last weekend but spending another week with Penny and Amy had just made their friendship stronger.

She was a bit worried about seeing Amy as her friend hadn't been at school for the past three days.

She was wearing her dark blue slacks, the pretty twinset that Grandma had given her last year, and her hair was long enough to put slides in. Her brothers had joined her in her attic bedroom, jealous that they weren't coming too.

'It's not fair, you get all the fun,' George said but he was smiling and not grumpy like he sometimes was when he thought he'd been left out.

'You need to find friends who live in Rowhedge; there might be a boy you haven't spoken to. I'm sure if you had somewhere to go then our parents would let you. I'll ask my friends when I'm there as they're bound to know. You can't miss a boy in a purple blazer.'

'Maybe this Penny or Amy have brothers our age. It wouldn't matter if they don't go to the prep school like us, they just need to be the same age,' he replied.

'Sorry to disappoint you, boys, but I know that Penny has two little brothers, about five, I think. Amy's siblings are grown up and don't live at home any more.'

She hugged both of them and they didn't flinch away which they did sometimes – they were getting to the age when physical contact with their sister wasn't always welcome.

Daddy was at work but he'd said he'd come and meet her from the ferry at five o'clock. As the shipyard was very close to where the ferry went backwards and forwards all day that made sense.

She'd got enough money to pay her fare and some extra for emergencies

– she wasn't sure exactly what emergencies there might be, but her mummy had said it's always wise to have something for them.

Her piggybank was satisfactorily full as she was now given a regular allowance for doing chores around the house. She'd already removed two threepenny bits and handed one each to her brothers.

'There you are, Mr Moore told me yesterday he was getting some sweets in today.'

* * *

There weren't that many people waiting to get on the ferry but she could see half a dozen housewives waiting on the other side. Emily hadn't realised that they came across to shop but wasn't surprised as Rowhedge was a much smaller place than Wivenhoe and didn't have as many shops – it certainly didn't have as many pubs.

She couldn't see either of her friends on the other bank but wasn't worried as they didn't need to be there until she actually arrived. It was a rising tide, easier for the ferryman to row the boat across but more difficult for him to bring it back.

She dropped her pennies into the pot and found a place on one of the wooden seats, just planks really. The ferryman immediately ticked her off.

'Not there, fill up from the other end. You're in the way.'

Emily scrambled to her feet, making the boat rock, and she expected to be told off again, but the man laughed.

'Careful, love, you'll have us all in the drink. Not been on the ferry before.'

It was a statement not a question and Emily nodded nervously as she stepped over the next two planks and sat with a girl about her age – but not someone she recognised.

'Don't take no notice of him, he's all right really. You visiting friends?'

'I am, but I can't see them waiting for me and I don't actually know where they live so I hope they turn up.'

'You're one of them posh girls what go to the grammar school – there's only two what do the same. Penny and Amy – if they ain't there I'll take you to that Penny's house as it's on me way home.'

'That's a kind offer but I hope I don't have to take you up on it. I'm Emily

Roby and I'm pleased to meet you.' This didn't seem the sort of occasion to offer to shake hands so she just nodded and smiled.

'I'm Doris Jones, pleased to meet you, I'm sure.' The girl pointed to her full basket. 'Been over for a few things, always more to be found here than in Rowhedge.'

'Don't you have to be registered to shop?'

'Not for veg, bread and that. You've got two bakers, two greengrocers, two ironmongers so I come over to go to them.'

The boat rocked again and the ferryman pushed them off with his oar, making further conversation difficult. The crossing took ten minutes; it wasn't that far but with a boat full of passengers it must have been hard work rowing with just one man. It wasn't a very exciting journey but river water splashed in a couple of times and Emily was quite sure she now had a wet patch on the rear of her slacks.

She was facing forwards, watching Wivenhoe, and didn't dare swivel round and see if her friends had turned up. The boat banged against the hard and a boy waiting there grabbed the end and held it so they could clamber off without falling in.

'It don't look like them girls have come for you. Are you going to wait, get the ferry back or come with me?' Doris asked.

'I'll come with you, if you don't mind. I'm definitely not going home until I'm quite sure I can't spend the day with them. I've been so looking forward to today as I don't have any friends on my side of the river.'

Doris grinned. 'Well, I reckon you can count me as a friend from now on. I ain't posh, I ain't clever like what you are, but if I say I'm doing something then I do it.'

There was something about the way Doris said this that worried Emily. They'd walked away from the ferry and were now standing by the pub. It looked a bit rundown, not like the ones in Wivenhoe.

'I get the feeling that you know something about my friends that I don't. Would you mind telling me?'

The girl shrugged. 'You'll find out soon enough. That Penny has to look after her two little brothers so her ma can work. I reckon that's what's happened today. Amy's dad is something hush-hush in London and I reckon her ma's involved in that too. That's what my nan says.'

'I see, well, actually I don't. I can see that maybe Penny can't get away to meet me but not why Amy hasn't come. I don't understand why they didn't explain things to me before inviting me over.'

'You won't find out standing gassing to me. I live in one of the cottages opposite that Penny. You'll not find it on your own – did they give you an address?'

'They didn't, they said they would meet me so I didn't think it necessary. I'm beginning to wonder if maybe I'd be better off going home, I'm obviously not welcome.'

'You any good with nippers?'

'Nippers? Oh, do you mean children?'

Doris laughed. 'Course I do. Well, are you?'

'I am, I used to spend my weekend helping out at a farm with their three children. I've also got two younger brothers and a baby sister and I take my neighbour's six-year-old to school every day.'

'Then you'll be very welcome. Your friend will be that pleased to see you if you can help her with those little devils.'

That didn't sound very promising and wasn't at all the way Emily had hoped to spend her Saturday. Nevertheless, helping Penny with her siblings would probably be more interesting than going back to Harbour House.

Hopefully, she'd discover why Amy hadn't come as having parents who were doing something secret for the government didn't really explain why she hadn't turned up either. Then she remembered that Amy had been absent for three days so maybe was too unwell to come.

9

Patrick played early-morning chess with Mr Hatch using the new bedtable and arrived at the shipyard ten minutes early. He didn't like to be late, not for anything. He wanted to speak to the foreman before everyone else turned up.

'Right, what can I do for you, Paddy?'

'I'm wondering how I can wangle a Saturday off next month. I'm prepared to work extra hours and not have any time off until then.'

'Going somewhere special then?'

'I'm taking my wife and daughter to London for the day. I've got to collect my stuff as I'm staying here permanently.'

'London? I'd not go there for love nor money right now. Them blooming bombers are back and forth every day. It ain't safe up there.'

'I'd agree with you if I was going right into the East End, but my digs were close to Liverpool Street station. They've not blown up any stations yet. I was going to take them for lunch and then to the pictures in the West End.'

'Fair enough, but rather you than me. You hoping to get back with your missus, then?'

'I don't think that's on the cards, but I want to get to know my daughter and I can't do that without Lily's agreement.'

'Okay, I'll speak to Mr Roby. You get your team to knuckle down and get this lot finished before the end of the month and I'll see what I can do.'

Patrick nodded. 'You're on, there's a lot I can do on my own and I'll come in early and get started.' He thought for a moment before continuing. 'A bit cheeky to ask this, but could you mention the reason I want the day off? If he knows it's for Lily and Daphne he might be more ready to oblige.'

None of the blokes liked working weekends but the poor sods in the navy and the RAF didn't get time off at all. They had to be on duty, ready to fight without the luxury of trying to arrange a day out with their family.

If he worked through his lunch break every day as well as coming in half an hour early that would make a noticeable improvement on productivity.

The foreman was about to leave but Patrick called him back. 'If I get the others to do extra, no overtime pay, can they get an afternoon off or even a day next month?'

'Don't see why not, fair's fair, you get these lazy sods motivated, get them to work like you do and I guarantee the boss will be only too happy to oblige with a few hours off here and there. You've got my permission to tell them it's official.'

Patrick gathered the dozen who were working on this wooden minesweeper with him before they started and explained the deal he'd come to with the foreman.

'I'll be upfront with you lot, I get the first whole day off, but all of you will get an afternoon, that's definite. Then a day off in turn.'

They exchanged glances and then one after the other they nodded and shook his hand. 'We'd not have been able to make any sort of deal with the bosses,' one of them said. 'You lead from the front, mate, and we'll follow along behind.'

He didn't expect them to do the extra hour that he was going to do, all he wanted from them was that they kept their heads down and grafted all day. Now they had the promise of a free afternoon on the horizon, all the blokes buckled down and they accomplished more that day than they had in two days previously.

Patrick was taking bites from his sandwich whilst working, he had the flask balanced precariously on the waiting timber. He looked up and saw the boss watching and he nodded and smiled and got on with it.

His foreman worked as hard as everybody else and overseeing the work in progress had to be done as well. The men in Patrick's team returned promptly – another first – from their lunch break and he was satisfied they'd be able to complete the job in hand by the end of the month so he'd get his Saturday off.

Around five o'clock they stopped for a brew and he saw Mr Roby leave the yard. Not long after that, Mr Roby senior strolled in. Immediately Patrick put down his tools and walked across to the old man.

'Good afternoon, sir, your son's just left the yard. I'm Patrick, can I help you?'

'Thank you for the information, young man, I gather from the strange way you're talking to me that you've seen me when I'm confused. I can assure you that I'm compos mentis at the moment.'

'Glad to hear that, Mr Roby, but I'm still happy to help.'

'Excellent, I'm curious as to what goes on here. I thought it was war work but I wandered in without anyone asking for my ID. I could be a Nazi spy. Very slack, very slack indeed.'

There was usually someone at the gate but he was there to stop kids coming in and he never asked for ID from anyone.

'You're right, but somehow I think a German spy might be recognised in Wivenhoe, don't you? Not many strangers around in a place like this.'

'Good point, well made. I don't suppose there's a cup of tea going?'

Patrick was concerned that someone at Harbour House would be looking for old Mr Roby. 'Just a tick, I'll speak to the foreman and then see if I can get you one. There's an old orange box over there you can sit on.'

The others ignored what was going on and continued to work. Everybody knew Mr Roby's dad wasn't quite right. Just then Patrick spotted the foreman.

'Hey, Jack, I've got Major Roby here, he's fine, wants a cup of tea, but I'm worried they might be looking for him as he's not always okay,' Patrick said.

'Bloody hell, the boss has just gone out to collect his girl, she's coming back on the ferry. Get him a cup of char, keep him chatting and Mr Roby will be here to take him home shortly.'

Patrick's heart sank when he discovered the old bloke had already wandered off. Maybe he wasn't quite as all right as he'd seemed.

'Where'd Mr Roby senior go, Frank? I've only been gone a couple of minutes. He was sitting there.'

Frank grinned and pointed to the rear of the shed. 'One of the apprentices is making his tea and showing him around. Nice old geezer, pity he's not always like this.'

Patrick returned to what he'd been doing but kept glancing over his shoulder to check how the lad was managing. Half an hour at least had gone by and still no sign of the boss.

The foreman came across, looking worried. 'Something's up, I should take the old bloke home, Patrick. Someone will be looking for him by now.'

* * *

Emily was enjoying talking to Doris. 'Do you ever come to Wivenhoe? If you do, why don't you call in and I'll show you around? I live at Harbour House, it's opposite the Grosvenor Hotel on the corner of Alma Street.'

'Cor, that'd be a bit of all right. Are you sure your ma won't object to you inviting someone like me to come and visit?'

'No, of course she won't, anyone I invite will be welcome.'

They were now approaching a row of modest cottages on the right and a big red-brick Victorian house on the left which was set back from the lane behind a crumbling brick wall and a straggly hedge.

'That's me, the end one, the posh house over there's where that Penny lives. When can I come and see you then?'

'What about next Saturday morning?'

'Righto, I'll be there around ten. I've got chores to do before I can come out.'

They said their goodbyes. Emily fought her way through the overgrown hedge and collapsing gate and walked up the path, not sure that she should actually be there. It was very rude, whatever the reason, to invite someone to spend a day and then not bother to come and explain why it had been cancelled.

She knocked loudly on the door, but nobody answered it. She didn't like to look through the letterbox but she pressed her ear against the wood and couldn't hear anything. Having come this far, she thought she'd find her way to the back door and see if the children were playing in the garden or something. Although if they were, shouldn't she be able to hear them?

The house was eerily quiet, the garden deserted and there was obviously nobody here, not even Penny and her mischievous brothers. It then occurred to her that maybe there was a different way to walk down to the ferry and her friend had taken that route and they'd missed each other.

The house was at the top of a hill and she could see the river and the shipyard in the distance but no sign of a path or a track that might lead down to the ferry. She didn't want to go in search of Amy, one missing friend was more than enough to deal with at the moment.

She stepped back out onto the lane and found Doris waiting. 'It's never that quiet, Emily, you can always hear the little blighters yelling and carrying on.'

'Do you think they might have gone to Amy's house, hoping that she came to meet me and I'm there?'

'I ain't got a clue, but you could be right. There's a cut through the fields to the lane what her house is in, I'll take you there, shall I?'

'Yes, that would be really helpful. I must admit I was cross at first but now I'm rather worried. I don't actually think that Penny would let me down if she could possibly help it,' Emily said.

It was a ten-minute walk through a meadow which fortunately had no livestock in it today. Doris proved to be an entertaining friend and she was almost able to forget her concern about the other two.

'I know that Penny has to look after her little brothers when her mother works, but what does her mother do?'

'I ain't got a clue, she catches the first bus into Colchester and sometimes never comes home until after dark.'

'Golly, that's a long time to leave someone as young as Penny in charge of two small children.'

Doris pulled a face. 'She ain't that young, she were thirteen the other day. Same age as me, more or less, and I take care of me grandparents on me own.'

Emily was shocked. 'What do you mean? Doesn't your mother help you?'

'She buggered off when I was born and dumped me with my nan and grandad. They've been good to me, better than she would have been, I reckon. Only Grandad's a bit feeble now, Nan ain't too bad. I do all the shopping, laundry and half the cleaning and she does the rest.'

It seemed a lot of responsibility for someone only a year older than Emily but she was impressed with her new friend's attitude.

'Is it all right for you to come with me? I don't want to make things difficult when I know you've so much to do.'

'Grandad's pottering around the garden, he don't do much now but he likes to be out there. Nan's doing a bit of baking and she likes me to get out the house and enjoy meself when I can.'

Emily made a promise to herself that from now on she'd be more grateful for what she'd got and more understanding about those that didn't have as much as she did.

'Right, we nip over this stile and Bob's your uncle,' Doris said and pointed to a gap in the hedge.

Once they were over, Emily looked around with interest. There were only three houses, two as big as Harbour House and one twice the size so one of these must be where Amy lived.

'It's the one with the blue shutters. I've never been in, but I've walked past it as I come home this way sometimes.'

This house wasn't as old as her home but Emily thought it was probably Georgian as it had a central front door and an equal number of big windows on either side of that. She thought that Georgian architects liked everything to be symmetrical. It was a huge house.

'I wonder if Penny and Amy went to meet me with the children, could they still be down there waiting to see if I was late?'

'Could be, no point in us walking down if they're on the way up,' Doris said.

'Let's check at the house and then decide,' Emily suggested.

She smiled at Doris as they approached because there was the sound of children playing somewhere outside. 'She's definitely here as I don't think Amy has any younger brothers and sisters.'

Doris hung back. 'I ain't coming with you, I'm not one of you lot, they won't want me hanging about.'

'They absolutely will, I'd never have found this place without your help. I know you don't go to our school, but that doesn't matter. If I like you then I'm sure that they will too.'

'Then if you're sure, ta, I'd like to see what it's like round the back.'

They ran up the gravel drive but didn't go to the front door but made their way around the house until they came to a six-foot brick wall with a solid wooden door.

'I can still hear those boys running about. Do we shout?'

Doris grinned and lifted the latch on the door and it swung open. Emily still couldn't see the children as they were right at the back and this door was halfway down the left-hand side of the house.

She reached behind and felt the back of her slacks. 'Is there a muddy patch on my backside, Doris?'

'No, all tickety-boo. I'd like a pair of them, much easier than wearing a frock. I've got overalls but they ain't good enough to wear outside the house.'

Emily nodded. 'I'll get one of my two friends who make clothes for people to run you up some. It won't cost you anything, but I can't promise what colour they'll be as they'll be made from whatever they've got left over.'

'Cor, ta ever so. This is my lucky day bumping into you.'

They were now walking along a flagged path and emerged at the rear of the house. This wasn't the garden as Emily had expected but a courtyard with various outbuildings.

'No wonder we can't hear the children properly, they must be through the gate over there. Do you think those are kitchens and so on we've got to walk past?' Emily asked nervously, expecting someone to bang on the window at any moment and demand to know what they were doing trespassing.

'Can't see no one in there, not sure they even have any staff what with them being hush-hush people from the War Office,' Doris told her.

Eventually they saw Penny looking really upset and two little boys kicking a football around. There was no sign of Amy, which was strange as this was her house.

Penny saw them and ran across and grabbed Emily's hands.

'Thank God you've come. I was desperate and didn't know what to do. I'm sorry, we didn't forget you.'

'What's wrong? Why are you so upset?' Emily asked.

'My mother got a call to go into work unexpectedly. I brought them here to tell Amy I couldn't see you today but she wasn't downstairs. I couldn't take the boys in as they break things. I found her in bed. She's really poorly. Her mum and dad should never have left her on her own.'

* * *

Lily was at home catching up on her housework when the boys from

Harbour House banged on her front door. She thought the knock on the door was her daughter who was due back from work at any moment.

'Have you seen our grandad? He's wandered off again and Grandma sent us out to look this way and she's gone the other way,' George said.

'No, I don't think he'd come here as he doesn't know where I live. Just let me take off my pinny and dry my hands, boys, and I'll help you look. Do you think he might have gone into the woods?'

'I don't know, Lily, he could be anywhere. Grandma has gone along the river, it's low tide but if he fell in the mud he could still come to grief, he'd not be able to get out again on his own.'

She quickly scribbled a note to Daphne explaining where she was and then the three of them ran into the woods but after searching for half an hour they were certain the old man wasn't there. They'd asked a couple of bigger boys on their bicycles but they'd not seen him.

'Let's go down to the station, he might have wanted to watch the trains,' she suggested so that's what they did.

'What about the shipyard, Lily?' George asked. 'He could have gone to see my dad.'

'We'll try there next. Sammy, would you be a love and run home and make sure he's not turned up? We don't want to be on a fool's errand.'

It was now after five o'clock. She and George hurried along to the shipyard and as they got to the gate Patrick walked out with Major Roby.

'A search party? I should have left a note saying where I was going, how very remiss of me,' the major said. He was obviously having one of his good days.

Patrick smiled. 'I was just walking home with him. Now you're here, lads, I'm sure you can accompany your grandad as I don't like to be away from my work if I can avoid it.'

'Course we can, Grandma's going mad, she thinks you've fallen in the river. I don't think she'll be that pleased to see you,' George said, smiling up at his grandpa.

Sammy arrived breathless and smiling as they left the gates.

'Thank you for coming, boys. Can I rely on you to protect me from her rough tongue?'

The boys laughed and the three of them walked off, chattering. Lily thought how sad it was that such an intelligent, charming old man was slowly losing the ability to be independent. Then she turned to face Patrick.

'I can have Saturday off whenever I want it, Patrick, so can Daphne, so just let us know. Are you sure it's safe with those bombers going over every day?'

'So far it's been the East End that's copped it, and we won't be there for long. I promise we won't go if it's dangerous.'

She nodded. 'I'll leave it to you then. Mrs Roby said she just needs to know a few days in advance – will you have that much notice?'

'I expect so. Can't wait to spend the day with you both. My treat, all of it, I'm putting all my wages away.'

Lily wasn't sure how she felt about that as allowing him to pay for a day out might give him the wrong idea. She was smiling as she walked home though. Having him around was proving not to be such a bad thing after all.

10

Emily turned to speak to Doris, who was backing away, looking worried.

'There's measles in the village, I reckon that's what she's got. I ain't taking it back to kill off me grandparents. Sorry, but I'm off.'

'Of course, I understand. Please come and see me next week if you can. Thank you for your help,' Emily said.

Doris nodded. 'I will, sorry, ta ta.' She waved a hand and was gone back around the side of the house, leaving her to speak to Penny.

'I'm so glad you're here, I've got to take the boys back. If you call the doctor I'm sure he'll be here soon and he'll tell you what to do,' Penny said as she beckoned for the little boys to come to her.

'You can't leave me here, I don't know the house. I'm only just twelve years old and you're thirteen – you've got to stay here. I'm the one that's going.'

'I'd stay if I could,' Penny said. 'I can't take the boys in the house and I'm terrified one of them will run away if I stay here much longer. Please, do it for me and for Amy. I'm really, really sorry, I'll explain everything if you get a chance to come and see me later.'

'All right, I'll ring the doctor.'

Penny was almost in tears. 'Thank you so much, you're such a good friend.' Then she grabbed the hands of the two small boys and vanished around the corner.

Emily was horrified as not only did she not know anything about this house, she also didn't want to be responsible for Amy if she was very poorly. She was tempted to run off herself but decided she had to call for the local doctor, whoever that was. She didn't know a lot about measles but did know it could be serious.

She hesitated, not sure what would be the best thing to do. Before she made that telephone call, she'd better see just how ill Amy was as the doctor would want to know. She'd wait for him but wasn't going to go into the sickroom as she was quite sure measles was very infectious and she definitely wasn't going to bring it back to her house when they had a little baby and two elderly people living there.

Decision made, she headed into the kitchen. It was twice the size of the one at home, but didn't have a lovely modern gas cooker. She thought that someone who lived in such a grand house should have staff – then there'd be someone to deal with emergencies like this.

The house was quiet apart from the ticking of a loud clock somewhere in the passageway outside the kitchen.

It felt wrong creeping around in this house, even though she was being a good Samaritan. She walked down the long passageway and eventually emerged in a huge hall. Why would anybody want to live in a house this size? It was freezing and dark and gloomy.

At least she'd found the stairs and tiptoed up, although she knew that wasn't necessary. She was faced with alternative routes, and could count half a dozen closed doors on either side. It occurred to her that if Amy was unwell then the door of her bedroom would be open.

She remembered that at the big house in London where they used to live there were smaller stairs which led to the nursery floor and then more that led up to the attics where the servants slept. Before she started knocking on these closed doors she was going to investigate further.

The stairs she wanted were where she expected and like those in their London house they weren't carpeted and were much narrower than the main ones. She flew up them and emerged on a landing, wider than a passageway, but with no carpet or rugs on the floor and no furniture, although it was big enough to have loads. Fortunately, there were windows so it wasn't as dark as downstairs.

There was an open door halfway along and she hurried towards it. She didn't go in but looked through and saw a huddled shape in a large old-fashioned metal bed. This must be Amy but it was impossible to tell how ill her friend was and she certainly wasn't going in.

Penny must have done the same and then run back downstairs. She was puzzled that whilst she was in the house her friend hadn't made the call herself.

Emily was about to call out but there was no point as even if Amy wanted something she wouldn't be able to help her unless she risked catching whatever the girl had. Doris had done the sensible thing and she wished that she'd left with her, then Penny would have had to stay. There was something strange about the situation with the boys and Emily decided she'd go and find out after the doctor had been.

She ran downstairs and went in search of the telephone. It wasn't in the hall where she thought it might be but after opening and closing a dozen doors eventually she discovered an office and there was one on the desk.

She didn't know the name of the local doctor or his number but she did know how to ring Dr Cousins. Even if this wasn't his practice, she thought he might come over on the ferry or at least contact the doctor who should come.

She asked the operator to connect her and Mrs Cousins answered the telephone.

'Mrs Cousins, it's Emily Roby. I came across to Rowhedge to spend the day with friends and instead I find myself alone in a huge house and one of the girls I came to see is very poorly in bed. I'm sure she needs a doctor.'

'Good heavens, where are the girl's parents? Why have you been left to deal with this?'

Emily quickly explained the circumstances and Mrs Cousins was outraged. 'I know the house you mean, Dr Cousins is here. Quickly tell him what you've just told me.'

The doctor listened. 'You're quite right to remain outside the room, good girl. There's a measles epidemic in Rowhedge. The child shouldn't be on her own. Dr Radcliffe is away so I'm actually covering his patients this week. I'm leaving now and will be with you in half an hour hopefully.'

'Thank you.'

The line went dead and she'd been going to ask if she should try to contact Amy's parents. She was going to do this anyway – she certainly wasn't going to stay here so she needed to find someone to look after Amy.

Opening desk drawers in somebody else's office was something she'd never do under normal circumstances, but this was an emergency. It didn't take her long to find a notebook with numbers in it and one of them was a London number and Penny had said Amy's parents did something important in London.

* * *

Half an hour later, the doctor arrived and she had good news for him. 'I managed to speak to somebody who knew Amy's parents. They said that they'd get word to them and one or both will come home immediately.'

'Excellent work, I was going to do that myself once I've examined the patient. Why don't you make a nice pot of tea? I could certainly do with one and I'm sure a hot drink would make you feel better too.'

Emily explained where Dr Cousins would find Amy and he rushed off with his battered bag tucked under his arm. The tea was made by the time he returned, looking grave.

'I've called for an ambulance, my dear, your friend has pneumonia and needs to be in hospital. I really don't understand how her parents could have left her alone – she must have been extremely unwell this morning.'

'I don't think they were here last night, Dr Cousins. I remember that Amy told me she's often left by herself overnight when they have to work.'

'Good God, that's child neglect. She might be thirteen years old but she's not old enough to rattle around in this place on her own. Did you find any food in the pantry?'

'Not much, bread and a few eggs. I don't understand any of this. Why was I invited to spend the day here if her parents were away?'

'Probably because they *were* away, my dear, as it would give their daughter some company. It's just not good enough. They might have important jobs in the city but nothing is more important than the welfare of your own child.'

'Is pneumonia catching?' Emily asked.

'Yes, but if you've not been in the room you're in no danger.'

'What about you? You've been in there.'

'Part of my job, my dear, I think we medics become immune after a while.

Good – I can hear the ambulance coming. The note I've left on this table will be enough to tell the parents what's going on.'

'I'm not expected home until five o'clock so I'm going to walk over to my other friend and will spend the rest of the day there. Thank you so much for coming.'

* * *

Emily didn't wait for Amy to be brought down on the stretcher as that would be too upsetting. She supposed that the doctor would go in the ambulance with the girl as she could hardly go on her own, even if she was used to managing by herself.

She was able to dash across the lane and scramble over the stile into the field before the ambulance turned onto the drive. The sun was out, birds were singing, and if it wasn't for the sound of distant explosions, the roar of fighter planes in the sky, one could almost imagine it was a normal year.

As she was walking across to Penny's house, Doris called her over. 'Did the doctor come? What did he say? Is it the measles?'

'No, it's pneumonia, which is more serious. I left as the ambulance arrived. Pneumonia's catching as well so it's a good thing neither of us went into the bedroom.'

'It would have been quicker for you to get to the ferry from where you were, Emily.'

'I know, but I want to see Penny. I'm glad you called me over because I'm hoping you can tell me a bit more about those brothers of hers. From the way she was talking they are a bit out of control.'

'They're twins. They don't seem to understand what's dangerous or listen when it's explained to them. They'll climb on things and jump off, pick up glass and that, it ain't fair leaving that poor girl to look after them on her own.'

'Oh, I wondered if it might be something like that. She was desperate to get home, I suppose it's easier for her to keep them safe in their own surroundings. She asked me to call in – why don't you come with me? She's really nice.'

'No, ta, I ain't good with kiddies, even ones what behave proper.'

Doris pointed to a window that could just be seen above the unkempt hedge. 'I've heard your friend crying at night.'

'Golly, she must be crying really loudly if you can hear it from here,' Emily said.

* * *

This time when she knocked on the door it was opened almost immediately by one of the little boys, who seemed quite normal.

'Come in, big girl. Penny's in the garden.'

'Yes, thank you, I'd love to come in and help if I can. How old are you?' Emily asked and turned to shut the door.

'We're five. I'm Toby, he's Thomas.' The boy scowled and tried to dash past her.

She stopped him and slammed the door behind her. 'You can't go out on your own, Toby. Can you take me to Penny and your brother?'

He pointed towards the back of the house. 'They're in there. I don't like you.'

He stomped off, leaving her to find her own way. It wasn't hard as she could hear the other child screaming and Penny trying to calm him down.

Emily pushed open the door so hard it slammed against the wall. The noise made both of them look round. It had the desired effect as the little boy stopped screaming.

'Hello, I'm Emily, I've come to play hide-and-seek but I don't think I can because you make so much noise I'd be able to find you immediately.'

Toby crept past her and joined his brother. The boys sidled up to her.

'What's hide-and-seek? Tell us, we want to play it, Emily,' Toby said.

'I need to ask your sister's permission first as she's in charge.'

They turned to Penny. 'Please, please, can we play this game with her?'

'Yes, but I'm sure there are rules. Do you think you can follow the rules?'

Thomas nodded and after a few seconds Toby did too.

'Good, then Emily will explain how it works. I have to follow the rules too, that's how games have to be played.'

Whilst the boys and Penny had been talking, Emily had worked out a way that the game could be played that would entertain the children but still keep them safe.

'We're going to play a very special game of hide-and-seek – it's a team game. This is what happens. Penny and Thomas are one team and Toby and I are on the other.'

'Can Penny and I hide first?' Thomas asked, giving her a beaming smile.

'Yes, one go and then we'll change over,' Penny said.

Emily was now smiling. 'That'll be super. How long shall I count for? Where can you hide and where can't you?'

Penny spoke up quickly. 'Inside only, not in the kitchen or in the study. Downstairs for the first go and upstairs for the second. If you don't find us in ten minutes we get a point, if you do then you get one. The first one to two points can then stay as a hider or change to be a seeker.'

The two little boys had listened carefully. 'Is it better to be a seeker or a hider, Penny?' Thomas asked politely.

'I think both are brilliant.'

* * *

The game was such a success that Penny agreed they could play three games outside as long as they stayed in the back garden. Lunch was sandwiches and cake washed down with squash and every morsel vanished. There'd been the occasional moment when one or other of the twins had, for no apparent reason, become upset but this was quickly smoothed over.

They had boiled eggs and soldiers for tea and apple crumble and custard for dessert. The little boys were flagging and Penny begged Emily to help with bedtime.

'Of course I will, I really don't think you should be on your own with them. Does it happen very often?'

'No, not having them all day like this. The extra money really helps – we don't get a lot from the government to compensate for Dad not being here but in the army.'

'What time will your mother be back?' Emily asked.

'In about an hour – she's something important at the Britannia Works, Paxman's, on Hythe Hill. She'll be so thrilled to find the twins asleep in bed. I can't thank you enough, especially after what happened at Amy's.'

'I feel guilty that we've not thought about her at all. I think I'm going to go home past her house and see if someone's there and can tell me how she is.'

'What time do you have to be back?'

'My daddy's meeting me at the ferry at five o'clock.'

Penny looked absolutely appalled. 'It's nearly six. I didn't realise it was so late. Will you get into the most dreadful trouble?'

'I hope not when I explain. I'd better go, I'll see you at school on Monday.'

Emily was halfway down the lane when she saw her father approaching. She was over an hour late now. He was too far away for her to see if he was furious or upset or both.

Then she didn't care how he felt, she just needed a hug after spending such a stressful day. Forgetting she was supposed to be quite grown-up she flew towards him and he opened his arms and she jumped in.

'Sweetheart, I've been tearing my hair out, where the hell have you been? Didn't you wear your wristwatch today?'

He hugged her tight and kissed the top of her head before putting her down and looking at her sternly.

'I didn't wear it in case I got it wet on the ferry. I'm so sorry, didn't Mrs Cousins tell you what happened this morning?'

'Yes, she did, but in case you haven't noticed it's now after six o'clock in the evening. I checked next door and they said your friend is seriously ill but not critical. Her parents are with her at the hospital.'

'That's good. Am I in the most dreadful disgrace? Can I tell you what's been going on today and then you can decide if I might be forgiven?'

They walked down the hill, he still had his arm around her shoulders which she thought was a good sign. She told him everything and he listened without comment. He was very good at listening and being fair about things.

'On the one hand I'm immensely proud of the way you behaved today, how you helped out your friend in difficult circumstances. On the other, at no time did you think about your family worrying because you were missing. Why the hell didn't you ring us?'

This was the second time he'd used bad language and he only did that when he was very upset or very angry.

'They don't have a telephone, Daddy, I'd have had to go down to the village post office where the telephone box is. I'm sure I would have remembered if they'd had one. I have to be honest, until the boys were asleep I didn't think about the time.'

'Well, water under the bridge now, I suppose, I am proud of you but you have to do a great deal of apologising to your family. Your brothers wanted to come with me, thinking you might have fallen in the river, they'll be waiting at the other side.'

'I'm so sorry, I should have thought about my responsibilities at home and not just about helping Penny with hers.' They walked in silence for a bit but it wasn't a cross silence, just a friendly one.

'We're so lucky to be living at Harbour House, Daddy, I'd never have guessed that my new friends had such difficult home lives. I know I've only been friends with them for two weeks but I should have known how things were. I don't think I even asked. Isn't that dreadful?'

He squeezed her shoulder. 'No, sweetheart, it's perfectly normal. If your friends didn't mention it and seemed happy, why would you suspect there were difficulties at home? I expect they didn't want you to know.'

'The older I get, the more I realise I have so much to learn. I keep thinking that I'm quite adult and then this happens. Will I be allowed to come over and help Penny again?'

'I'd prefer it if you came over to rake about with her, that you didn't have to do what you did today, but I'll leave it up to you. As long as you make sure you catch the ferry home when you say you're going to then you can come again.'

Whilst he was being so kind, she thought she'd tell him about inviting Doris to come next Saturday. 'Is that all right? She isn't a grammar school girl, but she's kind and funny and she doesn't have an easy life either.'

'Of course Doris can come, if you like her then she's welcome. Your mother thinks you should learn to swim if you're going to be going over on the ferry, what do you think about that idea?'

'Absolutely not, the water's dirty and cold. I asked one of the people waiting to cross this morning and they said nobody has fallen in since somebody went home drunk from the pub ten years ago. He was fished out wet, sober and glad to be alive.'

Daddy laughed. Emily was just so happy to be going home after the stressful day she'd had.

Lily saw nothing of Patrick for two weeks and began to think that the trip to London had been forgotten. The blooming Germans had been bombing London every night so it was probably not a good idea to go there anyway.

After the kerfuffle with the major the other week he'd been in his right mind since which was a relief to everyone. He was such a nice old gent, really polite and the children loved him. Emily was happy as she'd got friends of her own and it was lovely to see her with the grammar school girl and the local one called Doris. The three of them got on well, if the laughing and mucking about was anything to go by. The other one, Lily couldn't remember if she'd been told her name, had recovered from pneumonia and was out of hospital but wouldn't be able to play or return to school for a few more weeks.

On Thursday, the first one in October, Patrick came round to the house. She knew it was him because Daphne sounded really excited. Frank had already pushed off to the Greyhound and she didn't mind that her daughter brought her dad in.

'Do you want a cuppa? I've just made it,' Lily asked him.

'No, ta, I had one before I came over. Sorry to come late but first chance I've got today to come round. Can you come to London on Saturday?'

'Please, Mum, say we can go. I know them blooming bombers are there every night but Dad reckons it's safe enough during the day,' Daphne said.

'I'm not sure there's any point, love, as with so many bombs being dropped and that there'll be nothing open, no restaurants or cinemas anyway.'

Patrick shook his head. 'I promise there'll be plenty to see and do. I know the museums and art galleries are closed as everything's been moved away, but Nelson's Column and the lions are still there, the Tower's still there and so's the Palace.'

'Crikey, are we going to see all those? We'd better put comfortable shoes on, Daphne love, as it'll be a lot of walking.'

'The underground's working just fine, we don't have to walk everywhere. I was thinking we'd have a bit of a look around then go to Piccadilly Circus. We can get a decent lunch there and then go to the pictures. They'll all be open.'

Daphne giggled. 'As long as they've not had a bomb dropped on them. What do we do if the siren goes off when we're there?'

'Go down the nearest tube station along with everyone else. Safe as houses down there, better than the other shelters,' Patrick said.

'Houses aren't safe, that's why we go into a shelter,' Lily said with a smile.

'Very droll. I always loved your sense of humour. I'll call round at nine o'clock Saturday and we'll catch the quarter past train. As long as there's been no bombs dropped on the line we should be at Liverpool Street around ten thirty. Plenty of time to enjoy ourselves.'

Daphne walked him out and he heard her asking when he was going to collect his things as that was the main reason they were going up to London. She couldn't hear the answer but she expected her daughter would tell her as they didn't have any secrets.

* * *

Mrs Roby was ever so good about her having Saturday morning off even with such short notice. 'I'm not sure if I envy you, Lily, or am worried about the risk involved. We seem to be rather protected in Wivenhoe, we hear the bombers, see the fighters, but so far they've not dropped anything on us.'

'That puzzles me too, Mrs Roby, as I'd have thought the three shipyards would be ever so easy to see from up there. All of them are doing war work too. I know they've been camouflaged but reckon some of the shipyards must be visible.'

'Nobody takes any notice of the siren any more which I'm not sure is sensible. Did you know that where Mr Roby works they've got a giant metal tube and the men can sit in that instead of going into the shelter?'

'To be honest, I don't know much about any of the shipyards. I can tell you a lot about canning fish and catching it but not about building ships.'

Lily went back to work and thought there were things she didn't know about what went on in Wivenhoe and she'd ask Patrick when they were on the train. She'd noticed the other day when he came round that he was looking ever so fit, he'd filled out so that Mrs Hatch must be feeding him well.

* * *

Fortunately, Saturday morning was fine and bright and Lily and Daphne were dressed in their Sunday best and waiting by the door, she was wearing a hat and gloves but Daphne refused to put on either. Patrick strolled up, looking very handsome in smart creased trousers, polished shoes and a nice jacket and tie.

'You scrub up well, Dad, wouldn't have recognised you as the bloke who came round a few weeks ago,' Daphne said.

'You look just the ticket too. I've never seen your mum with a hat and gloves on before.'

'That's because I didn't go to church back then and that's when I put these on. I didn't want to let either of you down. Do you think it's a bit much for a day trip to London?'

'Crikey, no, I'll be the proudest man on the train.'

Daphne giggled. 'Only on the train? I reckon Mum's the prettiest anywhere, not just on the train.'

He nodded, his eyes twinkling. 'Absolutely, love, I'll be fighting the blokes off with a stick.'

Now Lily laughed at his nonsense. 'Then you'll spend the entire day in police custody. Give over with your flattery, we both know I'm no oil painting.'

To her surprise, Daphne and Patrick stared at her as if she'd said something shocking.

'Don't be daft, you look smashing, even more beautiful than you were when we first met.'

'What, with these horrible glasses? You must be joking,' Lily said.

'There's nothing wrong with them. You don't need fancy glasses, they suit you just fine,' Patrick said sincerely.

'I don't believe you, but I appreciate you saying so. Now let's stop nattering and get on that train.'

The businessmen had already left hours ago but there were still plenty of passengers waiting on the platform. This train came from Clacton-on-Sea where the army had a training base all along the front which meant there'd be plenty of khaki already in the compartments.

Patrick seemed to know exactly where to stand and when the train rattled to a stop they were standing right in front of the door. There were a couple of blokes getting off but they were first to get on.

This was one of the trains with the narrow corridor and individual compartments. The second one they passed had three empty seats and even though the window seat was taken they could all sit together comfortably.

'I prefer to be facing the way I'm going,' he told them. 'What about you two?'

'I've never thought about it as I've only ever been to Colchester and you're not on the train long enough for it to matter,' Lily said.

'Same here, Dad, only one stop from St Botolph's station and I usually stand by the door, don't bother to sit down at all.'

Lily wasn't sure she was entirely comfortable with her daughter calling Patrick 'Dad' but she couldn't really complain. A bubble of happiness swelled in her chest. This was the first time they'd been out as a family. It hadn't happened when Daphne was little, and she and Patrick were working too hard for the three years they'd been together.

She caught a glimpse of herself in the window and smiled at her reflection. They were both right – why hadn't she realised she'd grown into her glasses?

The ticket inspector appeared at the door and clipped their tickets. The other four passengers were all soldiers but not men, they were ATS girls. They looked ever so smart and as the train steamed out of Wivenhoe one of the girls, she had stripes on her arm so must be a corporal or something, smiled at Lily.

'If we're going to be spending the next two hours together, why don't we get to know each other? We've got four days' leave and are going to Town to have a jolly good time. What about you three?'

'We're going to do the same. Our daughter's never been to London – where do you think we should go?'

One of the other girls chimed in. 'Trafalgar Square and Piccadilly Circus. You don't need to go anywhere else.'

Patrick nodded. 'In case you're wondering, I'm in a reserved occupation, I'm also medically unfit to serve.'

There'd been no need for him to say anything but she was glad that he did. She wouldn't want anyone thinking he was shirking his duty.

* * *

Patrick sat back and let the girls talk – he didn't feel uncomfortable being the only bloke with seven women. He couldn't believe his luck. When he'd been told he had to go back to Wivenhoe he'd not anticipated he'd be sitting in a train with his wife and daughter going on a jaunt to London – what a lucky bastard he was.

They huffed and puffed towards Chelmsford, occasionally having to shunt out of the way to let a troop or goods trains go past, but on the whole they were making good progress.

They'd just left Chelmsford when the unmistakable whine of a German bomber flying low directly overhead stopped the conversation. Daphne was sitting between him and Lily and she clutched his hand.

The ATS girls were silent, listening, probably thinking the same as he was. Were they hearing a lone dive bomber, a foolhardy pilot chancing his luck or was this the start of a massive raid?

He bit his lip. He should never have suggested this excursion. If anything happened to his precious family he'd not be able to live with himself. The noise of the engine faded. No further bombers followed.

'Bloody hell, I thought we were a gonner,' one of the girls said with a nervous laugh.

'They follow the railway into London,' another one added, although this was something they all knew.

'Dad, I wish we hadn't come. I don't think it's safe to be in London.'

'It's on its way back to Germany, Daphne love. It won't be dropping any bombs on us,' Patrick reassured his daughter.

'I agree with Daphne, Patrick, we'll get the next train back,' Lily said firmly. Then she looked across at him and smiled. 'I wouldn't mind having a wander around Chelmsford instead, Patrick, I've never been there either and neither has Daphne.'

The knot in his chest unravelled. 'Fair enough, Chelmsford it is. We should be at Ingatestone in ten minutes.' He glanced out of the window and recognised the landscape. 'We'll soon be approaching the station, can't be more than a few miles from here.'

'Why don't we get off there, Dad, and catch the next train back to Chelmsford?' Daphne suggested.

'We might be sitting on the platform for a bit, but if that's what you want to do, love, we'll do it.'

Patrick was about to get up when there was a hideous screeching. The carriage rocked violently, passengers were screaming further down the train, then the carriage started to tilt.

He threw himself across the seats in which his wife and daughter sat, braced his feet, gripped an armrest with one hand and the door handle with the other and prayed. At first the movement was slow, then gravity took over and the carriage plummeted sideways.

The ATS girls were flung from their seats. He hung on for grim death and even the bodies crashing into his back didn't make him lose his grip. The carriage was on its side, the windows on the ground, and the corridor side was now the roof. It continued to slide for several minutes.

He blotted out the crying, screams, the moans from the other occupants and prayed that the only two he cared about were unhurt. The movement stopped with a jolt that even his iron grip couldn't compete with.

Patrick crashed into the glass, his head ricocheting against it. There was a stabbing pain in the back of his head and for a second he blacked out. He breathed in a few times, trying to control his panic, knowing that as the only bloke in the carriage it was down to him to help the injured and get them to safety.

The compartment was full of dust, making it hard to see. Being deaf in one ear made it more difficult to know where the groans and moans were coming from.

Slowly he elbowed himself to a sitting position then struggled to his feet. 'Lily, Daphne, speak to me. Are you hurt?'

He reached out as he spoke and to his relief the hands of his wife and daughter entangled with his own.

'You saved us, Patrick, we're bruised and shocked but you kept us in our seats. Are you all right?'

'Same as you, love, battered and confused, but not hurt.' He wasn't sure that was true but he wasn't going to worry them. The moans and screams from injured passengers further down the carriage made it difficult to concentrate. But the ATS girls weren't the ones making the racket.

He rubbed the grit from his eyes, slowly scrambled to his feet, hearing the broken window crunch beneath them, and looked around. 'Are any of you seriously hurt? I've got a first-aid certificate; I can stop bleeding and splint a broken arm.'

His heart sank when he saw that one of the girls was lying at a peculiar angle, her head twisted against the window. He knew at once that she was dead. He didn't want his daughter to see this.

Carefully he lifted Daphne down so she was standing beside him and then Lily joined him. 'Keep very still, I'm not sure how stable this bloody thing is.'

Two of the ATS girls seemed unscathed, the other two were injured but not seriously, probably a broken arm, concussion, cuts and bruises, nothing fatal. No worse than him. The one in charge was getting them organised.

The carriage was rocking alarmingly. It could continue to slide or tip over completely at any moment.

'I'm going to try and open the compartment. The carriage door's just outside so it should be fairly easy to get out. I can hear rescuers coming. They'll have ladders. We need to get out of this compartment sharpish,' he said, his voice loud in the compartment.

Patrick was a tall man, just under six foot, he should be able to wriggle out of the door if he could get it open. The senior ATS girl spoke to him.

'If you give me a bunk up, I'll get out quicker than you can.'

That made sense. Better he stayed inside to deal with anything that might happen whilst they waited to escape.

'Right, up you come.' He cupped his hands and she put one foot in them and he lifted her so she could stand on his shoulders.

'Golly, this isn't as easy as I thought it would be. Just a minute, it's moving,' she said.

A much-needed blast of fresh air came into the compartment but also the sounds of the injured passengers, the weeping, was now much clearer and more distressing for all of them.

The girl wriggled through the door and moments later called back. 'You're right, the door's here. I can't see anybody but I can hear them. If you give another of my girls a bunk up she can join me. I think I'll be able to get her through the door so she can call for help.'

A second ATS repeated the process, a bit harder for him as she was shorter and heavier, but she managed to join the NCO outside in the passageway.

'Dad, I think this one's dead,' Daphne whispered to him.

'I know, love, don't look at her. Everyone else in here is more or less okay which is a blooming miracle in itself.'

Lily pushed what looked like a bit of torn material from her petticoat into his hand. 'You've got a massive cut on your head, Patrick, it's bleeding every-where. You need to hold this on it until a first aider can sort you out.'

Until she'd mentioned this he'd been ignoring the fact that he was injured. He did as she suggested but more to appease her than anything else as he didn't think it would make much difference. He could feel the sticky wetness running down the back of his neck.

Then help arrived. The two injured ATS were lifted out first, they wanted to take him next but he refused.

'Ladies first, take my wife and daughter. I reckon I can get myself out and you can deal with passengers who are seriously hurt.'

'Sir, you need immediate medical attention. From the amount of blood on your person you're seriously hurt yourself.'

Lily pushed him forward, as did his daughter. 'Go, Patrick, they'll take us next. You need to get that gash cleaned and stitches put in it.'

He stopped arguing as if he was honest he was feeling a bit lightheaded, probably due to the loss of blood. He slipped the loop of rope under his arms and then used his feet to help him scramble up whilst somebody on the other end heaved.

There was broken glass everywhere, injured people were being lifted out and those that were able to were scrambling out on their own. Presumably there were ladders against the side of the train for them to climb down.

Willing hands guided him to the ground and after that it was a bit of a blur. He wanted to say he was fine, that he'd wait for his family to be rescued, but his mouth was full of cotton wool and he couldn't form the words.

From a distance he heard a man talking to him but he didn't understand the question and wasn't able to answer him. He wasn't going to pass out until he was sure Lily and Daphne were safe.

'We're here, love, let them look after you. You're a hero, I'll make sure everybody knows what you did for us.'

That was the last thing he heard before everything went black.

12

Lily saw Patrick's eyes flicker then he flopped back unconscious. The doctor seemed unbothered by this and smiled up at her as he expertly tied a temporary bandage over the large cut.

'He'll do, ma'am, a nasty cut, substantial blood loss and concussion. He'll go in the next ambulance. You and your daughter travel with him – it'll be absolute chaos at the hospital and you don't want to get separated.'

'Thank you, doctor, he saved our lives. He'd have gone back to help others if he hadn't felt so poorly.'

'I'm sure he would have; he's a brave man. Fortunately, there have only been two fatalities amongst the passengers so far plus the engine driver and the stoker. A lot of broken bones, cuts, bruises and shock. It could have been so much worse.'

The man was grey-haired, probably nearing retirement, but none the worse for that. He got to his feet, nodded and moved on to the next stretcher.

Only now did she fully take in her surroundings – they'd been guided down the embankment, through a field and into what looked like a farmyard. The farmer and his wife and half a dozen land girls were inviting those that didn't need medical attention to go into the open-fronted barn.

People were arriving with blankets, garden chairs, and some WVS ladies had set up a tea stall and were doling it out to those able to stumble over to them.

'Daphne love, you're very quiet, are you all right?'

Her daughter nodded, but tears were trickling down her grubby cheeks. 'I never want to go on a train again, Mum, I'll stop at home in future.'

Lily thought now wasn't the time to point out that she wouldn't be able to get to work if she didn't travel on a train or at least a bus.

'Your dad's going to be all right, love, the doctor said so. Why don't you go over and get us both a nice cup of tea? I could do with a drink, I'm that cold and shivering.'

Immediately Daphne perked up. Having something to do when you were scared and upset was always a good thing.

A kind lady came up and put a blanket over Patrick then wrapped one around Lily's shoulders. 'There you are, it's shock, you know, it makes you cold. Is someone getting you a hot drink?'

'My daughter, ta. Do you know what caused the accident? Blooming bomber flew over us a few minutes earlier so it has to be something to do with that.'

'You're right, the wretched Nazi dropped a bomb on the railway line and the engine driver didn't have time to stop.'

The warmth of the blanket was beginning to make Lily feel a bit better and when Daphne came back with two piping-hot mugs of tea, more sugar in them than she liked, she took it gratefully.

The two of them finished the tea and her daughter ran back to the table with the mugs so somebody else could have a hot drink. It had certainly made Lily feel a lot better.

She was sitting beside Patrick, listening to his breathing, which sounded ever so quiet. Sometimes she thought he wasn't going to take another breath.

She scrambled to her feet and looked around for somebody who might know when the ambulance coming for him would be arriving. Then three drove into the yard, bells clanging, and her panic subsided.

The two ambulance drivers in the first vehicle jumped out and ran across to them with the stretcher.

'Is this Patrick Turner?'

'Yes, and I'm his wife and this is our daughter. The doctor said we must travel with him so we can be checked out. We both feel poorly.'

'Fair enough, I've no quibble with that,' he replied.

'What hospital are we going to?'

'High Woods in Brentwood. Not far from here. Follow us, love, as we've got to get a move on so the others can come in.'

* * *

Lily watched Patrick anxiously, praying that he'd wake up, open his eyes, but he remained unconscious, his colour deathly pale and the bandage around his head was already blood soaked.

An ambulance wasn't very comfortable for her and Daphne and must be even worse for the patient. Luckily, they arrived quickly and white-coated doctors were waiting with a trolley to take Patrick away.

They scarcely had time to shake out their skirts before the ambulance had driven away to collect the next patient from the train wreck. She and Daphne were ignored, and as she'd never been in a hospital in her life, thank God, she'd no idea where relatives should wait.

'Come on, Daphne love, we'd better go in and see what's what. I think it would be better to get a once-over from a doctor, don't you? I'm pretty sure I've got bits of glass stuck in my arm. What about you?'

'Just a bit bruised, I'm sure I haven't got anything wrong with me.' Daphne clutched Lily's arm. 'Dad's going to be all right, isn't he?'

'He didn't look at all well, but he's in the best place now. Remember the doctor who treated him at the farm said he'd recover.'

Until she'd mentioned her arm, Lily hadn't thought about it but now she looked down and saw the sleeve of her best cardigan had holes in it but strangely no sign of any blood.

A student nurse came up to them with a clipboard. 'I can see that your arm needs attention, ma'am, come with me and I'll take you to someone who can look at it. Did you come in the last ambulance?'

'We did, I'm Mrs Turner, my husband, Patrick Turner, was the emergency. They rushed off with him on a trolley and we didn't know where we should wait.'

'When your arm's been seen to, Mrs Turner, then somebody will show you where the relatives are waiting.'

The ward they were taken to was full of passengers from the train – most didn't appear to have serious injuries, just cuts and bruises like her. The doctors dealing with these things were so young she thought they were probably medical students.

'Sit there, Mrs Turner, somebody will get to you as soon as they can.' The student nurse pointed to empty chairs and Lily sat down gratefully, Daphne plonked beside her.

'I reckon we're in for a long wait, love, but I'm just thankful so few people died in that accident – it could have been much worse.'

'How long do you think it will take them to fill in the hole that the bomb made, Mum?'

'They'll have people doing it right now. They have to keep the railways running, troop movement and so on. Probably be normal service resumed by tomorrow.'

'I need the WC, I'm going to look for one,' Daphne said and dashed off to ask one of the nurses where she should go.

Before her daughter returned, a nurse called Lily over to one of the curtained cubicles. The young man waiting to look at her arm seemed competent enough.

'Let's get your cardigan off, Mrs Turner, and see what's made the holes.'

Moving the arm was painful so the nurse took over.

'Mmm, you've got bits of glass embedded in your forearm. Not dangerously deep, so I can remove them. You might need a stitch in a couple of them. If you're a bit squeamish, Mrs Turner, look the other way or close your eyes. This might sting a bit.'

Lily did what he suggested, gritted her teeth, and listened out for Daphne.

'My daughter won't know where I am, would you please have a quick peek and see if she's back from the you know where?'

The nurse nodded and looked out of the curtains but shook her head. 'I noticed her when you were sitting together and she looks just like you. You could be sisters.'

'I've been told that before, I was ever so young when I got married and had her. My husband's the one who's hurt really badly. He was unconscious when they brought him in. Is this going to take very long as I want to find out how he's doing?'

The nasty pain and tugging had now stopped. 'All done, I'll just put a stitch in the biggest one, then the nurse will put on a dressing and you can go in search of your missing family.'

* * *

Emily should have been going over to Rowhedge this Saturday but as Lily was going to London with Mr Turner and Daphne she couldn't go. Her parents had said that her friends could come over to Wivenhoe instead as long as they were happy to help out.

It wasn't possible for her to contact Doris to change the arrangement but Penny had agreed to call in on the way home from school yesterday. Doing domestic chores wasn't going to be nearly as boring if she had her friends with her.

George sidled up to her as she was collecting the dirty plates in the dining table. 'Emily, we want to go to Alresford on the train. We don't have enough money for the fare, can you lend it to us?'

'No, you'd have plenty of money if you did chores like I do and got an allowance. Anyway, I'm quite sure that our parents wouldn't allow you to go unsupervised.'

George pulled a face. 'Just because you're twelve now doesn't make you in charge. Sammy is ten next week and I'll be ten in November. You'll only be two years older than us then, not three.'

Emily laughed at his convoluted logic. 'It doesn't matter how old you are or how old I am, I'm not lending you any money. However, if you go and ask Mummy right now if you can both go then I'll give you the money because I'm a generous, kind sister.'

'You're the best. We'll go and ask right now, won't you, Sammy?'

'I'm not asking, it's your turn,' Sammy said and nipped behind Emily so George couldn't pinch him.

'Oh, blooming heck, I'll do it.' George stomped off and immediately Emily turned to her other brother.

'What's going on? Why do you want to go Alresford so urgently?'

Sammy shifted from foot to foot and wouldn't meet her eye.

'I'm waiting, I'm not giving you the train fare until I know what's going on.' It was always easier to prise information from Sammy than it was from George.

'Don't tell him that I told you, but we're going to see Nancy and take the dog out for a walk. George thinks that it would be easier to get permission to go to Alresford rather than Colchester on market day.'

'Good grief! Why do you two make things so complicated? Clear the rest of this table for me and take it into the scullery and I'll sort things out if I can.'

George was still hovering outside the sitting-room door, trying to pluck up the courage to go in. Emily wasn't surprised as none of them liked to lie to their parents.

'Thank goodness I've caught you, silly sausage, why do you think you won't be allowed to go to Colchester?'

'It's further away and it'll be busy, not like going after school on Wednesday.'

'I'll speak to her, as long as you're only going to Nancy's and are back here for lunch I don't see that'll be a problem.' She came to a decision, possibly not a wise one, but it would be far easier having the boys out from underfoot for the morning when she had her friends with her.

'Here, this is enough for a return ticket each and a few pennies to buy a lolly if you can find one. Do you promise to be back by lunchtime?'

'We do, we promise. Are you giving us permission?'

Emily nodded. 'I am, you two get off and then I'll speak to Mummy; it'll be too late for you to be called back.'

They didn't need telling twice but wisely left through the back door where they wouldn't be seen from the sitting room. She gave them a few minutes and then took a mug of tea into the sitting room.

Her baby sister was now crawling and everything had to be put out of the way of her eager little fingers. Even Ginger stayed off the floor when he saw the baby approaching.

'Mummy, do you want me to take Grace with me when I go and meet Doris and Penny in half an hour?'

'Yes, that would be lovely, thank you.'

'Also, I told the boys they could go into Colchester for the morning so they can take Nancy's dog out for a walk. I gave them the train fare from my allowance.'

'Making sure they're out of the way for some of the time that your friends are here – I don't blame you, darling girl, but you really should have asked me first.'

'I know, but if I'm old enough to replace Lily this morning then I decided I'm old enough to make little decisions like that sometimes.'

'Fair enough. I'm going to give the pram to Nancy, if I'd known the boys were going into town they could have taken it with them on the train.'

Emily giggled. 'Golly, that would have been worth seeing. I think Nancy said she's coming to see her family on Monday and I'm sure she'll call in. Are you sure that just using the pushchair for Grace is enough as it'll be winter in a few weeks and it's not nearly as cosy.'

'You're right, I haven't really thought this through. Nancy's baby isn't due till March so I'll keep the pram until after Christmas at least. Are you going to use that or the pushchair today?'

'The pram, she can see more from that because she's higher up.'

* * *

Grandma and Grandpa were going to be out for lunch as they'd made friends with some older people who lived at the grand end of Wivenhoe. Emily was smiling as she pushed the pram down to meet the ferry, thinking how lovely it was that both her grandparents were well and happy. She didn't like to ask if this was temporary or if her grandpa would become confused and agitated again at some point.

This was the second time that Penny and Doris had come over to Harbour House and although it was sad that Amy hadn't been able to join them, Emily was relieved that her other school friend was making a steady, if slow, recovery.

She didn't have long to wait as the ferry was already halfway across the river and she could see both of them. They had their backs to her so couldn't see her but that didn't matter as they'd be on terra firma in a few minutes.

She turned the pram so her sister could see and the baby was waving her arms and laughing and pointing.

'Yes, sweetheart, that's the ferry and it's bringing my friends. You like Doris and Penny and I promise that we'll play with you.'

Suddenly her hands clenched on the pram handle. There was the unmistakable drone of a German bomber approaching. She stared into the sky as she saw it flying overhead. The sirens didn't go off, this one must be on its own and going back to France or Germany.

She prayed it hadn't dropped its deadly cargo on anybody – so many people, women, children, old people, had not only had their houses blown to smithereens but hundreds of them had also been killed and thousands injured.

Mummy and Grandma had been involved in sending spare clothes, furniture, and so on to London. So far no bombs had been dropped anywhere near Wivenhoe or on Colchester. The London train had left a little while ago and she knew that Lily and her family would be on it. Going to London when there were German bombers around was very dangerous and she was concerned for them.

Penny and Doris loved the baby and Grace recognised them – or seemed to – and chortled and seemed to be actually waving, although she was too little to be able to do that.

'We've got the house to ourselves some of the time, girls,' Emily told them. 'My brothers have gone into Colchester for the morning, my grandparents are going out for lunch and my mother's taking this little darling with her when she goes for lunch somewhere very grand.'

'Where's that then?' Doris asked.

'Wivenhoe House – it's a huge house at the top of the village but the grounds run almost down to the woods. Mrs Cousins, the doctor's wife, is going too so I think it must be a ladies-only sort of thing.'

'So only us for lunch,' Penny said.

'Yes, we can listen to the wireless in the sitting room, read the magazines and generally pretend we're ladies of leisure. I think the wealthier women of Wivenhoe are getting together to talk about how they can help the families that have been made homeless by the bombing in London.'

Doris liked to push the pram as she'd had no experience with babies, being the youngest in her family, and was now walking slightly ahead. Emily was happy to let her friend do this and she'd dropped back to walk next to Penny.

'Have you been in to see Amy recently?'

'She's not there, none of them are. Mum said the parents are now living in London and she's been moved to Kent to live with her grandparents. We won't see her again, which is sad, but much better for her.'

'Goodness, I wonder who'll move into that huge house. I've got an idea; I'm going to suggest that Amy's house is requisitioned. I was only in it for a few minutes but I think there must be a dozen bedrooms, there's certainly a huge garden so plenty of room for children to play. I think they could get two or three homeless families living there.'

Doris stopped pushing and turned round to join in the conversation. 'That'd be grand, maybe I could do a bit of babysitting and earn some extra.'

'I doubt that those sorts of families could afford to pay anybody to do anything for them,' Emily said.

Doris shrugged and continued to push Grace. They'd now reached the end of West Street and were about to turn into the High Street. This was where most of the shops were and any day apart from Saturday there'd have been lots of eager housewives on the ferry. Today they'd have gone on the bus to Colchester as it was market day.

There was something going on and from the faces of the group of women blocking the pavement it wasn't anything good.

13

Patrick was disorientated. He could hear sounds, voices, but wasn't sure where he was or why he was there. He had a bloody awful headache – he knew that much. Then he heard a voice he recognised.

'Mum, I think Dad's moving, waking up again. I'll fetch the nurse,' Daphne said.

'It's all right, I can deal with it,' Lily answered.

He forced his eyes open and saw her sitting by his bed, her arm in a sling, her face pale and anxious. Daphne was standing next to her, looking down. She'd been crying.

The light hurt his eyes. He was going to throw up. Lily calmly held a basin in front of him as if she'd done it before. He couldn't apologise. He'd do that when he felt better. He flopped back on the pillows, closed his eyes and the welcome blackness overwhelmed him again.

* * *

The next time he came round he was aware he was in hospital, remembered the train accident, but had no idea how long he'd been there. His head hurt but not too badly and this time he wasn't going to be sick.

Lily and Daphne had gone, and he didn't blame them. They must have stayed until a doctor told them he was out of danger. The curtains were drawn on either side of his bed but open at the front so he could look across the ward.

A bloke about his age, in hospital pyjamas, was sitting up in his bed reading a paper. There was a cradle over his legs so obviously that's where his problem was.

Slowly Patrick used his elbows to lever himself into a sitting position, waiting for the nausea to overwhelm him, but it didn't. The light didn't hurt his eyes as much this time either.

'Excuse me, mate, what's the date today?'

The bloke looked up from his paper. 'I ain't sure, this is a week old at least. I know it's Monday – that much I can tell you.'

'Ta, that means I've been out of it for two days. Have you been here since I came in on Saturday?'

The man nodded. 'I lost me leg playing silly buggers on me motorbike. I've been here three weeks and it'll be another week at least before I can have crutches and start getting about a bit.'

'I'm sorry to hear that. I was in a train crash.'

'Crikey, we all know that. Man of the hour and all that, the newspapers wanted to take a photo of you but your missus wouldn't let them. You're a lucky bugger having those two. Cracking pair of girls you've got.'

Patrick knew he should explain how things really were but just for a day or two he could pretend they were the happy family this man thought they were.

A memory of Lily having her arm in a sling came back to him. A nurse walked briskly into view. 'Excellent, Mr Turner, I'm glad to see that you're now fully functioning. I expect you'd like—'

'I would, I don't think I'll get to the bathroom.'

The girl smiled, whipped across the curtain, giving him privacy, and then handed him the necessary item. She turned her back until he'd finished and then took it from him and discreetly covered it with a cloth.

'Mrs Turner and your daughter will be back soon. They'll be so pleased to see you awake.'

He didn't have time to ask any further questions as she whisked out of the curtains, somehow managing to flip it open so he was able to talk to the bloke opposite.

'I'm Patrick, pleased to meet you.'

'Sid, right back at you. It'll be grub time soon, ain't too bad considering it's a hospital. I reckon you'll be starving, not having eaten since you got here.'

Sid was right, Patrick thought he could do with something to eat but what he wanted more was to see his wife and daughter. He wanted to know why Lily had her arm in a sling.

He didn't have long to wait as he heard them coming. He was pretty sure hospitals had very strict policies about visitors and as nobody else had anyone by their bed they must be making an exception for him. He wasn't anybody's hero, but if it meant he could speak to Lily and Daphne then he'd go along with it for now.

His daughter arrived first and her joyous smile made him feel that he really was her dad, not some stranger who'd just turned up in her life.

'Dad, I'm so happy to see you awake and not being ill all the time.' She rushed across and hugged him. He returned the embrace. It was worth getting hurt for just that one hug.

'How are you still here? Where have you been sleeping? What about work?' He'd intended to say how delighted he was that they were there, to thank them for remaining with him, but he blurted out his worries instead.

Daphne sat on the bed which she knew would be forbidden. Lily pulled up the chair so she was sitting close to him.

'Mrs Roby sends her best wishes and hopes you make a speedy recovery. I popped round to Mrs Hatch and told her what had happened and she was really upset that you were hurt.'

'Right, but you haven't answered my questions, love. I don't want you getting into trouble on my account.'

'The Red Lion have been very understanding and Daphne can have the rest of the week off if she needs it, Mrs Roby has said the same to me.' She smiled and for the first time since he'd come back he began to believe that maybe there was a chance for him after all.

'The hospital have been amazing. We shouldn't be in here as it's not visiting time and Matron has just told us we can't stay. Daphne curled up on the end of the bed and I slept in this chair – well, tried to.'

'I'm sorry you had to be involved with my care,' Patrick said. 'You need to get home and get a decent night's sleep.'

Daphne giggled. 'We do, Dad, and we could both do with a wash.'

He laughed and they joined in. 'You're not the only ones, love. You get off home.' Then something occurred to him. 'How are you going to do that? Are the trains running now?'

'The army got the hole filled and the line mended in less than a day. We're getting a bus to Ingatestone station and will catch the train from there.'

Daphne pulled a face. 'I said I'd never go on a train again but that would be silly. When you're better and you can get another day off, Mum and I want to spend the day together like we planned before the accident.'

'Then that's what we'll do. I've still got to collect my things but they'll have to wait until I'm fitter. Did you say you've both got the rest of the week off?'

'Well, if you're well enough to leave then we should go back to work really,' Lily said. She was smiling as if understanding what he was thinking.

'If you go home, get a good night's sleep and a wash, then go round to my digs and get me something clean to put on, we can go to Chelmsford for the day. I don't reckon I'm up to traipsing around London just yet.'

The ward sister came up and pulled the curtains back with a rattle. Before she could complain about his family still being there, he asked the all-important question.

'Will I be discharged tomorrow? I've got to get back to work.'

'You can't be discharged until the doctor has seen you. You have a concussion, Mr Turner, that can be a very serious thing. Also, you won't be able to work until you've had your stitches out and your local doctor has agreed that you are fit enough.'

'Fair enough.' He winked at the girls and they grinned. 'Off you go then, ladies, I'll see you here bright and early with my clean clothes. I intend to leave whatever the doctor says.'

Sister was scowling at them so they waved at him and hurried off. He could hear them laughing and talking as they left.

They'd not been gone long when the welcome rumble of the food trolley could be heard entering the ward. It didn't matter how awful it was, he'd eat it; he was lightheaded from lack of food.

He realised he still didn't know what had happened to Lily's arm but that could wait until tomorrow.

* * *

Lily was still smiling when they arrived at the bus stop outside the station. They'd been told that the buses were supposed to go twice an hour so the most they'd have to wait was thirty minutes.

'What an adventure, Daphne, who'd have thought just going to London could end up the way it has?'

'Do you think that Dad's going to be well enough to come out with us tomorrow?'

'I don't, but we can just find somewhere nice for lunch. We don't have to go to the pictures or anything.'

'Why don't we stay overnight? Dad will feel better by the second day, won't he?'

'We'd have to stay in one room; we can't afford to get two. I'm not sure that would be a good idea.'

Daphne shook her head. 'Come on, Mum, after what we've been through together I'm sure you can manage to sleep in the same room. I'll take the double bed with you, and Dad can sleep on the camp bed or whatever it is they'll be putting up for me.'

'Got it all planned then? It gave me a such a shock when he was so ill, I didn't know I still had feelings for him, not after what he did.'

'Then that's all right then. I'm going to have my very own dad like my mates. I know it won't happen overnight, but I've seen the way he looks at you so I'm sure he feels the same.'

'Sometimes having feelings for each other isn't enough to make a marriage work. I've spent the last fourteen years wanting to be free of him, it's going to take me time to get used to how things are and how things might be in the future. Promise me, love, that you won't say anything to him. It's early days yet, we need to get to know each other again before we can think about being a couple.'

To her surprise, Daphne pulled a knowing face. 'He fancies you and you fancy him. I reckon you won't be able to stay away from each other. That'll suit me just fine.' Her daughter pulled a face. 'Mind you, being good-looking isn't everything and especially after what he did.'

'That's right, love, it's going to take a while for me to trust him again.'

* * *

The next morning they were fortunate and the bus was waiting at the station when they got off the train. Daphne was carrying their overnight bag as well as a larger one with Patrick's things. Men's clothes took up far more space than women's and he needed clean everything and they only needed night things and a wash bag.

They got off the bus and Daphne squealed, making those in the queue waiting to get on stare at her.

'Look, Dad's already here. How can he be dressed when we've got his clothes?'

'I expect the hospital laundry sorted him out. He certainly looks smart, not quite as smart as he did on Saturday, but he'll do.'

He'd obviously been waiting at the bus stop and he came forward with a smile that warmed her. He was a hundred times more attractive than he'd been when they'd first married.

'Here, Daphne love, give me the bags. I should have told you that the hospital had sorted out my clothes but I didn't know how. I could hardly ring Harbour House as then they'd know you were taking an extra day off.'

'Quick, I can see a bus coming the other way. Things are working out so well today,' Lily said.

He tucked his suitcase under his arm and held their overnight bag in his right hand. Now she was up close she could see he still looked a bit pale, but the stares they were getting were not because of his complexion but the impressive bandage that was wound around his head.

'I had to discharge myself. The doctor said I should remain where I was until the weekend.'

'In which case we're going straight back to Wivenhoe,' Lily said firmly. 'We can go to Chelmsford another time. I'm not having you collapse whilst we're galivanting around the place.'

She expected Daphne to complain, but her daughter nodded. 'You look a bit peaky, Dad, let's get you home. Here, you're not carrying anything.'

'Hang on a minute, I was looking forward to spending the day with my girls,' he protested but handed over both bags without argument. In fact, Lily thought it might be best to take him straight back into the hospital.

'I'm all right, love, don't you worry, just a bit dizzy. I'm not going back in. Mrs Hatch will look after me better than they can. I'll go straight there.'

'No, you won't, you're my husband and I'll look after you. We'll get you home and then you can go to bed in the spare room.'

Both of them looked at her as if surprised by her suggestion – she was shocked that she'd just claimed him as her husband. She hadn't meant to move things on so speedily, but she was stuck with it now.

'If you're quite sure, love, there's nowhere I'd rather be than back with you and Daphne. I just need a bit of kip; I'll be right as ninepence in a couple of days so neither of you need to look at me as if I'm at death's door.'

* * *

By the time they got off the train at Wivenhoe Patrick was no longer chatting, was deathly pale and the sooner he was in bed the happier both she and Daphne would be. Lily had to take his arm and guide him up the steps that led from the path beside the station to Clifton Terrace.

Daphne didn't need to be told to run ahead and get the door open. Only as they were approaching the front door did Lily remember they already had someone in the spare room.

'He can go in my room, Daphne, I'll share with you. He won't want to be with Frank, not when he's so poorly.'

If Patrick heard this exchange he didn't say so. She was pretty sure he was only moving one foot in front of the other by sheer willpower. If he collapsed out here they'd need to fetch help as there was no way she and Daphne would be able to shift him.

Somehow they pushed him up the stairs and into her bedroom. He wouldn't care that the sheets weren't fresh on, but she did.

'Sit on the edge of the bed, Patrick, we'll get you undressed. You can sleep in your underwear for now.'

He flopped back on the pillows and was either unconscious or asleep, she wasn't sure which. She didn't have to tell Daphne – her daughter shot off and the front door banged moments later. Hopefully the doctor would be at home and come at once.

Dr Cousins arrived promptly and checked Patrick thoroughly. 'He really should have stayed where he was, concussion can be very nasty. You've done the right thing bringing him here where you can keep an eye on him. Let him sleep, but I should have a receptacle ready just in case he vomits when he wakes up.'

'He was determined to come back to Wivenhoe, Dr Cousins, he didn't want us travelling all that way to visit him.'

'He can't be left alone today, Mrs Turner. I'll inform the Robys for you.'

'Ta, remember that they said I could have as long as I needed. Are you sure he shouldn't be back in hospital?'

'No, he'll recover more quickly in familiar surroundings. I'll call in again tomorrow morning. Don't hesitate to send for me if you're concerned.'

Daphne came in and straightened the covers. 'I heard what the doc said, Mum, I'm sure he knows what he's talking about but why's Dad still unconscious?'

'Your dad's asleep, Daphne love, he overdid it coming out of hospital too soon and then walking about and catching buses and trains so he could come home.'

'Well, he's home now, isn't he, Mum? You'll let him stay when he's well, won't you?'

They were interrupted by a quiet voice from the bed.

'I'll go when I'm well, don't worry. I'll not have Frank turfed out of his digs.'

Lily sat on the edge of the bed and looked down at him. 'You can stay here as long as you need to, love. Our Daphne can nip around to Queen's Road and tell Mrs Hatch what's what.'

He smiled, then his eyes flickered shut again.

'You sleep, Dad, you'll soon be better if you do,' Daphne said and leaned down and kissed Patrick on the cheek.

Lily knew then that whatever her feelings might be he was in their lives to stay. She'd not separate her daughter from the man she now loved or stop him from becoming a good dad to her.

14

Emily didn't just have her homework to do when she came back from school but also extra chores. Even Mummy had to do things she'd not done before because Lily was away looking after her husband. She was rather dreading the weekend as she wouldn't be able to spend time with her friends because there was so much to do at home. She was busy boiling eggs for breakfast before she and her brothers headed out for school when her father walked in.

'Emily, sweetheart, you've done sterling work this week and we all appreciate it,' Daddy said as he hugged her. 'Mr Turner is now well enough to return to his digs and Lily is going to work over the weekend to make up for the time she's missed.'

'I'm so glad he's better. Does that mean I can go to Rowhedge after all?'

'We thought that maybe you would like to take your friends out to lunch in Colchester and then go to the cinema as a thank you for everything you've done without complaint.'

'Goodness – thank you so much. That will be absolutely spiffing. Penny and I can make the arrangements at school today. She can tell Doris.'

'Excellent, make a day of it. Go in around ten o'clock then you can potter about the market and spend a bit of your pocket money if you want to. I'm sure Nancy will be pleased to see you, especially if you take her dog out for a walk.'

'If there's three of us then we can take Rusty, Annie's dog, as well as Boyd. She brings him with her when she comes to work. I can't wait to get to school and tell Penny.'

* * *

On Saturday morning, Emily was up and dressed in her new slacks and was ready to go, too excited to eat breakfast today. The only people not happy were her brothers, who thought it very unfair. They were told in no uncertain terms by Grandma, Grandpa and their parents that if they were as helpful then they would have got a treat too.

She promised to bring them back something and grudgingly they agreed not to make a fuss. She felt a bit mean dashing across the road and heading down towards the station when they were hanging over the front gate looking fed up.

It was standing-room only on the train as it was packed with housewives clutching baskets going in to seek bargains at the big Saturday-morning market. Emily thought that the Wivenhoe shops, and there were dozens of them, sold everything anyone could possibly want. She wasn't exactly sure how buying from a market stall worked as you wouldn't have your ration book with you as it would be lodged with whichever general store you decided to use.

Doris and Penny were meeting her at Nancy's shop in Head Street and she couldn't wait to collect both dogs and take them down to the river. That was going to be almost the best part of the day.

She went around to the back gate and as expected it was unbolted. She called out to the dogs so they would know she was coming in as they tended to knock her over if they hadn't been warned to behave themselves.

'Good morning, love, did we know you were coming?' Dan, Nancy's husband, who was captain on a Thames barge, was sitting on a chair outside the kitchen door drinking a mug of tea.

'Good morning, Mr Brooks. No, I've come unannounced but I hope not unwelcome. My friends are meeting me here and we were hoping we could take Rusty and Boyd down to the river.'

He grinned. The dogs had wandered over to greet her but were on their best behaviour. 'I was about to take them myself but I'd be happy for you and your friends to do it instead. I've got a bit of carpentry I need to be getting on with.'

'Should I go up and ask Annie if she minds?'

'No, she'll be happy for him to get some extra exercise. Everyone's talking about the train crash. I heard that Lily Turner's husband was a bit of a hero and badly injured. Is he all right now?'

'He is, thank you for asking. Lily's back at work and staying all day today which is why I can have the whole of Saturday to myself. I'm usually doing chores in the afternoon.'

The dogs alerted and turned to face the gate, wagging their tails. 'I think that must be my friends.'

Dan clipped the leads on both dogs and handed them to her. 'Be as long as you like, love, the more exercise these two get the better. Do you want to have lunch here?'

'That would be smashing, I don't really like going into restaurants and cafés without a grown-up. It was probably going to be a bag of chips and a bottle of pop.'

Nancy appeared. 'Morning, love, my mum's here today so she'll make sure there's something better than a bag of chips.'

Emily could hear Penny and Doris outside the gate. 'I'm just coming, girls, be ready to be licked to death.'

* * *

The dogs behaved impeccably and none of them minded being a bit damp after the dogs had shaken river water all over them.

'I'm right starving, but I've had a lovely time,' Doris said. She was leading Boyd and he was walking to heel as he always did. Penny had Rusty, who was also well behaved when on the lead.

'I wish we could have a dog,' Emily said with a sigh. 'I might ask if I could have a puppy for Christmas but I don't suppose my parents will agree. That's why I love coming here – obviously to see Nancy and Annie who both used to work at Harbour House – but also to be able to take out the dogs.'

'Are you quite sure they want to provide lunch for the three of us?' Penny said.

'Nancy wouldn't have offered if she didn't want to do it. My brothers and I come for tea every other Wednesday evening and we always bring a few extras if we can. The good thing about when I used to go to the farm and help out with the Peterson children was that the farmer's wife rewarded me with cracked eggs, cream and bacon.'

'Did you fancy that Peterson boy?' Doris said with a smirk. 'He sounds a bit of all right.'

'Good heavens, nothing like that. I know you two are now thirteen but I was only twelve last month. I look two or three years older but I'm really not at all grown-up inside.'

They were now in the narrow track that led behind the houses and had to walk single file. 'Cor, would you look at that? There's a blooming cat come to meet us,' Doris said.

'That's Tabby, he belongs to Nancy and Dan. He followed Boyd home a few weeks ago and now he lives there too. He catches rabbits and brings them back to feed the dogs,' Emily told them.

She dashed ahead so she could open the gate, almost tripping over the cat as he jumped on top of it a few seconds before she got there.

'Silly animal, it would be much easier for you to walk through like we do. You're just showing off,' she said and reached up and stroked Tabby, who purred loudly and remained where he was as she carefully opened the gate.

Dan was in his shirtsleeves and making what was quite obviously a baby's crib.

Mrs Bates, Nancy's mother, had been housekeeper at Harbour House before Lily took over which meant that Emily knew everybody very well but her friends hadn't met any of them.

She carefully introduced her best friends and after a few moments of awkwardness both Doris and Penny were joining in the chatter.

The house where Nancy and Dan lived had four floors, the haberdasher's shop at the front, a big kitchen and scullery at the back. There were lots of bedrooms and a sitting room upstairs but she rarely went up there.

Over lunch, Emily asked Nancy which cinema had the best film showing but none of the adults had been recently so couldn't give them any advice.

'There are four in Colchester so you've got plenty of choice. You're bound to find something that you want to see,' Mrs Bates said.

'I ain't never been to the pictures,' Doris said. 'I can't tell you what a treat it's been today to be out with me mates and doing things like this.'

'That makes it even better,' Emily said. 'So, it really doesn't matter where we go as it'll all be new to you.'

* * *

They emerged from the cinema blinking and giggling. They'd watched two old films, one with Charlie Chaplin and the other with the Keystone Cops – Emily had never laughed so much in her life and Doris swore she'd wet her knickers.

'The cartoon was all right too, but I ain't keen on the newsreel. Too blooming depressing,' Doris said. 'Ta ever so for taking me out today, Emily. Nan says would you both like to come for tea next Saturday?'

Emily didn't hesitate. 'I'd love to. I'll do my chores in the morning and come across after lunch. What about you, Penny? Will you be able to come or is your mum working?'

'I'm coming, I do more than enough and deserve a few hours to myself every week. Shall we meet you at the ferry at two thirty next Saturday?'

'Super, can't wait. Thank you both for coming. Daddy gave me enough for lunch but we didn't spend it. I'm going to try and find something for the boys in that little shop in Eld Lane.'

'Crikey, I wouldn't go in there on your own. It's dark and spooky, I bet it's full of spiders and things,' Penny said, laughing.

'Probably, but I don't mind either of those. It's also full of knickknacks, bits and bobs and other interesting second-hand items.'

Doris nudged her. 'What's a knickknack when it's at home? My nan uses the other one but a knickknack's a mystery to me.'

'I don't know the actual definition, but as far as I'm concerned a knickknack is the same as a bit or a bob,' Emily said.

'And both of them are the same as a thingamabob,' Penny said.

Emily hugged them both and then they went to find a bus to return them to Rowhedge, although it wouldn't take them much more than an hour to walk back if one didn't come.

She headed for the second-hand shop and pushed open the door. The glass on it was so grimy she hadn't been able to see into the interior. The bell rang noisily and Emily looked around and immediately regretted coming in.

A strange creaky voice called out from behind a beaded curtain. 'Just a tick, little girl, I'll be there in a minute. You have a look round.'

'I'm not sure that I want anything, sorry to bother you,' she called back and moved swiftly to the door.

The owner of the voice hobbled into the shop and her heart stopped pounding and her hands unclenched. The shopkeeper wasn't anyone to be frightened of, he was a tiny, wizened man with a lovely friendly smile.

'You came in for something, my dear, tell me what it was and I bet I can find it for you.'

'I wanted to buy something for my two brothers. They're mad about the RAF and are also obsessed with playing war games with their lead soldiers. I don't suppose you have anything like that?'

'Just a minute, I know the very thing. I've got a jigsaw puzzle somewhere with a Tiger Moth on it and three of the lead soldiers.'

'Goodness, how exciting. I'm not sure if I have enough money for both. I've got exactly half a crown but I need some of that to pay for my train fare home.'

'The jigsaw puzzle was given to me so you can have it for nothing. Soldiers are ninepence each.'

Emily did a quick sum in her head and realised she'd only be left with threepence and that wasn't enough to pay for her ticket.

'Could I please have just two of the soldiers?'

The old man rummaged about, firstly under the counter and put the jigsaw in front of her. Then he tottered over to the back of the shop and opened a drawer to remove two somewhat battered and faded Napoleonic soldiers.

'Here you are, that will be one shilling and sixpence please, young lady.'

Emily thanked him and dropped the soldiers into her trouser pocket and clutched the jigsaw puzzle in one hand. George and Sammy would be delighted with these gifts.

She was right and her brothers put the precious soldiers in the box with the others and then tipped the jigsaw out onto the dining-room table.

'This is absolutely spiffing, Emily, you must have spent all your money to buy such terrific gifts. These are better than birthday presents any day,' George said and actually gave her a hug.

'I'm glad you like them. I paid ninepence each for the soldiers and he gave me the jigsaw for nothing as somebody had given it to him. Next time we go to Nancy's for tea I'll take you there. It said on the door he doesn't close until six o'clock so we'll have time to call in on the way past.'

They spent the rest of the evening assembling the five-hundred-piece wooden jigsaw puzzle and Daddy and Mummy came in to help as it was so difficult. The boys didn't even mind that the aircraft on the front wasn't one of their precious fighter planes – anything to do with flying was good enough for them.

* * *

Patrick had had the stitches out but the doctor had said he couldn't go back to work until Wednesday at the earliest as he was still slightly concussed. Hammering and banging would be very bad for his head, Dr Cousins had insisted. This would mean he'd missed twelve days' work and he wasn't proud of that. He should be doing his bit like all the poor sods actually fighting, risking their lives for King and country.

It was Monday night and Mrs Hatch had invited his girls around for tea as today he could eat when everybody else did and not at some God-awful hour like eight o'clock or even later. He couldn't wait as although Mrs Hatch and Lily and Daphne knew each other in passing they'd not been formally introduced as his wife and daughter.

Since the train crash, things had changed and Lily no longer talked about him signing the divorce papers. Daphne was calling him Dad, and he couldn't believe his luck. He didn't deserve to be taken back, but he was going to do everything he could to make that happen.

They were coming at six, immediately after Lily finished at Harbour House, and it was almost that now. He was as nervous as a boy taking a girl out for the first time.

'Is there anything else I can do, Mrs Hatch? The table's laid, the garden's looking tidy, and I've just had a shave.'

'No, love, everything's ready. My old man's had his tea, that table thing you made to play chess on works a treat for his meals as well.'

'I can hear them turning into the passage. Ta ever so for inviting them, it means the world to me.'

'I know that, love, I'll do everything I can to smooth things over for you so you can get back with your wife and daughter. Mind you, I don't want to lose you, you've been an absolute treasure helping out like you have.'

Patrick didn't have time to answer as Lily and Daphne arrived at the back door. He wasn't sure if he should go forward and hug them and didn't want to overstep.

Daphne flew into his arms, which made things easier. Then Lily was standing beside him and he hugged her too and she didn't seem to mind.

'Lovely to see you both,' Mrs Hatch said from the back door. 'Come along in, everything's ready on the table.'

'Thank you so much for inviting us,' Lily said, 'we really appreciate you looking after Patrick so well.'

There was rabbit stew first and then apple pie and custard for afters. Every plate was cleared, every mouthful enjoyed.

'As always, Mrs Hatch, the meal was delicious,' Patrick said as he stood up and started collecting the plates. This was something he always did, initially his landlady had protested but she now let him do it.

'I'll make the tea and bring it through,' he called out.

'I'll help you,' Lily said and to his surprise and delight she arrived at his side.

He needed to speak to her privately and this gave him the perfect opportunity.

'I'm not clear to work until Wednesday so I'm going up to London tomorrow to collect my things. I can't leave them there much longer or my landlady will flog them off to someone.'

'I wish we could both come with you but I'm working. You won't be there when it's dark, will you?'

'Fat chance, I'm not stupid. Those blooming Nazis will be dropping bombs and incendiaries all over the East End by then and I don't intend to be there when they do.'

'Daphne and I were wondering if Mrs Hatch would agree to Frank swapping over with you? He's a nice bloke, I'm sure he'll do things for her like you have. Then you could come home.'

Boiling water slopped out of the kettle, luckily missing both of them. 'Crikey, are you sure? It's what I want more than anything in this world. I know I've got a lot of fence-mending to do before you'll even consider me being your husband again. But being your lodger will do me for now.'

Patrick carefully didn't draw attention to the fact that she'd said he was coming home, he didn't want to rock the boat and make her change her mind. She ignored what he'd said and just nodded.

'Then I'll leave you to speak to Mrs Hatch after we've gone.'

Later Lily was talking to his landlady about the impossibility of getting any kitchenware, that no shops had anything new as it was all going into the production of things needed for the war. He went outside to pump some water – he always did that before it got dark.

'Dad, can I come with you tomorrow? I could meet you at Colchester station. I can be there by one o'clock.'

'Don't see why not, we won't be stopping long but at least you can tell your mates you've been to London.'

Soon after that, the two of them left and he didn't think any more about the conversation. He was more concerned about how to break it to Mrs Hatch that he intended to move.

She nodded when he told her, was happy to have Frank instead of him living there.

'I'll come round and play chess with Mr Hatch when I can, I promise you I won't leave him in the lurch.'

'Go along with you, we don't expect you to keep on helping once you've moved.'

'It isn't helping, I enjoy the matches as much as he does. Frank's a good bloke; he'll do as much as I've been doing to help out. So, you're okay with this changeover?'

'I was expecting it, love, you should be with your family. You come whenever you want for a natter and a cuppa, you're always welcome here.'

'It'll be getting darker early in a few weeks so I'll have a bit more time. I'll definitely be around more often then.'

'Good, that'll be grand.'

'I'm fetching my things from London tomorrow so I'll take those straight to Clifton Terrace. I'll pack up everything else and move that before I catch the train.'

It occurred to him that maybe Frank wouldn't be as happy about this new arrangement as he was, but he'd not get a better billet than with Mrs Hatch – he'd be spoilt rotten like Patrick had been these past few weeks.

Patrick had heard the bombers heading for London for yet another devastating attack and realised it would be foolhardy to take his daughter to London in the circumstances. There could be a daylight raid as well as the regular night-time attacks and Daphne didn't have to be in the city.

'I'm just popping round to speak to Lily, Mrs Hatch, I won't be long.'

Daphne, luckily, was standing outside talking to a couple of her friends. She saw him approaching and ran across.

'Sorry, love, you can't come tomorrow, not with what's going on up there. Your mum would have my guts for garters if we got caught in an air raid.'

Instead of being cross, she looked relieved. 'I've been telling my mates and they said I'd be mad to go anywhere near the East End. I'd have come if you wanted me to but I'm glad I'm not going. Do you really have to fetch your things? Couldn't you just let them go?'

'No, everything's in short supply, I know clothes aren't rationed yet, but you still can't buy what you want. I've also got personal items I don't want to lose. As you're not coming, I'll probably go up earlier and should be back before there's anything to worry about.'

To his surprise, she stepped in and threw her arms around him. 'I'm so glad you came back, Dad, and although she won't admit it Mum's really pleased too.'

'Give her time, love, I treated you both appallingly and I don't deserve to be forgiven too easily. Tell your mum I'll be round in the morning with my stuff.'

'You'd better come before seven o'clock as that's when she leaves for work.'

'I'll be there. Good night, love, see you tomorrow evening.'

He stepped away and she ran back to her friends, who were watching the exchange with interest.

15

The air-raid siren wailed as Patrick was getting into bed but like most of the people in Wivenhoe, he ignored it. There'd been no bombs dropped within five miles and only the one German fighter plane shot down at the farm in Anglesea Road several weeks ago.

Patrick was up at six, played a game of chess with the old bloke, and then tucked into his last breakfast.

'Ta for everything, Mrs Hatch. I'd better get my things to my new digs before Lily goes to work.'

'You do that, son, and don't be a stranger. You and your family are welcome here any time.'

With his gas mask and haversack over one shoulder and his battered suitcase under his arm – carrying it by the handle was no longer possible – he walked the short distance to the end of the road, crossed the High Street and was at his old family home in good time.

The front door was open and he stopped and called down the passageway.

'Come in, Patrick, you'll have to leave your things in the front room until I've had time to tidy up there. Frank's packed up his stuff.'

'I'll bring it down and leave it by the door then he can grab it easily when he finishes work. Don't worry about cleaning the room – I'll do that.'

He was wondering why his daughter hadn't come up to speak to him when Lily joined him in the hall.

'Daphne was asked to go in really early this morning and do breakfasts. She's a hard-working girl and is saving for her bottom drawer.'

'Crikey, isn't sixteen a bit young to be thinking about putting things away for when she gets married? She's not courting already, is she?'

'Over my dead body,' Lily said with a smile. 'No, I should have called it saving for her future. She puts money away in her post office account every week, keeps back a couple of shillings for herself and gives the rest to me for her keep.'

'Good for her. Mind you, we married young so we can't really criticise if she wants to do the same.' This was the wrong thing to say as her happy smile vanished.

'And look what happened to us! I wouldn't wish that on anyone.'

'I'm sorry, that was a stupid thing to say. I'm a better and wiser man now, Lily love, and just want to prove it to you both. Do I come round to Harbour House to get the key when I get back from London?'

'No, I've got the spare one waiting for you.'

It didn't take him long to transfer his belongings to the empty chest of drawers and wardrobe – he didn't have much – but by the time he'd put Frank's two bags by the front door Lily had gone to work. He thought it significant that she hadn't said goodbye.

Patrick wanted to leave for London immediately but the trains would be packed with businessmen, people with more legitimate reasons to be using the train, so he decided to remain where he was until after lunch.

He left his ration book on the table for Lily to register it – he didn't know which shop she used for her groceries but thought it would probably be the one opposite Harbour House and not the smaller shop a few doors down from where he'd been living.

He looked out of the living-room window and smiled. The terraced garden was running wild. He'd make a start on that right now.

Patrick had managed to clear most of the weeds by one o'clock and they were now dumped in the compost bin. Tramping up and down the three lots of steps was hard work and he was hot, sweaty and knackered.

He stripped to the waist in the garden and tipped a jug of cold water over his head. He didn't want to go to London covered in dirt. His ablutions were interrupted by a neighbour calling out.

'Blimey, I'll go to the foot of my stairs, if it ain't Patrick Turner, large as life and twice as ugly, come back home again.'

Patrick grinned and turned to speak to Mrs Hobday – she'd been a friend to both of them when they'd first moved in and he'd always liked her.

'Good to see you too, Mrs Hobday. I'm lodging here, not living here, if you get what I mean.'

'I don't reckon it'll be long before your missus takes you back – you're twice the man you were when you left. If I was half me age I'd be there right now.'

He laughed and so did she. Mr Hobday was a fisherman and had his own boat down at the hard. A huge man and not a bloke anyone with sense would want to cross.

'Excuse me, I need to get dressed and catch the train.'

She returned to pegging out clothes on the line – the weather was still fine for the middle of October, which was good for the washing but not so good for those living in London – a clear day and night meant more bombing to come.

* * *

Patrick caught the train with a few minutes to spare and was fortunate to find a seat. He couldn't help tensing as they approached the stretch of track where the train had been derailed.

It steamed through and despite stopping at every station it arrived only half an hour late in Liverpool Street. So far the station hadn't taken a direct hit, but the Gothic tower and the glass roof showed signs of blast damage.

He walked out of the station into Bishopsgate and stopped, his eyes widened and he stared around in horror. There didn't seem to be a window that wasn't broken or a building that didn't have some sort of damage. Yet the market traders, the stallholders, the resilient men and women of the East End were walking about as if there was nothing unusual going on.

He cut down Middlesex Street and turned left into Wentworth Street where his old digs were. By some miracle, most of the houses were still standing, although there were a couple of missing buildings on the other side of the road.

He stopped to gawp – one of them had only the outside walls standing but there were still curtains fluttering in the broken windows. Next to it there was nothing but a pile of rubble – it was as if a giant had reached in and plucked the house out. If anyone had been inside when the bombs dropped they'd have perished.

Patrick didn't see anyone he knew but that was hardly surprising as it was now teatime and the men would be at work and the women too if their children had been evacuated and not returned last October as many had done.

The front door of his previous lodgings opened onto the pavement. The doorstep was scrubbed clean as always, the door knocker polished, and even though the windows were crisscrossed with tape they were still sparkling in the autumn sunshine.

The door opened and his previous landlady greeted him with a friendly smile despite the fact that she'd had to hang onto his stuff for far longer than he'd expected.

'Mavis, I've finally come to collect my things. I'm sorry it's taken me so long.'

'Never mind that, love, you come along in and have a bite to eat. You can tell me how you got injured – I can see a nasty cut just healing on your head.'

'If you've got the time I'd love to catch up. I'm not going for the train until after the rush-hour, so I've got a couple of hours to spare.'

He followed her into the familiar house, the narrow passageway was as immaculate as always and there was an appetising smell of something meaty cooking in the kitchen at the rear of the building.

These terraced houses had running water in the house but they shared an outside privy with their neighbours. There was no room in the communal yard for more than a few washing lines.

'Did they finish building the shelter for this neighbourhood, Mavis?'

'They did but me and my Bobby don't use it, we go down the station and into the underground tunnels. It's a lot safer there.'

'I'll get my stuff and put it by the front door. Where is it?'

'It's behind the sofa in the front room – we don't use that so it was the best place for it. We've got another nice young bloke living here now, he's an auxiliary fireman and waiting for his call-up papers.'

'He'll be kept busy every night, I reckon he'll find it safer and quieter in the army,' Patrick said as he pushed open the front room door to fetch his belongings. He put them on the bottom stair, out of the way, but easy for him to grab when he left.

Sometime later, he glanced at the kitchen clock ticking noisily on the dresser. 'Good God, I'd better get going, thanks for the tea and sandwiches – I like a bit of spam and piccalilli.'

He hugged her and collected his things. He was halfway down Wentworth Street, almost at the junction, when the sirens wailed. He thought the raids didn't start until dark but obviously he was wrong.

* * *

Lily was happy to be at work where she didn't have to think about Patrick. She still wasn't sure if she was ready to become his wife again. She was doing it for Daphne, not for herself, at least that's what she'd tell anyone who asked.

Gladys, who came in to clean three times a week, and to see to the laundry, would be doing the bedrooms later. She'd got on with the washing and ironing whilst the family were still upstairs.

'Morning, Lily, you get out the wrong side of the bed this morning? Where's your sunny smile?' she said as she tied her pinny around her ample waist.

'Things on my mind, I'm fine, thanks for asking. I'll leave you to get on.'

The three children were down first, smartly dressed in their posh uniforms – the purple blazers the boys wore were very distinctive. Emily's was just plain navy blue.

'Remember, Lily, tonight we don't come home for tea as we have it with Nancy,' Emily said.

'I'd not forgotten, don't you worry. Do you want porridge or just scrambled eggs on toast?'

None of them wanted porridge and she didn't blame them; she wasn't fond of it herself, but the major loved it so she made sure he had it every morning.

Mr Roby had already left; there was a bit of rush on at the shipyard and he was working all hours at the moment. Mrs Roby was spending the morning with the doctor's wife, along with a few other mums and their babies who were knitting balaclavas and socks for sailors.

No new wool was available so they had to unravel old jumpers and cardies and then wind the wool into a ball and use that. Lily didn't think the sailors would mind as long as they'd something warm on their head and their feet.

The grandparents always came down later which made sense as it was noisy and busy first thing.

'Good morning, Mrs Roby, Major Roby. Are you both having porridge today?' She always asked, even though she knew the answer, as it was polite to do so.

'Not for me, thank you, Lily, but my husband will have it as usual. If you've got any cornflakes and some spare sugar, then I'll have that.'

'Are you going to be in for lunch?'

'Not today, we're going to catch the train into Colchester and will have lunch at the Red Lion.'

'Daphne's doing the pies today, you'll be in for a treat,' Lily said proudly.

'That's what I hoped, my dear, we've heard a lot about these pies and I can't wait to try one for myself,' the major said, and his eyes twinkled. He was a really attractive old gentleman and it was obvious where Mr Roby had got his good looks. She didn't remind him that he'd eaten a pie before as that was the last time he'd been confused.

She left them to their breakfast and finished the washing up from earlier before taking in their scrambled eggs on toast. The major was a slow eater and didn't like to be rushed. Lily had noticed that although he hadn't been unwell recently, hadn't wandered off and got lost, he did seem to be slowing down, taking longer to do things than he had when he'd first arrived. No one in the family appeared to be worried and it wasn't really any of her business.

* * *

Lily was laying the table later that day when Mrs Roby senior came in to speak to her.

'Something smells tasty, have we got jacket potatoes tonight, Lily?'

'You have, along with a nice bowl of cabbage, sausages and gravy. Afters is apple pie and custard.'

'Then I can dish that up for the four of us. Why don't you finish early tonight?'

'Are you sure? The sausages are cooked and in the slow oven with the cabbage. I was going to serve the pie and custard cold.'

'That sounds perfect, my dear. You run along; it'll be a treat for me to have something useful to do.'

Daphne was home and busy in the kitchen. 'Hey, Mum, see what Dad's done out the back,' she called.

Lily hung her coat on the rack by the front door and hurried into the living room. The window in here overlooked the garden and she beamed. Patrick had cleared all the weeds and the cabbages and sprouts she'd planted in the spring were standing proudly in the beds and no longer invisible under the nettles, dandelions and other weeds.

Her daughter joined her at the window. 'Now it's clear we could have a few chickens down there, or maybe rabbits. It would give us extra to eat.'

'Chickens for eggs, but not to eat and certainly not rabbits unless you're prepared to wring their necks. I'm certainly not.'

'Maybe Dad would do it – he's a bloke – it's the sort of thing a man could do, especially during the war.'

Lily smiled. 'You're right, if our menfolk can go out and kill other human beings then they should be able to do the same to a chicken or a rabbit. You can ask him when he gets home – as long as I don't have to be involved, the two of you can set up a menagerie at the bottom of the garden. Whatever you put down there will be covered in smoke as the trains go past so close – I wonder if that will change the taste of the eggs?'

'Shouldn't think so. I know that the Peterson farm have chickens – I'll walk up there after I've spoken to Dad and see if they've got some pullets for sale or failing that maybe half a dozen fertilised eggs we can have.'

'How would we hatch them out? You need a broody hen,' Lily said.

'Someone at work said you just put them in some cotton wool and put them under a lamp.'

'Well, we're not doing that, young lady, as I know who'd be the muggins looking after the eggs and chicks if we got any.'

Daphne grinned. 'Fair enough. I wonder what time Dad will be back – I doubt he left all that long ago. It would have taken him hours to clear the garden.'

Lily frowned. 'I hope he gets back before dark when the raids start.'

'He's not daft, Mum, he won't hang around any longer than he has to. I reckon he'll be back by eight o'clock at the latest.'

Lily glanced at the clock on the mantel shelf and saw it was already six – even with double summer time it still got dark by nine. The German bombers didn't always come in following the railway line to London but often did. The siren went off as they approached but nobody took any notice and just carried on as usual.

It would be different in London – the poor folk there were being bombed every night and sometimes during the day as well. She thanked God that in Wivenhoe so far the only casualties had been service people and no civilians.

* * *

Emily was the first to leave Greyfriars that Wednesday night as she'd arranged to meet the boys at the funny little joke and toyshop in Eld Lane. Nancy wouldn't mind if they were half an hour later than usual and her brothers didn't want to risk the shop being shut when they left to catch the train later.

Running in school uniform was absolutely forbidden and there was always the chance she'd be seen by a prefect from the senior school – she was pretty sure no junior prefect from Greyfriars would be on the prowl just yet.

She hurry-walked down Queen's Street and turned into Eld Lane halfway down. She waved as she saw her brothers heading towards her. They met outside the little shop which looked as strange and deserted as it had the other day.

'It's like something from a fairy story – do you think the old man's a wizard?' George asked.

'You will have to decide for yourselves. Let's go in, we mustn't take too long here or Nancy will be worried. Did you bring your pocket money?'

They both nodded but looked less eager to go in than they had a few moments before. Emily smiled and pushed the door open. The bell jangled and the door seemed to close itself behind them, leaving them in semi-gloom.

'Hello, I've brought my brothers to see you,' Emily called out as confidently as she could.

The bead curtain rattled and the strange little man pushed his way through it. 'Ah, the young lady who bought the soldiers and took my jigsaw puzzle as a gift.'

George and Sammy emerged from behind her and rushed up to the counter, no longer nervous.

'Thank you so much, sir, for giving us the puzzle. It took the entire family a whole night to do it,' George said.

'It's back in the box now, but we're going to do it again at the weekend. Thank you very much for your generosity, sir,' Sammy added.

'Well, what a treat to have such polite young people in my shop. I'm glad that you enjoyed doing my puzzle. Did you come in to say thank you or are you looking for something else to purchase?'

'Do you still have the other soldier, the one Emily couldn't afford last time?' George asked.

'Not only do I have that one, young sir, but I have found three more. If you buy them all you can have them for – let me see, two and sixpence instead of three shillings.'

The boys turned to Emily. She nodded. 'I'll lend you sixpence as I know you only have two shillings.'

The transaction was completed to the satisfaction of all of them and ignoring the risks they ran all the way to Head Street, around the back into the alley behind Nancy's haberdashery shop.

'Rusty, Boyd, it's us, we're coming in,' Emily called out.

* * *

As they were walking back from Wivenhoe station, the siren began to howl. They ran along Station Road and burst into their front garden but didn't go any further. Even Emily wanted to see just how many planes the Luftwaffe were bringing across to bomb London this evening.

16

Patrick saw people heading for an aboveground shelter and was tempted to avoid it and head for the station and go down into the tunnels where it would be safer. Mavis hadn't explained why they didn't like these shelters but if they didn't want to go in one then neither did he. Then he was accosted by an irate ARP warden.

'Stop buggering about, mate, them bleeding bombers will be here any moment. Can't you hear them? You got cloth ears? Get in the shelter or you'll be blown to smithereens.'

Patrick joined the queue pushing their way in and gagged as he got to the door. The stench of crap was overwhelming. Someone should have emptied the bucket.

'No, sorry, I'm not going in there. I'll take my chances,' he said to the warden and dodged sideways so the man couldn't shove him in.

Seconds later, the door to the shelter slammed in his face, leaving him in the street to face the oncoming horde of German planes. He stared up into the sky, the black dots seemed too far up to be dangerous, the strange, unbalanced engines loud but not deafening. Then each one dropped a string of what looked like little black cylinders – bombs – and hundreds of them.

It was too late to run for shelter at Liverpool Street, he'd have to take his chances here. The street was empty, but the sky wasn't. He was opposite the bombsites and, like lightning not striking in the same place twice, he thought he'd probably be as safe hiding in there as anywhere else.

He scrambled into the pit left by the vanished house – he wasn't stupid enough to go anywhere near the one about to collapse – and cowered against the nearest pile of rubble clutching his haversack, holdall and suitcase.

From where he was crouched, he could watch what was happening. There were parachutes dropping but there weren't German spies dangling below them unless they were hidden inside the large black containers. These must be another sort of hideous bomb – he'd read about some sort of land-mines being dropped from the sky and had thought it nonsense until now.

The noise was horrendous. Screeching, banging, explosions – so far nothing had dropped on Wentworth Street. Hurricanes and Spitfires screamed over-head. Two of them shot down a bomber which spiralled in flames towards the Thames. If that dropped on any houses it would be as catastrophic as a bomb.

The air was full of dust, he could smell fire but could no longer see anything. Bombs must have landed somewhere in the vicinity. He dropped his head, covering it with his arms – not that doing this would protect him but it made him feel as if he was taking cover.

Hundreds of Junkers – he thought that's what they were but wasn't sure – released their deadly cargo and after doing so turned tail to run away from the RAF who were doing their best to shoot them down. Hopefully, they'd turned back as many as had got through the cordon.

The raid lasted only twenty minutes or so and then the sky was clear of German aircraft and the continuous wail of the all-clear sounded. Patrick heard bells clanging, voices shouting, the rescue services were already on the move.

He stood and brushed as much of the debris and dust from his clothes as he could. He recovered his belongings, tossed them over the edge of the crater and scrambled up after them.

Women were screaming and it sounded close by. He dropped his things back down the hole and ran towards the cries. Just then he stopped, his eyes widened. A bomb had dropped directly on the shelter he'd been going to go into.

For a moment he was frozen – he'd not expected to be facing such horror. Then he joined half a dozen blokes who were frantically pulling away chunks of concrete in the hope of finding someone alive. The screams hadn't been coming from the shelter but from the women who'd emerged from somewhere they'd been hiding and seen the total devastation of the building that was supposed to protect those inside.

The blast had blown the walls of the shelter out and the thick concrete roof had dropped on top of those within it, killing everybody instantly.

Someone gripped his shoulder. 'Leave it to us, it'll be body bits in there and you don't want to see that if you don't have to.'

Patrick straightened and saw the man speaking to him was a fireman. 'Why did this happen? They should have been safe. It's a shelter, for God's sake. What's the point of going in there if the bloody thing collapses on top of you?'

'It's why they call these sodding things "sandwich shelters". The government put them up too fast and without enough cement to hold the bricks together. The poor buggers inside are the meat and the concrete floor and roof are the bread.'

Patrick shook his head. What could he say? Fifty or so innocent civilians had just died because of government incompetence – he blinked back tears, swallowed bile in his mouth, and backed away. Bastard Germans! He wished he wasn't deaf in one ear and could kill some of them himself.

He stumbled to the bomb crater and collapsed on the edge with his feet dangling. For some reason he didn't have the energy to drop down and get his stuff. It could have so easily been him in that shelter and this thought kept running through his head. Twice now he'd been spared – was the big man upstairs trying to tell them something? Trying to tell him that his life was worth living and it wasn't his time to die?

'You all right, mate?'

Patrick glanced up and saw the sympathetic face of an elderly policeman staring down at him.

'I'm tickety-boo, ta, constable. I should have been in that shelter – just thanking God I wasn't.'

'You get on home to your missus, lad, there's hundreds of families lost loved ones tonight. Be thankful you weren't one of them.'

Ten minutes later, Patrick was getting onto a train along with dozens of others. No one was talking, many of them were as dishevelled as he was, he slumped into a corner seat, his bags and case balanced in his lap. This way he'd be able to hide behind them and not have to look at anyone.

The compartment filled up, not just with people but with fag smoke. This would have annoyed him normally but tonight he didn't care. He was alive – that was a bloody miracle and he wasn't going to take his life for granted again.

The train left eventually, he wasn't sure if it was late or not as he didn't know what the time was. The station signs had been removed but it was still just light enough to recognise where they stopped.

Patrick wasn't even sure if he was on a Clacton train or one that went to Norwich. He swivelled and asked the man sitting next to him.

'Clacton or Norwich?'

'Clacton,' the man replied.

There was no need for further conversation. Everybody in the compartment must have been involved in some way with the air raid. He couldn't help wondering how many passengers who usually travelled weren't on the train tonight.

* * *

Patrick shuffled out of the compartment as soon as they steamed through Hythe station as Wivenhoe was only a few miles down the track. He appeared to be the only person getting out of this door – the businessmen were probably all safely at home.

He unhooked the leather strap on the inside of the door, dropped the window and leaned out to turn the handle. The guard didn't ask to see his ticket, just nodded him through the gate.

Walking along the narrow path that led to Clifton Terrace gave him a few moments to breathe in fresh, untainted evening air. He hadn't decided what to tell Lily or Daphne, but they'd guess he'd been in some sort of situation because of his clothes.

The steps at the end of the path were almost too much for him. He didn't know why he was knackered, he'd not been blown up, hadn't done anything useful at all. Then as he approached his home he remembered he'd spent five hours digging the garden this morning. Small wonder he was aching and ready for his bed. He was also officially off sick so shouldn't really be doing anything strenuous.

* * *

When Lily had seen wave after wave of German bombers heading for London a couple of hours ago they'd given her a sinking feeling in her stomach. They were supposed to come when it was dark, not in the afternoon. Patrick was up there, in the East End, which was where most of the bombs were being dropped.

The radio crackled and hissed, the evening concert no longer audible, and Daphne got up to twiddle the knobs and put it back on the right wavelength.

'Dad should be home by now; there've been two trains go past in the last hour. I thought he'd have been on one of them.'

'Don't worry about him, love, he's been living in London for years. He'll know where to go to be safe.'

'He'd better. We've just got him back, Mum, I don't want to lose him again. I'm so glad that he can't be called up when it comes to his age group. We'll all be safe if we stay in Wivenhoe, won't we?'

'We will, love. Why don't you nip upstairs and see that his room's looking nice? There's a few marigolds and that growing along the edge of the garden, why don't you pick some of those and put them in a jam jar on his chest of drawers?'

Daphne dashed off, leaving Lily to process her feelings. Her daughter was assuming that she felt the same about Patrick, but she wasn't sure that she did. He was still legally her husband but they hadn't lived together for fourteen years and they were different people now. He didn't look like the boy she'd married and she didn't look like the girl she was back then.

She smiled. They'd met when they were about the same age as their Daphne – hardly surprising that the marriage hadn't lasted. If he'd stayed, no doubt she'd have half a dozen children, would have lost her figure, be scrimping and saving to put food on the table for the family.

As it was she was comfortably off, had found a job that suited her, was putting a bit aside every week and couldn't be happier. Daphne came in with a bunch of marigolds, a few straggly buttercups and a single pink rose.

'Blimey, I didn't know that was still alive. Your dad gave me that when you were born.'

'He's cut it back and what's left looks healthy. Imagine, this rose is as old as me.'

Lily laughed. 'The bush might be your age, love, but that rose will be no more than a few days old.'

'Do you think Dad will remember about the rose?'

'I'm sure he pruned it and made it look nice because it means something to him – to both of us.'

Daphne arranged the flowers in the jar and headed for the door. She turned before she left. 'I'm praying that you and he will fall in love again so we can be a proper family.'

Fortunately, her daughter didn't wait for a reply as Lily didn't have one that made sense. There was no doubt that she found Patrick physically attractive, that it wouldn't take much to entice her into his bed, but that wasn't the same as being in love. Maybe that would come when he was living under the same roof as her.

It was hard to concentrate on anything, even listening to her favourite programme, *It's That Man Again*, known by everyone as *ITMA*, as she and Daphne were aware that since the bombers had flown overhead no trains had gone past the bottom of the garden. Lily got on with some mending that didn't really need doing to occupy her fingers and her mind – her daughter was trying to immerse herself in a book she'd borrowed from a friend.

'Do you think Dad will want some supper when he gets here?'

'There's a nice bit of that pie you brought back left over from our tea. It's just as tasty cold as hot. There's some mash as well – that'll be good dusted with a bit of flour and fried in some lard.'

Lily could do all this herself but the book Daphne was pretending to read was upside down so better for her to keep busy. The next hour dragged. The blackouts were drawn so they couldn't see what was going on outside but the sound of a train stopping at the station made them both sit up.

This was the first one since the all-clear went hours ago – if he wasn't on it then maybe he wasn't coming home today. She shuddered.

'I'm going to walk to the steps. I can't sit here another minute worrying myself frantic,' Lily said.

Not waiting for an answer, or bothering to grab her coat even though the

October night was chilly, she slipped behind the blackout curtain that hung across the front door and ran across the small front yard and into the road.

She'd been in such a rush she'd not even thought to pick up her torch, but the moon was bright enough to see. Half a dozen shadowy shapes appeared and she wished all of them good evening as they walked past.

None of them was the person she was praying for. Then, a few minutes after the last passenger had disappeared into the darkness, Patrick was there. She ran towards him. He dropped his bags, opened his arms and she flung herself into them.

'We thought you were dead. We thought you'd been bombed. Daphne has made you a nice supper. I'm so pleased to see you—' Lily knew she was babbling and looked up.

'I'm here, love, I'm sorry you were so worried. I'll tell you what happened in a bit and why I've been so long. I'm fine but it could have been different.'

'Here, I'll take one of these bags. I can't see you properly in the moonlight, but I can tell you're in a bad way.'

'Ta, all I need is a wash – I'm covered in brick dust and God knows what. Then whatever's going will be lovely as long as there's plenty of tea.'

She'd left the front door ajar – no light got round the thick curtain so she wouldn't be shouted at by the ARP warden. As soon as they were inside she put his bag on the bottom of the stairs and turned to look at him.

Her eyes widened. 'My God, you've got cuts and scratches all over your face. Did you know that?'

'No wonder I got some funny looks – it's superficial, love, nothing to worry about.'

Daphne erupted from the back of the house and ran right into his arms. He hugged her.

'I'll fill a jug with hot water for you, Patrick, and fetch you a clean towel. I reckon you'll want to clean up in your bedroom.'

It would be good to hear him moving about upstairs. He was back where he belonged and they needed to try and make a go of it for Daphne's sake. Lily handed him the jug and he smiled and walked slowly up the stairs to his room.

'I'll just take his things to him, Daphne.'

Lily carried them up and put them outside the door. She knocked and called out to him. 'Your bags are outside in case you need anything, Patrick.'

Daphne was hovering anxiously in the passageway. 'What did he say to you when you were outside, Mum?'

'He said he'd tell us when he was cleaned up. He said it could have been different – I think he meant it was a near miss.'

'He looked dreadful, I'm going to make him promise never to go to London again, not whilst this blooming war's on.'

'You do that, love, I don't want him getting hurt either.' Lily paused and then decided her daughter was old enough to be asked her opinion. 'I do have feelings for him, and I want him to be a real part of this family like you do. But it's going to take a while for me to adjust to all this.'

'That's all right, as long as you're going to try, not going to send him away, then that'll do me for the moment.'

Patrick joined them in the kitchen later looking more himself. He told them what had happened and they listened in silence.

'Those poor people, it shouldn't have been like that. Promise me, Dad, you won't go up to London again until it's safe.'

'I'm happy to give you my word, love. I never want to be in that situation again. We're the lucky ones living here where it's safe. If I'd been allowed to, if I wasn't deaf in one ear, I'd already have volunteered.'

Lily was sitting next to him at the table and without thinking reached out and squeezed his hand. 'Then I'm glad you're not. Because of my poor vision I can't be called up either – who'd have thought that something we were unhappy about when we were young has turned out to be such a blessing?'

17

This Saturday, Emily was going to Rowhedge to spend the day with her friends. The last time she'd gone they'd had tea with Doris and her grandma and grandpa and that had been good fun. It had also reminded her that not everyone was as lucky as she was and made her even more determined to do her bit and not complain when things didn't go her way. Today George and Sammy were coming with her and they'd all be at Penny's house helping look after her little brothers.

'Can we go now, Emily?' George shouted from the bottom of the attic stairs.

'Don't shout, I'm coming. Doris is meeting the ferry at nine o'clock so we've still got fifteen minutes before we have to leave. I'm tidying my room – if you haven't done the same with yours then I'm not taking you. That was the deal.'

'We've done it,' Sammy yelled, completely ignoring her instruction not to shout. 'Come and see, it's never looked better. We've also done our home-work – we got up ever so early so we've got nothing to do for the rest of the weekend.'

'I'll be down in a jiffy. I'm impressed, boys, I've still got a couple of hours of mine left to do but I'll do it tonight.'

* * *

Lily had been quieter than usual these past few days and Emily hoped she wasn't going down with whatever people had been catching. Half her class were away with a nasty respiratory infection – she knew that's what it was called as Dr Cousins had told her so when he came to look at Grandpa, who was a bit under the weather.

She inspected the boys' room and praised them for their diligence. 'Why don't you wait in the garden, I've just got a couple of things to do and then we can go. I promise I won't be long.'

Her brothers rushed out of the front door – they couldn't do anything slowly or quietly but then that's what boys were like. Daddy was at the shipyard and Mummy was giving baby Grace her gloopy breakfast in the dining room.

'We're going in a few minutes, Mummy, are you sure you don't need my help this afternoon? Grandma's going to be busy taking care of Grandpa and Lily finishes at lunchtime.'

'No, darling, you go off and enjoy your day with the boys. It's so kind of you to take them with you as I know you enjoy being with your friends in Rowhedge.'

'Mummy, is Lily all right? She seems awfully quiet this morning – I hope she's not getting whatever it is that Grandpa's got.'

'Patrick, Mr Turner to you, was almost killed in the air raid when he went to London on Wednesday and it was the most dreadful shock for all of them. He's fine, back at work now, but something like that does make you think.'

'That's all right then, I was worried she might be unwell. Is Grandpa very poorly?'

Her mother shook her head and smiled. 'No, Emily, he's just got a cold, not this dreadful thing that's making so many people very ill here and in Colchester.'

'Good, I'm glad it's only a cold. I'd better go; Doris will be waiting on the other side of the river for us. We'll be back before dark.'

Emily kissed the top of the baby's soft downy head and smiled at her mother.

'Daddy's promised to be back earlier tonight. I hope the three of you aren't too late as we were rather hoping we could have a family game of Monopoly – we haven't played that for a long time.'

* * *

The tide was coming in which meant they'd be there quicker. This was the first time George and Sammy had been on the Rowhedge ferry and they were thrilled with the experience. Even when the boat rocked and they were splashed they just laughed.

Doris, as promised, was waiting to greet them. 'Morning, lads, are you looking forward to spending the day running around after the little varmints?'

'We are, Doris, we're going to play football, cricket, and hide-and-seek. It's going to be super fun for all of us,' Sammy said and George agreed.

Emily hugged her friend – she saw Penny every day at school but as Doris didn't go to the grammar school she only saw her at the weekend.

'How's your nan? I hope this horrible cold thing isn't running riot over here like it is in Wivenhoe.'

'She's tickety-boo, ta for asking. Penny's mum is going to be back by four o'clock – she's not working a full day today. Nan wants you to come to mine so she can meet these little tearaways she's heard so much about from you.'

'Will there be any of that yummy ginger cake you brought over the last time you came to Harbour House?' George asked.

'You bet, she's making scones as well and if you're lucky you'll get some of her strawberry jam to go with them. Can't promise no butter nor cream, so marge will have to do.'

'Sounds scrumptious,' George said, grinning and hopping from one foot to the other. 'I like old people; we've got two of them living in our house.'

He didn't wait for a response but raced after Sammy who was already halfway up the hill. Doris had given them directions to Penny's house and as they were able to find their way all over Colchester, Emily wasn't worried about them getting lost somewhere as small as Rowhedge.

* * *

Patrick kept his head down, didn't tell his workmates that he'd almost kicked the bucket. The near miss was playing on his mind – the what ifs, why nots and why not him, were keeping him awake at night, making him jumpy during the day.

His team's part on this minesweeper would be finished by lunchtime and the foreman had told them they could finish when they'd done. Patrick felt guilty having time off when he'd had so much off already because of his injury. He suggested to the foreman that he stayed and helped another team.

'You've made up for the time you had off, Paddy. Mr Roby said you were looking a bit peaky and he doesn't want you catching this nasty flu that's going around.'

'Kind of him to think of me. I'm just tired, I need to get my strength back and then I'll be fighting fit again.'

The foreman turned to go but there was something Patrick wanted to ask him. 'I want to go to church tomorrow – I don't want you to say anything to anybody else but I could have died in London on Wednesday.'

He briefly explained what had happened and the foreman patted him on the shoulder. 'Not surprised you want to go to church, I'm not a big God botherer myself, but even I would go after what almost happened to you.'

'Lily and Daphne go regular as clockwork, I've managed to avoid it because, like everybody else here, I'm at work at the weekend. I'll just give myself a brush down and join them there. We'll sit at the back so I can leave after an hour. I'll not be longer than that.'

'Then I can't see the boss objecting. Enjoy your afternoon off.'

* * *

Patrick was going to have to use his key for the first time as neither Lily nor Daphne were home from work. Doing this was going to make him feel he was part of the family. After brushing himself down outside the front door, he carefully removed his work boots and whilst holding them in one hand he pushed the key in the lock.

He wasn't going to change as he intended to finish the back garden. He'd managed to accumulate enough odds and sods of timber to build a chicken coop – keeping rabbits for the table had been abandoned as he wasn't keen on killing a little fluffy bunny.

Therefore, having hens was the plan. He was pretty sure if they got fertilised eggs and then had to wait for them to hatch then those chicks wouldn't be laying any eggs until next spring at the earliest. He hadn't liked to point out they were as likely to get cockerels as hens. He'd had to wring a few chicken necks when he was living in the country and thought he could do that again if he had to.

The hut was finished and in position by the time Lily and Daphne got home. He'd just completed cleaning his tools and was returning them to his canvas tool bag when they banged on the living-room window and waved. The two of them appeared delighted with his efforts.

They joined him in the garden to admire the hen house – he thought he'd done a decent job and was pleased they agreed with him.

'Look, Mum, there's a little ramp for them to walk up and this door goes up and down so they can go in and out and we can lock them up at night,' Daphne said as she examined it. Then she spotted the egg box at the other end. 'This is ever so clever, Dad, I can't wait to get some chickens.'

'I agree, love, it's just the ticket.'

Hearing this from Lily made the hard work more than worth it. 'Have a closer dekko. There's a perch inside and there's doors at the back which open right up so it can be cleaned out.'

'I'm not doing that,' Daphne said. 'I don't mind collecting the eggs but I'm not doing anything mucky.'

'Don't worry, I'll do it. A bit of chicken crap's good for the garden,' Patrick said.

'I think you've done a smashing job, love, and I'm so glad that you're here to help out,' Lily said. Her smile made him warm inside.

'I'm glad you girls approve. All we need now are some hens, straw, and maybe a bit of grain to feed them on.'

'That's a point, I haven't really thought about what they eat. Maybe I need to get a book about looking after chickens before we get any.'

'I lodged with a family for a year that had a dozen down the bottom of the garden so I know what's what when it comes to hens. Instead of putting your vegetable peelings in the pig swill bin from now on you'll have to cook them and that's what we'll feed to the chickens. They eat anything, they'll dig up worms, insects and other things from the garden. I don't reckon we need a run, we'll just let them roam about. They can't get onto the railway or into the gardens next door.'

Mrs Hobday must have come out whilst they were talking and overheard the conversation. 'Here, I can help you out with that. I know someone who's got chickens they want to get shot of. I don't reckon they'll want more than a few bob for them as they are that desperate for them to go as they move out tomorrow.'

'Crikey,' Patrick said. 'That's a bit of luck. We could go and get them now. What do you say, ladies?'

* * *

Lily found an old orange box and Patrick knocked up a lid to go on the top. He also added a couple of knotted string handles so they could carry it between them and hopefully the chickens would remain upright during the journey. The only thing needed now was something to put drinking water in, straw for the egg boxes, and the hens themselves.

The place where the hens were was one of the big houses along Belle View Road, they just had to walk up the High Street and turn right.

'I don't want a cockerel, Patrick, too much noise and the neighbours would complain. What do we do if there's one with the hens?'

'We'll have to take it, but I can wring its neck and we can have it for Sunday lunch. Or I could go up to the farm at the top of Anglesea Road and let it out when it's dark.'

Daphne giggled. 'I couldn't eat something that I've seen running about alive so if there is one then I'll come with you after blackout. Mrs Peterson will get a shock if she finds an extra cockerel wandering about in her yard tomorrow.'

The family was so relieved to find a home for their poultry they were happy to accept five shillings for all of them.

'I've got to finish packing as the removal men are coming at dawn tomorrow,' the lady said. 'I'll leave you to get them. Take whatever you want that's in the shed – I think there's half a bale of straw and a few other bits and bobs that will be useful.'

'Ta ever so,' Lily said. 'They'll get a good home with us. My husband's made a lovely coop for them and they'll have the run of the garden as we don't have much growing in it at the moment.'

'Go down the side and through the gate and you'll find their run behind the hedge.'

* * *

Patrick led the way holding the crate. 'Good God, there must be a dozen in that tiny run, all crammed together like sardines in a can. No wonder they look miserable and half of them have lost feathers.'

'Poor little things, they'll be a lot happier with us. The house you've made them is more than twice the size of the one they've got now,' Daphne said.

'I'm not sure we can let them out immediately, they'll need a few days to get used to their new home,' Patrick said. 'We won't get more than six in this crate so we'll have to make two journeys.'

Lily grabbed his arm. 'Over there, love, there's another box. I think we could take them all if we use that as well.'

'Right, I need to make a lid or they'll jump out as soon as we put them in. I can see a bit of chicken wire over there, luckily, I've brought my snippers with me and I can make something that'll do in a few minutes.'

* * *

The chickens were lethargic, skinny, and barely made a cluck when they were picked up and put gently into the boxes.

'I'm going to dismantle the run; it'll take me about half an hour but we're going to need to put something temporary up before we can let them out and you can't get chicken wire like this anywhere.'

Daphne was banging about in the shed. 'There's half a bale of straw, but nothing in here for them to eat. I don't think they've been fed very often, do you?'

'Lily, I think I saw a dilapidated wheelbarrow on the other side of this hedge. She said we could take what we wanted so I'm assuming that includes the barrow.'

Patrick was relieved the house owner didn't come out to see what they were doing as the three of them took over an hour to get themselves organised. The roll of chicken wire was balanced on top of the half-bale of straw in the wheelbarrow.

'Daphne, love, I need to push this as it's blooming heavy and awkward. Do you think you can carry the smaller crate on your own?'

'Course I can, they don't weigh hardly anything at all. Mum, can you manage the other one?'

Lily looked at it. 'I think if you put it in my arms, Patrick, I'll be able to balance it. You'll need to walk next to me in case it wobbles.'

* * *

Lily was surprised they made it without losing any of the chickens or knocking unwary pedestrians into the road. They'd certainly got a lot of funny looks and quite a few comments as they made their way slowly back to Clifton Terrace.

Patrick abandoned the wheelbarrow and took the box from her. 'I'll take these round but I won't get them out until we've got things sorted for them.'

In order to get to the back, built as the front a hundred years ago, he'd have to take the path at the far end that ran from one end of the cottages to the other.

'I'll get the vegetable scraps cooked and mix in the crust from the end of today's loaf.'

'Good idea, these hens look half-starved. Daphne, why don't you put yours down in the front yard and then see if Mr Moore has anything that the mice have been at that might do for these hens.'

'Right, that's a good idea, Dad. I'll grab my basket. I've got a few shillings in my purse so if I have to pay for any scraps and leftovers, I'll do that. I'll go to all the other shops, the bakery, the chip shop and the greengrocers in case they can help out.'

He set off, pushing the laden barrow easily and with hardly a wobble. The boxes of hens would have to be taken round the same way as Lily didn't want them going through the house.

* * *

Lily left Patrick to get on with things as he obviously knew what he was doing. She couldn't help smiling as she watched the potato peelings and other odds and sods boiling away in an old saucepan. It was lovely having a man about the house. She realised in that moment that this Patrick wasn't the same one who'd abandoned them over a decade ago. The handsome man outside in his shirtsleeves hammering away was a real man, a family man, a man any woman would be proud to call her husband.

18

Emily was happy to walk beside Doris, knowing that her brothers couldn't get lost as the lane they were walking up went right past Penny's house and ended at the stile. The trees were shedding their leaves, soon it would be November and maybe the river would be too rough and dangerous for the three of them to get together every weekend.

'I've been waiting to tell you this, Emily, I know you're interested in what happens to the empty house your friend used to live in,' Doris said.

'Go on, are there new people living there?'

'Not half, four families what were bombed out are there now. Only women and kiddies, obviously, the menfolk are all in the services.'

'That's exactly what I thought should happen. Are there any girls our age?'

'They ain't been there long enough for me to find that out. They only came yesterday – I was told that there are three nans, four mums and maybe more than a dozen children.'

'Golly, even that huge house will be packed to the rafters with so many living there. My mother and the Wivenhoe branch of the WI have been collecting clothes and other items for the homeless people. I want to call round there and see if they need anything.'

'Righty ho, why don't we do it now? I can see your brothers climbing on that gate – you'd better call them in case it breaks. The farmer ain't that partial to having his sheep all over the village.'

* * *

Ten minutes later, all four of them were marching up the drive. George and Sammy were as eager as Emily and Doris to discover exactly who was living in the huge house.

'Crikey, this is more than three times the size of our house,' Sammy said as they approached the front door.

'Imagine how much it must cost to keep it warm in the winter,' Emily said and then laughed. She sounded just like a fussy old lady, not a young girl of twelve.

'I wonder why there are no children playing in the garden, it's nice enough today,' Doris said.

'I was thinking the same thing,' Emily replied.

'If they've only just arrived from London I don't suppose they've ever seen the countryside – all they've known are streets and having bombs being dropped on them every night.'

George was right. It would probably take all of them a few days to adjust to their new surroundings. Emily thought that peace and quiet, being safe, might seem less welcoming than familiar streets even with bombs being dropped every night. When she and George – Sammy hadn't belonged to the family then – had arrived two years ago they'd never even seen a cow.

Sammy pointed to an upstairs window. 'Look, someone's staring at us. In fact, I think it's several someones.'

'You're right. We'd better knock on the door and explain why we're here.'

There was no need to do this as the front door opened before they got there. Emily had prepared a polite speech but didn't use it. She laughed instead. Facing them were not adults but three small children.

'Hello, I'm Emily, these are my brothers George and Sammy and this is my friend Doris. Welcome to Rowhedge. Could I speak to a grown-up, please?'

The three exchanged a look and then the one that looked the oldest, a girl of no more than five or six, nodded.

'Jimmy here had to stand on my shoulders to open the door. It's ever so heavy, you know.'

'I do know, I was in here once seeing a friend. Her family have moved away now which is why you can all live here and be safe from the bombs.'

'My mum's gone down the shops to register us. Auntie May and Auntie Alice went too and took the twins in the pram. Jimmy's mum's feeling badly again and she's in bed.'

'I see, but what about the grandmothers? Surely one of them is able to come and speak to us.'

'They ain't nowhere to be found. They was here last night but they ain't now,' the child said. 'None of them was pleased about coming here. They said there were too many cows and not enough pubs.'

'I see. The countryside's very different from the city and it will take a while to adjust. But you'll be safe here as we don't have any bombs. By the way, what's your name?'

'I'm Jenny. There's my big sister, Joan, and my big brother, Trevor, but they're looking for the nans. Jimmy's got two sisters but they never came with us after all – they said they'd take their chances with Hitler.'

Doris was looking as puzzled as Emily was. 'Okay, so you three are on your own. Nobody looking after you nor nothing?'

'That's right, miss, we were told to behave and stop inside. We saw you coming so thought we'd better open the door.'

George and Sammy thought it was a lark. 'Three lost grandmas – what a hoot! Shall we help you look, little girl? It'll be like a game of hide-and-seek.'

Before Emily could tell them this was a bad idea, that it was none of their business, the small children and her brothers had run off laughing.

'The missing women won't be hiding in the house. Jenny said that two of the older girls refused to come, that the old ladies didn't like it here either. I bet the three of them are back in London by now,' Emily said.

Doris wasn't so sure. 'They might have wanted to go home but there ain't no transport at night. No trains come here as we ain't got no station. No buses neither. I reckon they could be wandering about in the fields. People from London don't know how to go on down here.'

'I've got to find my brothers, otherwise I'd come with you.'

'Where am I going then?'

'You need to nip down to the village and let the mothers know what's going on. I'll see if I can find the one that's not well and see if she knows anything helpful,' Emily said.

It took her a while to find the bedroom which Jimmy's mother had taken for her own. The laughter and noise from the three little ones and the two boys meant they were happily occupied for the moment.

'Excuse me, ma'am, but I think you need to get up. The older ladies who came with you appear to be missing. They've not been seen since last night according to Jimmy.'

The blackouts were drawn in this bedroom but from the light filtering in from the passageway Emily could see there was a figure in the bed, although it didn't stir.

She found the light switch and turned it on. This had the desired effect but not one she was expecting.

'Turn that bleeding light off or I'll tan your bleeding hide. I told you, I need me sleep and you little sods have got to look after yourselves for now.'

Emily retreated and banged the door behind her. Jimmy's mother wasn't going to be any help. The boys appeared with the three little ones and she knew what they had to do.

'Come on, you lot, we're going across the lane to Penny's house. She'll be worried that we've not arrived.'

'We ain't had no breakfast nor nothing,' Jimmy said.

'Then you'll all get something to eat over there. I'll write a note for Doris and your mothers so they know where you are.'

'My mum's no bleeding use,' Jimmy said. His swearing shocked Emily and so did his comment. The little boy continued as they headed downstairs. 'She found some drink and had the lot. She'll not be up today.'

'Oh dear, I'm sorry about that. Please don't use bad language, it's not polite.'

He stared at her, puzzled for a moment. Then he nodded. 'Me mum uses that word all the time. I'll not say it again. Can I still come with you?'

Emily bent down and hugged him. 'Of course you can. Now I know where the study is, it won't take me a minute to write the note. George, will you and Sammy take the children into the garden and wait for me there?'

She watched the five of them dash through the still open front door and then ran along the corridor to the room where the telephone was. She'd only been in this house once a few weeks ago but remembered how to find her way.

Note written and with a drawing pin found, she hurried back to the hall and pinned the note prominently to the front door where Doris would see it.

Penny was waiting for them outside the front door. She was relieved to see them even with the three extra children. 'I thought you weren't coming, Emily. My brothers are going mad in the garden, they'll be so glad to see George and Sammy.'

'Boys, take our new little friends with you,' Emily said. 'I'll call you in when there's some breakfast ready for you three.'

Penny led the way to the side gate and reached over to unlock it. 'I can't risk my brothers getting out as they'd vanish.'

'Me nans have done a bunk, miss,' Jimmy said. 'We ain't seen them not nowhere.'

'I'm sure they'll be back soon. Grown-ups don't run off or get lost,' Penny told him.

* * *

Half an hour later, the children from London were fed and back in the garden playing a noisy game of football. Even the littlest one, a girl, was running up and down enthusiastically, even though she didn't go near the ball.

Emily flopped onto a deckchair and her friend joined her. 'Thank you for feeding them. Where do you think the missing grandmothers could be? There are no buses out of Rowhedge, according to Doris, at night.'

Penny clapped. 'I know where they might be. There's an empty cottage, it used to be lived in by a gatekeeper, and they might well be in there. It's furnished, no electricity or plumbing, but there'd be oil lamps and candles.'

'I hope you're right. However, I don't understand why they wandered off in the first place. Can you watch all of them for a minute whilst I dash back and add that information to the note I left?'

There was no need as Doris arrived. 'The old biddies have returned. Seems they got lost on the way back from the pub and slept in the cottage.'

Emily gazed expectantly at the path. But there was no sign of the other mothers. 'That's what we thought. Aren't the other ladies coming for their children?'

'I told them but they didn't seem bothered and said to send them back when we got fed up with them.'

'They are so happy playing with our siblings, shall we keep them for a bit longer, Penny? If that's all right with you,' Emily asked.

'I've been watching closely, you know my brothers can be volatile, unpredictable, but having children here that are younger than them seems to have calmed them down.'

* * *

Nobody from the big house came to collect the children and eventually, after a picnic lunch, Emily and Doris took them back. The front door was still open and the three little ones ran off and into the house without saying thank you or goodbye.

'Ungrateful brats,' Doris said. 'I bet this new lot are going to be trouble. I'm glad they don't know where I live or they'd be round mine all the time.'

'Never mind, they weren't much trouble and actually made things easier for Penny. I think they might well be banging on her door now they know where she lives.' She frowned. 'I think these mothers and grandmothers are not taking proper care of the children. Jimmy told us that there are two older ones but they haven't appeared either.'

'None of our business, Emily. Let's enjoy the rest of the afternoon before you and Penny come round to mine.'

* * *

Patrick shoved straw into the egg boxes, filled up the heavy iron water container and, satisfied he'd done as much as he could to make these pathetic chickens comfortable, he went to fetch the crates. Lily had called out of the kitchen door that he could come through the house but not the hens.

Daphne was watching over them, talking to the terrified birds as if they understood what she was saying. 'There you are, Dad, these birds need to be in their new home before they die of fright.' She pointed to her brimming basket full of unwanted but edible items she'd collected from the various shops.

'Sorry, love, I had to make the run. You've got enough to feed them for a few days – well done on getting so much. Let's get them in and see what happens.'

He picked up the smaller crate – the one that he'd made from an orange box – and handed it to her then scooped up the bigger one. Mrs Hobday saw them go past her window and came out to admire the new coop. She couldn't see it properly as it was on the lowest bit of the terrace and only the top of it was visible. Lily was waiting in the garden like an anxious mother.

Patrick put his box down and then removed the second one from Daphne. 'Right, girls, here we go. They look half-dead so don't be surprised if they don't survive the night.'

'I've mashed up the peelings and scattered them in the run. I don't mind if we don't get any eggs for a while, I just want them to recover. I know they're not like cats or dogs, but that woman was cruel to let them get like this.'

'I shouldn't think we'll get any eggs for weeks, if at all, but they won't cost much to feed and I'm still pleased we rescued them,' he said.

One after the other he gently lifted them out, shocked at how emaciated they were under their remaining feathers. It only took a few minutes to put the fourteen on the ground in the run. He backed out and hooked up the makeshift door, hoping it wouldn't fall to bits if the wind got up.

'Next door's got a big ginger cat, Dad, I hope he doesn't come in here looking for lunch.'

'We'll keep an eye on them – I'm sure we'd hear if the cat came in and bothered them,' Lily said.

'Do we watch from the window or stay out here in case they need any help?' Daphne asked.

'Go in, love, even though we're strangers to them I expect they don't trust humans right now,' Lily said.

'We can watch from here,' Patrick said when they reached the middle section of garden, 'we'll not see a blooming thing from the house.'

His eyes widened. 'Crikey, I don't believe it. The little beggars are already on their feet and drinking water. Not only starving but dying of thirst too. I'm glad we stole the wheelbarrow now. I wish we'd taken a few more things.'

Lily was pressed close to him on one side and his daughter was doing the same on the other. He was tempted to put his arms around them but thought that might be pushing his luck – with his wife anyway.

They remained where they were for half an hour. By then, every one of the birds had taken a long drink and most of them were gobbling down the scattered scraps.

'We've not had a bite to eat. Either we have a very late lunch or an early tea,' Lily said, 'which do you prefer?'

'Let's just have a cup of tea and eat at the normal time. I'm going to bring in what Daphne managed to scrounge. I think we're going to have to keep it somewhere in the kitchen or the rats will find it.'

'I've got the perfect thing, Patrick, an old bread bin. I meant to hand it in when they were collecting scrap metal to build Spitfires last year, but I forgot.'

'I'll get it, Mum, I know where it is. It's a bit rusty but hasn't got any holes even in the lid.'

Daphne opened the door quietly and slipped out, not wishing to upset the pecking chickens, although Patrick doubted they'd be aware of what was going on in the house. He followed her out, interested to see what reaction her appearance would have. He could hear the chickens in their makeshift run, but from here he couldn't see them.

The birds nearest to her looked up as she tossed in a couple of handfuls of broken biscuits and shrivelled currants. They ran to investigate as it landed on the grass, clucked and then got back to what was important – filling their empty bellies.

* * *

The sun set early now and it was dark when they'd finished their tea. 'I'm going to take my torch and see if I can chivvy them into the house, I don't think they should stay outside. It doesn't take long for local foxes to sniff out a run full of chickens.'

Daphne followed him. Negotiating the steep steps would be lethal without a torch. He shone the narrow beam into the run and chuckled. 'Blooming heck, there's not one outside. Unless they've got out and wandered off, they must all be inside.'

He moved quietly to the coop and crouched down to look inside the little door.

'Would you look at that! Not just inside but sitting on the perch.'

Patrick dropped the door and fastened it, delighted that the new residents had settled in so well.

Daphne went to the other end and lifted the lid on the egg boxes and hastily closed it again. 'Dad, there's three in here. Do you think they're laying us some eggs for breakfast?'

'I doubt it, but you never know. Miracles do happen – I'm the living proof of that.'

19

Patrick didn't need an alarm clock the following morning. He was so accustomed to getting up at dawn in order to be at work by seven thirty that somehow he managed to open his eyes at the correct time without assistance.

He ran his fingers over his jaw and scowled. Men working at the shipyard didn't bother to shave every day – most of them looked a bit rough if he was honest. However, today he was going to church so had no option.

The water in the big china jug was cold but he'd shaved in water he'd had to break the ice on many times so this didn't bother him. There'd been no sound from the other rooms which was how he wanted it. His intention was to be down first, get the range up to heat, have the breakfast waiting for them when they came down, even though neither of them had to work today.

With his last clean flannel shirt on, the only waistcoat he had which still had buttons, he pulled on his work jacket and was ready to go down. The blackouts couldn't be drawn back yet as without the light switched on he'd be falling over things.

'Dad, you shouldn't be doing things in here. That's women's work – you sit down and let me carry on,' Daphne said from behind him.

'I don't like to be waited on—'

'You're a paying guest at the moment, don't forget. Have you been out to see how the chickens are doing?'

'I was just going to let them out. It occurred to me after I was in bed that we should have picked up any food that was left. Rats would have been all over the run if there was anything there for them to eat.'

'Actually, Mrs Hobday's cat, Benny, keeps this terrace free of vermin. I've not seen a rat out the back since she got him two years ago.'

'Good to know, love. The tea's brewed – why don't you take a mug up to your mum? She deserves a lie in.'

Daphne grinned and did as he suggested. He checked the table in the living room was laid correctly, yesterday's bread was sliced and ready to be toasted, and the margarine and jam were out.

He filled a chipped enamel bowl with the remaining cooked vegetable scraps, added a couple of handfuls from the old bread bin. He switched off the kitchen light and then lifted the corner of the curtain – the sun was coming up so time to let the chickens out. He hoped none of them had died overnight but he wouldn't be surprised if they'd lost one or two.

Before he unlocked the door, he filled a saucepan with water to refill the container in the run and was then ready to investigate. Daphne arrived at his side, her eyes were shining, she grabbed his arm.

'I'm not sure I should have prayed that they survived, Dad, but I did. I reckon God's got better things to do than worry about our chickens.'

'He's supposed to be all-seeing and all-knowing. Maybe he can hear every prayer even if he doesn't have time to answer them all,' Patrick said half-jokingly.

'What about if the Nazis pray? He must be able to hear them but he won't answer any of their prayers.'

This was a bit too philosophical for him so he handed over the saucepan of water to distract her. Whilst she tipped the water into the container he unlatched the little door and raised it.

He barely had time to move back before a rush of clucking eager chickens poured down the ramp.

'Quick, love, tip out the food before they escape. We forgot to close the gate behind us.'

How could this bustling flock of birds be the same lethargic half-dead ones they'd collected only yesterday afternoon?

Some headed for the water and the rest nosedived into the food that

Daphne had just tipped out. They both had to watch their step in order not to tread on them.

'I'm going to look in the egg boxes to make sure they've all come out. I'm not sure exactly how many we got yesterday, Dad, are you?'

'Fourteen, I'm pretty sure that's how many there were.' He did a quick count and laughed. 'All out, love, and despite their lack of feathers and general scruffiness I think we got to them just in time.'

Suddenly his daughter squealed. For a moment he thought there might be a rat in the egg box.

'Dad, we've got two eggs. You said we probably wouldn't have any for weeks and now there's two.' She waved them in the air triumphantly.

'Why don't you take them round to Mrs Hobday, love, we wouldn't have them at all if it wasn't for her.'

There was no need for Daphne to go in search of their neighbour as she appeared on her back doorstep on cue.

'Here you are, Mrs Hobday, a gift from our chickens,' Daphne called and their neighbour shot down the steps and was holding out her hand before his daughter had finished speaking.

'Would you look at that? I've not seen nice eggs like this for weeks. We only get one a week each since the blooming rationing started. Ta ever so, me and Bill will have them for our breakfast.'

She vanished as rapidly as she'd appeared and Patrick smiled. 'I hope Lily doesn't mind that we gave away those eggs. Seemed right to do it.'

Daphne giggled. 'She was that tickled pink by having tea in bed she'll not mind about a couple of eggs. If we get eggs every day, do we have to give them over to the government?'

Lily was now in the kitchen making a fresh pot of tea and overheard this as they came in. 'Emily used to go up to the farm to help out with the children and she told me that they always have plenty of eggs because cracked eggs don't have to be given in. I'm quite certain that our hens will only be laying cracked eggs because they're so old and malnourished.'

Patrick told them that he was joining them at church as he put his bag, gas mask and cap on the side table ready for when he left. 'I can't stay more than an hour, but I'll be there. Can you sit at the back so I can come in and out without disturbing anyone else?'

Suddenly Lily was in his arms. He was so shocked he stumbled back, and they ended up in a tangle on the lino in the hall.

* * *

Lily tried to sit up but Patrick was holding onto her. She forgot their daughter was watching this pantomime and relaxed into him.

His kiss sent spirals of heat racing around her body. Her lips parted to allow him access and for a few seconds she was swept away by desire. Then he picked her up and put her to one side as easily as if she was a child.

'No, love, you need to be sure. You know how I feel but I'm pretty sure you haven't quite made up your mind about me.'

She leaned against the wall, catching her breath. 'Who are you? You look roughly the same but I never felt like this when you kissed me before.'

He grinned, rose smoothly to his feet and pulled her upright. 'I told you I've changed. I had a lot of growing up to do – I don't regret for one instant marrying you and having a lovely daughter, but I was still a boy, too young for the responsibility.'

'We're the same age. It was hard for me too but I didn't give up.'

'I know, I think girls become adults sooner than boys. I'll never stop apologising for abandoning both of you and wish I'd had the courage to speak to you when I came back the following year.'

She pushed him back against the stairs. 'I can't believe you came to Wivenhoe and didn't speak to me. But it's a good thing you didn't.'

'What do you mean?'

'It would just have made things worse. I wouldn't have forgiven you and then maybe we wouldn't be where we are now.'

Patrick pushed a strand of hair from her cheek before speaking. Even the gentle touch of his fingers brushing against her face made her tingle.

'We've changed, grown up, I think we can make a go of it but I won't pressure you,' he said.

Daphne spoke from the living room. 'After what I've just seen, Mum, it's a bit late to talk about making up your mind. Shocking behaviour, if you ask me.' She giggled. 'If you're going to have any breakfast, Dad, you'd better get a move on or you'll be late for work.'

She risked a glance at him and he was looking as bemused as she was by this sudden turn of events. He ate four slices of toast, drank two mugs of tea without pausing for breath and then was on his feet.

'I'm off, I'll see you at ten o'clock. I apologise in advance if I'm looking a bit scruffy – Sunday best's not an option for me, I'm afraid.'

'The Lord doesn't care what you look like – it's the people who run the church who make the rules. I can't tell you how happy it makes me that you're going to come to matins.'

His smile made her feel like a young girl again. 'I'll do anything to make you and Daphne happy, you know that.'

Then he was gone and the house somehow seemed flat and empty without him in it. Daphne jerked from her daydream.

'I'm going to see how the chickens are before breakfast, Mum.'

'You were just out there half an hour ago. I shouldn't think they've done anything different in so short a time.'

Lily was wrong. She'd scarcely got the dishes into the sink to wash when her daughter returned at a run.

'You won't believe it, Mum, another two eggs. I'm not giving these to Mrs Hobday. You and Dad can have one each for tea tonight.'

'No, if they're going to lay us four eggs a day we'll wait until we've got enough for all of us. Imagine, they looked so poorly and bedraggled and yet they've only been here a few hours and already laying us some lovely eggs.'

* * *

Saturday afternoon was usually the time when Lily did the washing and ironing but none of that had been done because of fetching the chickens. Either she'd have to do it on a Sunday – not something anyone approved of round here including her – or get up even earlier tomorrow and do it then.

Daphne arrived downstairs with a bundle of Patrick's laundry. He was a paying guest and laundry and ironing was part of the deal – if they were back together then she'd still have to do it but wouldn't get paid for it.

She laughed and her daughter shook her head. 'I never thought a pile of dirty clothes would make you laugh, especially these.'

Quickly Lily explained and instead of laughing as she'd done Daphne pounced on the suggestion that Patrick would soon be a genuine part of the family.

'There, I told you just now when he kissed you that things are different. I think I'll change the sheets on your bed so it's nice and clean for tonight.'

Lily's cheeks turned scarlet. 'You're only sixteen – how do you know so much about what goes on between a husband and wife?'

'You were expecting me when you were only a year older – are you telling me you didn't know about the birds and the bees?'

This was a very strange conversation to be having and Lily wasn't entirely sure she was comfortable with it. 'I knew absolutely nothing about anything. I was brought up by an elderly aunt who couldn't wait to get rid of me. It was someone at school told me about monthlies, otherwise I'd have thought I was dying.'

'What about Dad? Did he know a bit more about that sort of thing?'

'I think he knew even less than me. We were both so young. He was brought up by his grandparents which is why he had the house left to him. They loved him all right but obviously they were too old and set in their ways to talk about intimacy.'

'Crikey, it's a wonder I was ever born from what you're telling me. Do you think he's had other relationships since he left you? He's a very handsome man, has a twinkle in his eye, he must have learnt what's what from someone.'

The thought that he'd been with another woman shocked Lily for a moment but then she smiled. 'It's none of our business what he did whilst he wasn't here. I could have had an affair with someone but he's not asked and neither will I.'

'I'll put these things on to soak for you, Mum, then I can give them a good scrub this afternoon. I don't suppose Dad's got more than one change of clothes.'

'That reminds me, I said I'd give his room a clean and I've not done that. I'll go up and get started, you're a love to help me out so much.'

As soon as she stepped into his bedroom, she knew that he'd already done what was necessary. The furniture was shining, not a scrap of dust anywhere, the bed was made, and his shaving kit and his other things were set neatly on the washstand.

It was a strange feeling standing there looking at his personal items. She shouldn't really be in here but something prompted her to investigate a little further. There were a couple of photos in a silver frame on the bedside table. One was of her, the other with both Daphne and herself.

She went to his wardrobe and opened the door. He had his decent jacket, a waistcoat with no buttons, two flannel work shirts and one smart one. The collars and studs must be in his chest of drawers.

There were no spare boots so he obviously only owned the ones he worked in. For some reason this upset her. She didn't like to think of him clumping about in his heavy boots every day of the week.

She thought she'd check on his collars in case any of them needed to be scrubbed and starched. There were two small drawers at the top of the chest, and two big ones beneath. She pulled open the left-hand small drawer and her eyes widened. There were two post office savings books, battered and old, one with her name on the front and one with Daphne's.

Her fingers trembled as she picked them up. She really shouldn't be looking through his belongings – if he did that to hers then she'd be furious. She opened her book and saw that from a few weeks after abandoning them he'd been putting a few pennies in. She flipped to the last page that was filled in and had to steady herself against the chest of drawers.

There was more than £800 in her book and £600 in Daphne's. She was blinded by tears. All this time she'd been thinking he'd forgotten them and he'd been putting away money for them both. Every week for fourteen years – not very much sometimes – but he'd never missed a week.

Then Daphne burst in. 'Mum, I've been calling you. Why are you crying? What's wrong?'

Lily couldn't speak. She handed over the savings books and continued to cry. She watched her daughter's expression change to surprise and then she dropped the books back in the drawer and slammed it shut.

'Mum, we shouldn't know about this. You shouldn't have been sneaking into his things. It is that why you're crying, because you shouldn't have done it?'

Lily finally located a handkerchief up her sleeve, wiped her eyes and blew her nose before she answered. 'I'm crying because all this time I thought he'd forgotten us but he's been doing without himself in order to save up for us.'

'For us? What do you mean? I thought you'd found his savings and were surprised he had so much put by.'

'No, look at the names on the front, love. He can't touch this money even if he wanted to – only you and I can get any of this out from the post office.'

'I'm rich! I thought that having just over £10 saved was good but that money in that book could buy me a house if I wanted one.'

'I don't know how we're going to pretend we don't know,' Lily said as she ushered her daughter from the room they shouldn't have been in anyway.

'You'll have to tell him that you know.' Daphne grinned and gave her a saucy wink. 'Will it be before or after you've spent the night with him?'

* * *

At five minutes to ten, Patrick was heading for the church. Only then did he realise he wasn't the only one who had permission to attend the service. He spoke to one of the blokes.

'This is the first time for me. Do you come every week?'

'Not as often as I'd like, Paddy, but I come when things ain't too busy in the yard. The boss is good about this sort of thing.'

'He's good about all things. I've never been happier than I am working here. How long does the service last?'

'The vicar's an old bloke, often forgets what he's doing, where he is in the service book, but his sermon ain't never more than fifteen minutes.'

Patrick felt a bit guilty that he didn't know the man's name and yet he knew his. 'Sorry, I don't know who you are and to be honest I'm surprised that you know my name as there must a hundred or more working at the yard.'

'You're famous, mate, of course I know who you are. I'm Sid James, I ain't from Wivenhoe, I come across on the ferry every day.'

'Good for you.'

There was still a trickle of people entering the ancient building so they weren't the last. Patrick couldn't remember how long it was since he'd been inside a church – probably when he was living in Wivenhoe the first time.

Daphne was swivelled around in a pew at the back watching for him and he nodded to Sid and smiled at her. She'd left a space at the end and he slid into it. Lily looked round and gave him a warm smile but obviously didn't want to talk. A lot of the congregation were on their knees, and he thought he was probably expected do the same but that would be disrespectful as pretending to pray, in his opinion, was worse than not doing it at all.

The organist was mostly in tune, the choir more or less kept in time with the music but as the congregation sang with gusto it didn't really matter. Several times the vicar lost his place in the order of service but nobody seemed to mind.

The sermon was about forgiveness, vaguely linked to the Bible passages they'd heard, and the old bloke rambled on and then stopped abruptly. Patrick looked at Daphne, who was trying not to laugh. Lily was also smiling and when he glanced around the packed church he saw no one seemed bothered.

He reckoned they were all relieved they could get out and get home in time to have a decent Sunday lunch. This was one time that despite rationing, despite there being a war on, all families made sure they sat down to a decent meal.

The vicar shook hands with the congregation as they left, nodded and smiled, but didn't seem to know anybody's name. Lily had put her arm through his. She was making a public statement of intent and if they hadn't been standing outside the church he would have kissed her.

'I've got to go, love, I can't say I enjoyed it particularly but I'm glad I came. We finish at six on a Sunday – I expect you know that from having Frank living with you – so we'll be able to eat at a sensible time.'

'I'm doing a nice rabbit pie. The big cat at Harbour House brings in a rabbit most nights.'

'That sounds perfect.' Patrick turned to go but she stretched up on tiptoe and kissed him – not on the cheek but on the lips. Then Daphne hugged him.

He pulled them both close. 'I love you both and I won't let you down again.'

20

Lily took Daphne's arm and they hurried home, not wanting to stop and talk about what had just happened. They were almost running when they reached their front door.

'Crikey, Mum, Dad's face was a picture. I'm going to go round Sally's tonight, I don't think either of you want an audience.'

'No need to do that, love.'

Daphne grinned. 'I'm still not going to be here tonight.'

'Fair enough, thanks, probably be best if we have a bit of privacy. Why don't you move into the front room, quieter there? Let's get things sorted upstairs and then you nip round and speak to Sally and see if it's convenient for you to be there tonight.'

'Everybody will be talking about that kiss. And that you don't have to wait as you're already married.'

'Fair enough, you're a good girl. How would you feel if you had a baby brother or sister next summer?'

Daphne's face lit up. 'I'd just love it. Are you sure you want to go through all that again at your age?'

'I'm thirty-three, not forty-three, and I know of at least two other women who had more than one baby in their thirties. Mrs Roby's one of them. I wouldn't even consider it if it wasn't for what Patrick's put by for me. He earns good money, and with what you give me we'll be fine.'

'They won't be happy at Harbour House if you do get in the family way and leave next year. They've already had two housekeepers and they've only been there a couple of years.'

'They'll soon find somebody else, it's a lovely job and anyone who can cook, do a bit of cleaning and that could do it.' Lily couldn't stop smiling. She'd always wanted another baby but had resigned herself to having an only child. She sent up a quick prayer to the Lord that she and Patrick would be blessed with a baby.

Just thinking about what they'd be doing tonight made her dizzy with excitement. They'd been too young when they'd got married but they were ready now to make it work.

Things would be easier this time as Daphne would be like a second mother rather than an older sister. There'd be no money worries either and she still had all the baby things carefully packed away in the attic. She'd never had a pram, had had to carry Daphne everywhere until she was old enough to walk. Maybe this time they might be able to find a pushchair which would make things so much easier.

It didn't take long to remove Patrick's things as he didn't have much. 'Doing this means that he'll know we've seen the savings books. I won't have to tell him I was nosing through his personal things,' Lily said.

'I'm going to run round to Sally's. She's got twin beds in her bedroom and one's been empty since Brenda joined the ATS a few months ago. I can't see that Mrs Trent will mind.'

'Off you go then. Don't be too long as I've got soup and spam sandwiches for lunch. We don't need much as we're having a big meal tonight to celebrate.'

Daphne had to bang the front door twice to get it to shut and that reminded Lily that as Patrick was home to stay she could ask him to mend the door and do a few other jobs around the place.

* * *

When her daughter returned with her overnight stay arranged, both bedrooms were done.

Daphne decided she'd have tea with her friend so wasn't at home when Patrick returned. Lily had fed the hens, collected two more eggs, and laid the table for a late tea. She'd found a tablecloth from when they'd been first married, a little faded from being in a drawer, but still pretty.

'I've put hot water upstairs for you, love, and I've moved your things to where they belong.'

His eyes darkened and he looked different, almost dangerous, for a second. Was she making a mistake? Was this a man she actually knew? Never for a moment when they'd been together before had he looked so formidable, so masculine, so desirable.

It belatedly dawned on her that once they'd shared a bed she was committed to the marriage. She couldn't divorce him, couldn't throw him out, he'd be back as the man of the house. Before she'd been in charge, she'd made all the decisions and he'd gone along with it. Was this why he'd left? Had it been her fault for wearing the trousers?

He took the stairs two at a time and she made the final adjustments to the meal she'd spent so long preparing. He wouldn't take more than five minutes to wash and change his shirt. The plates were warm and waiting on top of the range, the roast potatoes and parsnips crispy and brown, the carrots perfectly cooked and the gravy thick and rich just as it should be.

Ten minutes dragged into fifteen. Where was he? After twenty she went to the stairs and called his name but he didn't answer. Something was wrong.

* * *

Patrick stripped naked; he wasn't making love to his wife for the first time in years smelling of the shipyard. He scrubbed from top to toe and found his underpants and vest. No, no vest, the fewer things to take off the better.

Tonight was the night for his smart shirt so he needed the collar and studs. He pulled open one of the small drawers and his world fell apart. He'd forgotten about the savings books, but Lily must have seen them when she moved his things. She'd kissed him because of the money. Why else had this happened so unexpectedly?

His doubts flooded back, he wasn't good enough, she wouldn't have taken him back without the money. Half-dressed, still clutching the tell-tale books, he slid to the rug and drew his knees up, hugged them and dropped his head. Whatever she said, he'd never know if her love was real or because of the savings.

Then she was beside him, her arms around him and she was crying too.

'No, darling, it's nothing to do with the savings. I love you and just loved you more when I saw that you hadn't forgotten us as I'd thought but had been putting a little aside every single week since you left.'

He raised his head and looked at her. She was as distraught as him, her cheeks were wet, and slowly his world righted and his panic and heartbreak began to subside.

He still couldn't quite believe that he'd got it so wrong, that he'd almost thrown everything away for a second time. She saw the uncertainty on his face and grabbed his arms and shook him.

'Patrick, think about it, I'd already thrown myself into your arms, kissed you, before I even thought about moving your things over. We've both changed but you know I've never lied to you and never would.'

The constriction around his chest slackened and he was finally able to breathe. 'I'm sorry, I don't know why I immediately thought the worst.'

'It doesn't matter. I expect we're going to have a lot of misunderstandings before our marriage runs smoothly. Now, get dressed and be down in three minutes as I'm dishing up right now.'

As she whisked away, he saw that she'd dressed for the occasion. She was bare legged but wearing a pretty floral frock which emphasised her shape. Dinner was going to be very, very short.

* * *

The table had a cloth on which he recognised. 'That was a wedding present from Mrs Hobday. It looks as good as the day she gave it to us.'

'It was only for high days and holidays and there weren't any of those. However, today is one of them. In case you're wondering where our daughter is, she thought she'd rather spend the night with a friend than be here getting in our way.'

'Then let's make the most of it.'

She laughed and shook her head. 'Absolutely not, Patrick Turner, I've spent a lot of time and effort making this meal so we're going to sit down like civilised people and enjoy it.'

'So, if I tell you I'm not at all hungry, that I'm tired and ready for bed that won't make any difference?' He'd attempted to make his tone light, to disguise how he really felt and appeared to have succeeded if her answer was anything to go by.

'There's no need to rush things, let's just spend time together, talk about the future and enjoy the meal I've prepared for us.'

She gestured towards a chair that was already pulled out and he sat down. The last thing on his mind was eating or talking. For the past fourteen years he'd dreamed about making love to her again and waiting even half an hour was going to be difficult.

She stood on the other side of the table and looked at him. 'Actually, everything is in the slow oven, it won't spoil for half an hour.'

He was on his feet so fast his chair tumbled backwards. In two steps he was next to her, she was in his arms and he was up the stairs like a rat from a drainpipe. It was she that slammed the door shut behind them.

Clothes were almost torn off, flung in all directions and they fell, naked, onto the bed. 'I love you, Lily, I've never loved anyone else and I've not been with anyone else.'

'I love you too, Patrick, and I've been faithful too.'

* * *

Eventually they got dressed and made their way downstairs. Making love to Lily had never been like this before. Neither of them had gained more experience in that department but somehow they'd known what to do to please each other, there'd been no nervousness, no embarrassment and certainly no clothes at all.

'I can't believe the pie's still edible, the vegetables are crisp and tasty and the gravy's heated up a treat,' Lily said as she put a plate in front of him.

'Smells delicious. I hope there's seconds as I'm starving.'

'Try it first before asking for any more. It should have been eaten an hour ago.'

Even if it had been burnt he'd have eaten and enjoyed it. They talked about the weather, the chickens, their daughter as they munched their way through the entire pie and all the vegetables.

'I don't want any afters, love, if that's all right. But I could do with another cuppa. I'll help you clear and make the tea. You put your feet up.'

'Don't be daft, I'm your wife and it's my job to look after you.'

There were three comfortable but dilapidated armchairs grouped around the fire, facing the mantelpiece where the precious wireless sat. Whilst Lily was pouring out tea in the kitchen, Patrick pushed two of them closer together.

'That's a good idea, love, I should have thought of that. There are things we need to talk about before we go to bed.'

'You're right. I didn't use any protection – are you all right with the idea that we might have another child next summer?'

'I hope we do; I've already talked to Daphne and she's all for it. I've got everything we need upstairs.'

'Crikey, that's a surprise but a good one. Our Daphne will be leaving us in a few years and have a house of her own. It'll be good having a little one running around. I missed out when she was growing up and I'll be a better father this time if we're blessed with a baby.'

'I'd have to give up my job as housekeeper but with what you've put by for us we'll manage just fine on your wages alone.'

'You take the savings book, love, you do what you want with it. I'll keep putting money aside for Daphne and she can have it when she gets married or when she's twenty-one.'

'No, she doesn't need any more than what's already in there. I think I'll have to stop getting the allowance from the War Office as you're not a lodger.'

'I've already thought of that, love, and they deduct ten shillings from my wages to go towards what you get, so my money will go up. Also, Mr Roby's putting me in charge of my shed – I'll get a few bob more for that as well.'

'I don't think I was ever really happy before. We got married because we were friends, different from the others we knew, I was fond of you but it was nothing like I feel now. Is that the same for you?'

Patrick leaned across and took her hand. 'I've always loved you, but you're right, it's different now. I can't believe that you've taken me back, that we've fallen properly in love, that my daughter's forgiven me and accepted me. If a bomb dropped on this house right now then I'd die a happy man.'

Lily pulled her hand back. 'Don't talk about dying, you've almost done that twice already.'

'Sorry, love, you know what I mean. I didn't come to Wivenhoe expecting more than to see you both, to give you the post office books and sign any papers you wanted me to.'

'I was so angry when you turned up on my doorstep. I can hardly credit that in just a few weeks we've not just got back together but are truly in love. I wonder if we could say our vows again and get our marriage blessed.'

'Like a fresh start? I'm not sure we can do that, but if the vicar's prepared to let us then I'm all for it.'

'We don't have to have a wedding breakfast or anything like that, it could just be the three of us. As we're already married then we don't need any witnesses,' Lily told him.

'Next time I get an hour off we can go and see him.' He yawned loudly and she giggled.

'Go on with you, you're not tired.'

'I do want to go to bed though. Are you coming?'

* * *

It took time for her to wash up, for him to shut up the chickens and after that they still had to use the WC and do all the other pre-bedtime things.

'I shaved this morning, love, do you want me to do it again before we turn in?'

He was standing right beside her and she reached up to run her fingers over his cheeks. Just touching him made her pulse race. His eyes darkened and his eyes blazed.

'No, you're fine, love,' she just about managed to say, her vice husky with passion. He reacted instantly, pulled her hard against him and his mouth covered hers in a kiss so fierce, so passionate she couldn't breathe.

They scarcely made it up the stairs. An hour later she was resting her head on his shoulder and he was gently stroking her hair off her face.

'If we don't have another baby, love, we're certainly going to enjoy trying.'

'If I'd known doing this could be so exciting, so wonderful, then I'd have found someone to do it with and not waited all these years.'

'It's only because of how we feel about each other that it was like this. It's called making love for a reason.'

'I need to find my nightie as I'm not going outside in my birthday suit later.'

'Use the po under the bed in the other room. No need for a nightie, love, I'll just be taking it off again in half an hour.'

21

Emily always looked forward to half-term break and holidays from school but this half term was going to be extra special. Grandma and Grandpa were going back to their own house in Kent and she was going with them. Not to stay forever, of course, but to stay for two weeks.

Daddy had written to her headmistress and got permission for her to be absent from school for an extra week. Her parents thought that having her travel with her grandpa would make things easier for her grandma. Her brothers were moping about, fed up because they weren't coming too. Sammy wasn't being too bad but George was plain awful.

'It's not fair, it's jolly well bad form for you to go and we can't. We've never been to Kent, we'd be able to see loads of dogfights and battles from there,' George moaned for the hundredth time.

'Shut up about fighter planes, you horrible little boy,' Emily said. 'Sometimes I want to shake you and do you know why?' She didn't wait for him to answer and told him anyway. 'Glorifying death is just despicable. It doesn't matter if the people who die are Germans, English, Polish or any other nationality – they are still somebody's relative.'

'Killing Germans is a good thing, so there. You're just a silly girl so don't understand about war,' George replied.

Mummy had overheard this argument and called out from the sitting room. 'If I hear another word from you, George, then you'll be confined to the house for your entire half-term holiday.'

George rushed to the door. 'I'm sorry, I won't say anything else. But I still don't see why—'

Sammy grabbed George's arm and pulled him back before he could make matters worse. 'You just don't know when to shut up, do you? I'm going out to play football in the park. I don't care if you come with me or not as you're getting on my nerves too.'

Both Emily and George were silenced by this outburst. This was the first time since he'd been adopted into the family that he'd spoken up.

'Good for you, Sammy, he needed to hear that.' Emily smiled at him and the little boy – not so little really as he was almost ten and growing like a weed – opened the front door and rushed out, not waiting for George to follow.

'I don't care; he's not our real brother anyway.'

Before he could stomp off, Mummy appeared in the doorway looking very cross indeed. 'I warned you, young man, about your poor behaviour. Go to your room and remain there until I give you permission to come out.'

Her brother scowled. Emily wanted to warn him not to make things worse but he was too far away to nudge and wasn't looking at her.

'I wasn't talking about fighter planes or the war so it's not fair to be sent to my room for saying something that's true.'

For a horrible moment, Emily thought he was going to get a smack. It was a very close thing judging from Mummy's expression.

'Get out of my sight. I have four children; I love them all equally but at the moment you're my least favourite.'

He gulped and fled up the stairs and Emily turned to follow him. She hated to see him so upset, even when it was his own fault.

'No, let him be. I don't know if you noticed that he's very upset about your grandparents leaving. The fact that you're going to go with them for a while is just making it worse.'

'I know that, Mummy, but that's just him being selfish. Grandpa isn't happy here, he misses the quiet, the countryside, his dogs and his garden. Do you know what he said to me the other day when we were walking along the river path?'

'No, tell me.'

'He said that he wanted to end his days somewhere familiar. That he loved living here, but it was too noisy and the house was too small and too full for him to be comfortable. Haven't you noticed that since they decided to leave he's been a lot brighter and less forgetful?'

'I had noticed that and that's why Daddy and I are happy that they're going home. We are going to miss them most dreadfully but it's right that they go. I'm sorry he said something so sad to you.'

'Is he going to die soon, Mummy?'

'He's ten years older than your grandmother, so he must be in his seventies, which is very old. I think he might be around for a year or two more but it's in God's hands.'

'Don't say that, please, I don't like to think that there's a God somewhere deliberately ending the lives of thousands and thousands of people. That would make him a most monstrous God, don't you think?'

'I'm sorry, I said that without thinking. It's the sort of thing you say in the circumstances but we both know when people die has very little to do with a celestial being. I find it a comfort going to church, praying for my family and friends, praying that the war will end soon and that Hitler won't win, but like you I'm not entirely sure there's anybody or anything actually listening.'

Impulsively Emily stepped forward and hugged her mother – neither of them were physically affectionate by nature. 'I look like you, Mummy, but I hadn't realised how alike we are in so many other ways.'

* * *

The following day, before the boys were up and Daddy hadn't even gone to work, a taxi, one of the few still in service, was waiting outside Harbour House to take Emily and her grandparents to the main station on the other side of Colchester. They didn't have a lot of luggage considering that they'd been living with them for ages which was fortunate as carrying it would have been difficult.

'I'm so excited, I've never been anywhere except London or here,' Emily said as she squeezed into the corner of the back seat.

'It's going to be a long journey, I expect, my dear, but Lily's made us a nice picnic so we've only got to buy a drink at some point,' Grandma said. 'Although I think that beverages are included if you travel in first class.'

'We're going at this God-awful hour of the day, Emily, to avoid the businessmen and the German bombers,' Grandpa said with a cheerful smile.

'You can't reserve seats but I'm hoping that travelling in first class will ensure we have somewhere to sit,' Grandma said.

'Are we going on the underground to Charing Cross or in another taxi?'

'Taxi, if possible, I don't think we could manage our suitcases on the underground, Emily,' Grandma replied.

* * *

A porter wheeled their cases out of Liverpool Street station and by some miracle found them a very ancient taxi. The luggage was put beside the driver but there was no door on the space and Emily thought it quite likely they'd lose their suitcases before they reached Charing Cross.

The back of the cab was like a pram hood and could be folded down which she thought was very odd. Inside there was faded orange prickly matting underfoot and a slippery leather seat. Grandpa recognised the strange old vehicle and said he was tickled pink to travel in this old taxi.

Emily wasn't exactly sure what tickled pink meant as she'd never heard the phrase before but guessed it probably meant that he was pleased. She rather liked it too. What she didn't like was seeing the devastation they passed through. She'd known that London had been horribly bombed over the past few weeks but seeing the results was just awful.

She couldn't speak, couldn't look away, couldn't understand how her grandparents could chat about this and that as if there was nothing wrong at all. Emily was relieved when they pulled into the forecourt of Charing Cross and she didn't have to see bombed-out houses, ruined pavements and streets, and in one place there'd even been a burnt-out double-decker bus.

Grandma paid the fare whilst Emily went in search of a porter. Luckily there was one lurking not far away and he brought his barrow over immediately.

'What platform?'

Emily didn't know and she wasn't sure that either of her grandparents knew this either. 'We need the train that goes to Hastings, but we don't know the exact platform and I hope that you do.'

He nodded but didn't answer. He was a bit grumpy but then he was old and probably thought he wouldn't have to work again and now there was a war on and he'd no choice.

He didn't tell them where he was taking them and they had to almost run to keep up as he charged through the station, almost flattening other passengers.

They arrived at the platform to find the train already there. 'You ain't got long,' the porter said. 'It'll be going in five minutes. First class?'

'Yes, thank you, we are,' Emily said, surprised that neither of her grandparents were taking part in the conversation.

He trundled their cases to the correct carriage and to her surprise even carried them in for them. Grandma gave him something large and silver – Emily wasn't sure if it was a two-shilling piece or half a crown, but he seemed very pleased with what she gave him.

A steward – she thought that's what a waiter on a train was called – stowed their cases for them and then conducted them to a compartment which to her surprise was empty.

'No one else expected, I reckon you'll have this to yourselves. I'll bring you a nice tray of coffee as soon as we're underway.'

Grandpa took the bench seat on one side and Grandma sat opposite, leaving the other window seat for Emily. 'Wake me up when the coffee arrives, Emily, I'm going to have forty winks. Travelling's exhausting.'

'Is Grandpa all right?'

'Yes, darling, he's perfectly splendid. I'm so glad you told me how he felt. I was being a selfish old woman keeping him in Wivenhoe. He loves the country and will be so much better in his own home. I can't wait to show you where your father grew up.'

'I can't wait to see it. Is it safe so close to the coast, Grandma? To be honest, I was rather surprised my parents allowed me to come with you because of the bombs being dropped in London and on Hastings.'

'We live inland, Emily, ten miles away, in the middle of fields and woods. Absolutely safe, I can assure you. I've arranged for our gardener-cum-chauffeur to collect us so we won't be in Hastings for very long.'

Emily smiled and settled back with a sigh, this was going to be a real adventure and she wasn't going to worry about exactly how she was going to get back to Harbour House on her own when her holiday was over.

* * *

Lily lay awake listening to her husband breathing beside her. He seemed to fall asleep more easily than she, but she couldn't remember if that had been the case before. She smiled in the darkness. After Daphne had been born he'd moved, at her request, into the room Daphne now had, and they'd rarely been intimate at all.

She couldn't hold back a bubble of laughter and giggled. Instantly he was awake.

'Why are you giggling, love? Did I fart?'

'No, don't be vulgar, even if you had you shouldn't mention it.' She snorted and between giggles tried to explain. 'I think we've made love more tonight than in the entire time we were together.'

She could just see his outline reflected under the door from the night-light on the stairs.

He'd pushed himself up onto one elbow, was on his side and even in the darkness she knew he was staring at her intently.

'Then we've got a lot of time to make up for.'

Eventually, they slept and when she opened her eyes she was alone. Then she heard his footsteps outside on the landing and he walked in – not a stitch of clothing on – holding two mugs of tea.

'You shouldn't walk about the house like that, love, what if Daphne had been home? You'd have given her the shock of her life.' It was a bit of a shock to her too as she'd not seen him like this until last night. She was pretty sure few men wandered about the house with nothing on so where had he got these risky ideas from?

He grinned, unabashed. 'Well, she isn't, and I won't do it when she is. I'd happily come back to bed with you but I've got to get moving. I have to be at work in half an hour.'

All thought of tea in bed and romance vanished. 'If you've got to be at work in half an hour then so have I. I've never been late for anything in my life and I don't intend to start today.'

Ignoring the tea, she scampered about the room searching for her under-wear, then her frock and pulled both on whilst he smiled in a superior way. Despite the fact that she'd started getting dressed first he was ready before her.

'I'll make toast and boil a couple of eggs for you. Do you have time to let the chickens out or shall I do that whilst you eat?'

His smile made her heart flutter. She was certain that in future – even when their daughter was just across the landing – they weren't going to get a lot of sleep.

'I think I'd better just close the door, love, we don't want Daphne seeing the state of the bed.'

She was halfway down the stairs when he called this out and turned, putting her hands on her hips like a fishwife. 'I'm telling you now, Patrick Turner, and I'm only telling you this once. What happens in our bedroom is between us and I'll have no mention of it anywhere else. Is that quite clear?'

He nodded solemnly and raised his hand as if in surrender, but his eyes were dancing with mischief. He was irresistible and he knew it. Thank goodness she hadn't been in love with him when they were together as they'd now have a dozen children instead of just the one.

She nipped out to the WC and heard him go down the steps to the bottom of the garden to let the chickens out. The kettle was put to simmer on the range first thing so it wouldn't take her long to bring a saucepan of water to the boil and pop in a couple of eggs whilst she made the toast.

'Three eggs today, love, and I've left the gate open. The hens are obviously settled or they wouldn't be laying so well. We'll let them have the run of the garden. They won't need as much food if they're finding insects and worms for themselves.'

'I need to protect the few veg I've got growing or they'll be gone by this evening.'

'Already done it, Daphne's rose and your veg are safe.'

He left a few minutes later and he was whistling. If she could whistle then she'd be doing it too. For the first time ever she left dirty breakfast things in the sink as she didn't have time to wash up.

This morning old Mr and Mrs Roby were leaving Harbour House and she'd wanted to be there early enough to say goodbye but she saw the taxi drive past the end of the terrace as she was locking her front door. Emily had gone with them for a visit so she'd only have the two boys and Mr and Mrs Roby to cook for. The baby just had whatever they were having mashed up with a bit of gravy.

There was a bit of an atmosphere in the house, which was unusual.

Hardly surprising as the older Robys were much-loved members of the family and would be missed. It was unlikely that she'd ever see either of them again, which was why she'd been so keen to say goodbye before they left.

Mr Roby ate his breakfast in silence and left without saying goodbye to Mrs Roby. As it was half term, the boys would probably have a lie in, which gave her time to start sorting out the empty bedrooms whilst she waited to finish cooking and serving breakfast.

Sammy appeared just after eight o'clock. 'George's in disgrace, Lily, he has to stay upstairs. I don't like it here without Emily – I wish she hadn't gone away too.'

'Never mind, love, she'll be back in a couple of weeks. What are you going to do with yourself this morning?'

He shrugged. 'Don't know. I'll go up the park and see if there's anybody there and if not I'll come home again.'

Lily was certain there'd be no children anywhere so early but didn't have the heart to tell him.

The two rooms were spotless, the sheets had been removed and must have already been taken down to the laundry room, the blankets were folded up neatly on the bed. All the furniture was dust free, and she couldn't see a speck of dirt anywhere. When had Mrs Roby done this? She must have been up at dawn.

Lily knocked on George's door and received a grumpy reply. She opened the door and found him sprawled on the floor surrounded by his little soldiers.

'What do you want for breakfast? There's no porridge as your grandpa's gone, but I've got everything else.'

'Not hungry, don't want anything. I don't see why Sammy didn't stay up here with me and play war games – I don't like being on my own. It's not fair that Emily got to go away for an adventure.'

'Life isn't fair, George, a lot of the time. But I think you're lucky to live in such a lovely big house, go to a posh school, have regular meals cooked for you – there are dozens of boys who'd give their right arm to be you.'

He didn't answer for a minute but then nodded. 'I'm just fed up; we'd all got used to having our grandparents here and it won't be the same without them. Do you think that Sammy and I might be able to go and stay with them next summer?'

'Nobody knows what we can do next summer what with there being a war on and all that. To be honest, love, just be grateful that you live somewhere safe and don't worry about next year until it comes.'

He managed a feeble smile. 'Maybe I am a bit hungry, Lily, so I'd like a bit of breakfast but I'm not sure I'm allowed to have it up here.'

'Go on with you, you might be in disgrace but you're not going to be starved, are you?'

Lily had heard Mrs Roby coming out of her bedroom with the baby and knew that what she'd just said would have been heard by her employer.

'Well said, Lily, nobody goes hungry in this house even when they've been misbehaving. However, as we're all a bit sad today I've decided to rescind your punishment, George. Come down with me and we'll have breakfast together. I heard your brother going out which is a pity as I'd like to have had him there too.'

'So would I, Mummy, I apologised to him and we made it up. He's my brother and I love him.'

None of them had heard the front door open and close but they certainly heard the thunder of Sammy's footsteps as he hurtled up the stairs.

'I love you too, George, and I don't like being on my own.'

Lily exchanged a smile with Mrs Roby as the boys hugged awkwardly and then followed them downstairs.

* * *

When Mrs Roby suggested that the boys come with her to a WVS meeting Lily was surprised that they agreed so readily.

'Will we have jobs to do, Mummy?' Sammy asked.

'Your job will be to entertain your little sister whilst I take part in the meeting. There are toys provided and in return you'll be given at least one slice of cake and a cup of tea.'

'Sounds all right to me,' George said. 'Will there be other children there or just us?'

'As it's half term there might well be quite a few but I'm sure none of them will be as well behaved and polite as you two.'

The boys swelled with pride and Lily hid her smile. There weren't many nine-year-olds who were so good, helpful and friendly. She thought that if she was lucky enough to have another baby she'd like him or her to grow up just like the Roby children.

At ten o'clock the house was empty apart from her and the cat. Ginger would be asleep somewhere comfortable, so he didn't really count as he was no company.

Gladys would be working outside in the laundry room this morning and so wouldn't really be in the house much. She'd come in for elevenses, and to use the WC if necessary, but otherwise stayed in her own domain.

Lily was just making the tea for them both when the telephone jangled. She waited to see if it would ring a second time which meant the call was for this house and not for the doctor's next door. It was for them and with some reluctance she wiped her hands and hurried to pick it up.

'Good morning, Harbour House, housekeeper speaking. How can I help?'

This was what Mrs Roby had trained her to say and she said it in her poshest voice.

'Golly, that's a problem. I only have a few pennies for the telephone and I really need to speak to Mrs Roby or Mr Roby at a pinch.'

The voice belonged to someone young, someone very well spoken, and Lily wasn't sure if it was her place to ask this girl to identify herself.

'Who shall I say is calling?'

'Oh, silly me, I'm Lucinda Somiton, I'm Mrs Roby's cousin. Can you please tell her that I'm coming to stay with her and I'll explain everything when I arrive later.' The pips started to go. 'Sorry, can't tell you anything else. I'll be there after lunch.'

The phone disconnected as Miss Somiton's money ran out. Lily put the receiver back on the hook, surprised, but quite pleased, by this unexpected information. This Miss Somiton sounded like the sort of young lady who would really liven things up and that's just what Harbour House needed at the moment.

Emily would be surprised to find an unknown family member living in one of the vacant rooms when she came back at the end of next week.

Mrs Roby received the news about her cousin arriving without invitation with a sigh and a smile. 'There's a fourteen-year gap between us so we've never been particularly close, but the occasions we have met have been amicable enough. Lucinda's always been a wild girl, rebelling against everything; she was expelled from her boarding school twice. One can be quite sure that she's coming to us to escape whatever nonsense she's got herself into.'

'Which room shall I get ready for her, Mrs Roby?'

'Either, it doesn't matter. How fortuitous that my in-laws decided to leave and on the very same day Lucinda decided to come.'

'If they hadn't gone, I could have cleared out the other attic room easily enough. Do you think she'll be staying long or will this be a flying visit?'

'Until I know what trouble she's got herself into it's impossible to say. Assume she's going to be a semi-permanent visitor, Lily.'

22

Emily enjoyed the train journey and especially the free hot beverages and sandwiches that were brought to their compartment. The picnic lunch wasn't necessary but they ate it anyway.

'How does your chauffeur know when to come to the station at Hastings when the trains are so erratic at the moment?' Emily asked.

'He'll come at the time it's supposed to be there and just wait until we arrive,' Grandpa told her. 'I expect he'll get himself a pint of beer and enjoy not having anything to do.'

'I hope he doesn't have more than one, Gregory, we don't want to be driven home by someone who's inebriated,' Grandma said.

This was the first time Emily had heard that her grandpa was called Gregory. She wondered what her grandma's name was but didn't like to ask.

'I'm sure he won't, my dear, he's a sensible fellow.'

'What does he do when he's not driving you about the place? I didn't think that civilians had petrol any more,' Emily said.

'As I was temporarily in charge of the Home Guard, I had an allowance and we'll use the car as long as some of that remains. Smithers looks after the kitchen garden, the chickens and other poultry. He finds local boys to help him as it's too much for one person. His wife is our housekeeper and she has someone from the village come in and help as your mother does at Harbour House.'

'I see. I can't tell you how excited I am to be visiting somewhere new, to be able to see where my father grew up. As it's near the sea I always thought it must be why he became an Admiralty surveyor.'

Grandma nodded. 'A bike ride away, and he spent a lot of time when he was on holiday messing around on boats. He went away to school – we thought that best as he was an only child and didn't have any friends in the neighbourhood.'

The closer they got to his home, the brighter Grandpa seemed. Emily hadn't noticed until then how thin he was, how frail-looking, and she was quite certain he'd looked more robust when he'd come to them a few months ago.

Sadly, she turned away from him and stared out the window. Kent seemed to have more hills than Essex, lots of cows, lots of fields and she was thrilled to have seen several land girls working.

She wondered if the war would still be going on when she was old enough to enlist in one of the services. She thought she'd rather be a WAAF than anything else, but it would probably be safer to work on the land although a lot harder.

Seeing so many farms made her think about Jimmy Peterson. He would be fifteen soon, three years older than her, and he could very well be called up if this beastly war didn't end soon. Somehow it would be much harder thinking about someone she liked, someone close to her own age, having to fight the Germans.

After hours of stopping and starting, shunting on and off the main track to let troops and goods go past, the novelty had worn off. Neither of her grandparents seemed in the mood to speak to her – in fact they weren't even speaking to each other; they appeared to be lost in their own thoughts. Emily was getting rather bored and was eager to share some of her ideas with them but thought she might leave that until later.

Having never been away from home before it belatedly occurred to her that maybe she didn't really like new experiences as much as she'd expected to. Thank goodness she hadn't insisted on being evacuated with her school as she'd have absolutely hated that.

Eventually her grandparents perked up. 'We'll be at the station in around ten minutes, Emily, I notice you've been shifting uncomfortably so I expect you'll be pleased to know that there's a ladies' room at the station you can use.'

Grandpa winked at her and that made Emily laugh. 'Sorry, I've been getting a bit desperate. I didn't like to ask if there was anywhere on the train.'

'Actually, my dear girl, there's a perfectly adequate WC in the first-class compartment. You've still got time to use it as Hastings is where this train terminates. It won't steam out with you still on board.'

Emily was out of her seat and through the door seconds later. The steward saw her look of desperation and pointed to the necessary door. 'Don't flush the chain if we've actually stopped in the station, miss.'

There wasn't time to admire the little room, but it was a lot cleaner than the one she'd had to use a few times at school. She quickly dipped her hands in water, dried them on the towel and was then out again and back to her compartment before the train slowed to enter the station.

'Excellent, I shall avail myself of the facilities at the station. I find peeing when on a train is a highly unsatisfactory experience,' Grandpa said.

She wasn't sure if she should be shocked or laugh as she'd never heard a grown-up say anything about that sort of thing. Grandma pretended he hadn't spoken which was probably the best thing to do.

* * *

Half an hour later their luggage was stowed in the boot of a big black car and Emily was on the back seat. However, neither of her grandparents had yet to emerge from the station. This gave her an opportunity to speak to the middle-aged man who was driving the smart car.

'Mr Smithers, I'm Emily Roby. I'm pleased to meet you. I'm going to be staying for two weeks.'

He was standing just outside the open rear door, waiting to assist her grandparents into the car.

'Pleased to meet you, Miss Roby. Do you like dogs?'

This seemed a strange question and wasn't one she could really answer. 'I certainly do and I regularly take a friend's dogs out for walks. We've got a big cat and I like that very much. I didn't know my grandparents had dogs as they've never mentioned them.'

'Well, Othello and Caliban, big black labs, are Mr Roby's – Mrs Roby doesn't have much to do with them.'

'I don't know what a lab is apart from being somewhere scientists work.'

He chuckled. He was really a nice man – obviously too old to be called up, but not so old he wasn't still fit enough to work.

'Labradors – gundogs – not that either of them is a working dog as Mr Roby isn't one for hunting.'

'I like their names. I hope they're friendly as I'd really like to get to know them.'

'If you can throw a ball or a stick they'll be your friends for life. Daft pair, nothing they like better than fetching things for you, particularly if you throw it into the river.'

'Rusty and Boyd, the two I take out, swim in the river and also love to fetch sticks.'

'What breed are they, miss?'

'Boyd looks a bit like a wolfhound and Rusty like a large red setter. They are big dogs but really well behaved.'

'Then our boys will be no problem for you, labs are big but not as big as either of your two, I shouldn't think.'

She hadn't known there was a river and was just about to ask him more when her grandparents came out. They were walking arm in arm and looked quite different – not like the people they'd been when they were living at Harbour House.

This surprised her as she thought her home was the best place in the world and that everybody would think the same. She'd once heard someone say, 'home is where the heart is' and hadn't really understood its true meaning but now she thought she did.

They drove through narrow country lanes with high hedges so she couldn't see anything but greenery. Autumn was late this year and most of the trees had all their leaves even though they were turning a bit brown in places.

'We're almost home, Emily, just a few minutes more and you'll see the entrance to our drive,' Grandpa said and even his voice sounded different since he'd got off the train.

'I expect your dogs will be really excited to see you home, Grandpa. Mr Smithers told me about them but he didn't say how old they are.'

'They're from the same litter, they'll be five, I think. I'm not exactly sure – Eloise, my love, do you remember when we got them?'

'I do, mainly because of the puddles and other unpleasantness they brought with them. You're right, my dear, they would have been five a couple of months ago.'

'How long do dogs live?' Emily asked.

'Not long enough, if you ask me,' Grandpa said immediately. 'Smaller dogs seem to live longer and can even get to the grand old age of fourteen or fifteen. Unfortunately, bigger dogs don't usually survive much more than eleven or twelve years.'

This was the longest sentence she'd heard him speak. 'Then they've got a lot more years in front of them than they have behind which is very good indeed.'

He chuckled and reached out and ruffled her hair – again not something he'd done before. She began to wonder what had happened earlier in the year that had made her grandma rush down to Kent and bring him back to Wivenhoe.

She smiled. Eloise was a lovely name and it suited her lovely grandma.

* * *

Patrick went to speak to Mr Roby during the half an hour they got to eat their lunch. He explained that he was no longer a lodger but the man of the house.

'Good for you, Patrick, I imagined that was on the cards. I'll inform the War Office and have the stipend for Lily terminated. As you've just been promoted you'll have the five shillings from that, plus the ten shillings that was being deducted.'

'Thank you, sir, I appreciate you sorting this out for me.'

Patrick missed the flask of stewed tea that Mrs Hatch had provided with his lunch but he had a bottle of water with a drop of squash and that was almost as good. The arrangement that had been made when he first arrived to have sandwiches prepared for his shed meant he always got something decent to eat and it was worth the tanner a day.

'You're a cheerful sod, Paddy, you won the pools or somethink?' Trevor, one of his team, asked.

'Even better, mate, my Lily and I are back together. I reckon I'm the luckiest bloke alive – I'm doing a job I like and am good at, getting decent money, not in any danger from being bombed or shot at, and my wife has taken me back.'

'Lucky sod, your Lily's a cracker. Small wonder you're looking cock-a-hoop.'

'About the pools, Paddy, we was wondering if you'd like to join the syndicate. We put in a tanner each week and we've more than had our money back over the months,' Billy said.

'Not a lot more, I expect. I used to do them and once won £10. I'm in. Ta for asking. It'll be the Unity pools now as they've merged because the post office didn't want all those different coupons every week.'

* * *

They finished earlier that evening as it was too dark to work safely because of the storm. Patrick didn't mind getting soaked on the way home for two reasons. One, because he was going to see his wife and daughter and for the first time in over fourteen years he would be entitled to sit at the table with them. Two, because tonight there shouldn't be any air raids in London.

He had to put his shoulder to the front door to open it – next time he had an hour off he'd sort that out.

'Bring your coat through, love, it'll dry better in the kitchen,' Lily called.

Patrick had already put his boots in the box just inside the door and padded through in his socks. Daphne was sitting at the table reading what looked like a soppy romance book.

'Evening, Dad, you're dripping on the floor.' She stood up and held out a hand for his coat, cap and scarf.

'Here you are, love, my jacket's not too bad so I'll hang it over the back of the chair. It'll be fine by the morning.'

He stepped down into the kitchen and Lily walked into his arms, which was exactly where she belonged. Several minutes later they were both hot and bothered and he could hear his daughter sniggering in the living room.

'That's enough of that, Patrick Turner, I told you this morning we're keeping things decent down here for our daughter's sake.' She spoke quietly but he thought Daphne had probably heard.

'Fine. Did you shut the chickens up? Had they all found their way back to the coop?'

'Daphne did it. They went in a bit early as it was tipping down. We've now got eight eggs in that bowl. I think I'm going to have to tell somebody as we're not supposed to have more than three a week between us.'

'Let's enjoy another week of having fresh eggs. Give some to our neighbours – I reckon they'll be pleased to have a couple of fresh eggs each and won't be snitching on us to the Ministry of Agriculture.'

'If it stops raining I'll get Daphne to take another two to Mrs Hobday and a couple to old Mrs Hughes and her daughter on the other side.'

'You didn't say, love, did the chickens get in safely after wandering around the garden all day?'

Daphne called out from the living room. 'All present and correct, Dad, I counted them. They look like different hens to the ones we got a few days ago. Pity I can't say the same about the garden.'

He grinned and went to join his daughter. 'There's not much growing in it at the moment, although now I'm back I'll try and find time to plant spuds next year. They don't dig those up.'

'I couldn't believe how much ground they'd scraped up looking for worms and that. You won't have to dig much as the chickens are doing it for you.'

They were settling down in the living room for the evening when Lily remembered she'd got news to share with them.

'I never told you two what happened this afternoon,' she said. 'There's a new resident at Harbour House – Miss Lucinda Somiton. She's Mrs Roby's cousin but a lot younger than her.'

Patrick wasn't listening, he was fiddling with the wireless, but Daphne was all agog.

'Go on, Mum, what's she like and why's she there?'

'She's ever so pretty, very posh, very smart and seemed nice enough. I don't know why she's come. Mrs Roby said earlier that she thought her cousin was in trouble of some sort but obviously they're not going to tell me what that is. As soon as I hear anything you'll be the first to know.'

'Maybe she's in the family way, that'll be a turn-up for the books.'

Patrick frowned. 'That's enough of that gossip, young lady, mud sticks and none of us know why the girl's come and anyway it's none of our business.'

Daphne apologised and Lily smiled. After all these years there was a man in the house again and she couldn't be happier.

* * *

Their daughter went up at nine o'clock, saying she was on the early shift again but would be home by three – two hours earlier than usual. Ten minutes after she went, he and Lily tiptoed after her.

They were just settling down after a passionate hour or so when the siren began to howl. Patrick sat up.

'There shouldn't be any raids tonight because of the weather. Stop where you are, I'm going to pull the blackout out of the way and see what's going on out there.'

She didn't argue. He stubbed his toe a couple of times on pieces of furniture – he wasn't familiar with the layout of the room yet. He pulled the heavy black curtain aside and pushed the window up.

Immediately, he heard the distinctive, uneven drone of German bombers flying overhead. The rain had stopped, the storm cleared, it was now a bomber's moon.

'Close the curtain, come back to bed, love, you know they'll not be dropping any bombs here,' Lily said.

'I know that, but where do you go if you do want to take shelter? If bombs started falling in Wivenhoe where do folk go?'

'There's an Anderson shelter at the end of the terrace – I took a look in when it went up last year – nasty, smelly place. You'd be sitting with your feet in several inches of water. It's never been used.'

'Remember there's another much larger cellar as well as the one where the coal's stored under the kitchen. I'm going to investigate the bigger one and see if I can turn it into a shelter we can use if necessary.'

'I never went down there when you were here so why would I go down when you'd gone? It'll be full of mice, possibly rats as well, spiders and God knows what.'

He dropped the blackout and hopped back into bed. 'I never looked when I lived here as a child with my grandparents – they said the stairs were too dangerous – I can't think why we never at least had a poke around to see if there's anything worth having stored down there,' Patrick said, slightly disappointed that she'd put her nightie on as he wouldn't have minded making love a third time.

Patrick couldn't sleep as he was now eager to explore under the house. It was a mystery he wanted to solve – there could possibly be valuable antiques from his grandparents' time stored down there, forgotten for all these years. They'd bought the house when it was new so there couldn't be anything older than mid-Victorian. He slipped out of bed, collected his clothes and took them onto the landing. He dressed at speed just in case Daphne had heard him and came out to investigate.

There'd be no electricity down there but there was a lamp in the front room which would give him more light than his torch, but he'd take that with him anyway. He had to move two chairs in order to roll back the rug and reveal the trapdoor.

The living-room light was enough for him to look down the steep stone steps. He sniffed. He wasn't going to find anything unpleasant, no dead bodies, as he'd have been able to smell them even after all this time.

It didn't take him long to remove the glass mantel and trim the wick of the lamp. He soon had it burning brightly. He'd not use his torch unless he had to as batteries were hard to find. You could buy paraffin at the back of old Mr Chaney's shop just across the road so replacing that wouldn't be a problem.

There was a rope attached to the wall and he hung onto that as he descended with the lamp in front of him. His breath hissed through his teeth when he reached the brick floor without breaking his neck.

The cellar appeared to be huge, to stretch under most of the house. No reason why it shouldn't as this row of cottages were built on the top of the slope made when the Victorians had dug the cutting for the trains to run through.

He shuffled forward a few steps. The lamp didn't allow him to see into the pitch darkness that surrounded him on all sides.

'Crikey, Dad, what are you doing down there in the middle of the night?' Daphne called down the steps.

He almost dropped the lamp. 'What are you doing up? I nearly had a heart attack, love, I could have dropped this and set the house on fire.'

'Good thing you didn't then. I'm coming down – never knew this was here. Why are you investigating now?'

'We need our own shelter just in case. Wivenhoe's been lucky so far but it's only a matter of time before the Nazis discover that the shipyards are here.'

'No, I don't reckon they'll ever notice. It was ever so clever of them to paint the roofs of the sheds and buildings to look like ordinary houses.'

'Never mind that, did you bring a torch, love? I think we're going to need yours and mine as well as this lamp. I'm going to put it on the floor, it's hot and heavy and not meant to be carried around like this.'

'Hang on, I'll get a couple of candles. I know where Mum keeps them.'

23

Lily turned to cuddle Patrick and found his side of the bed empty – not only empty, but cold. She reached up, switched on the bedside light and saw his clothes had gone too. She scrambled out of bed, pulled on her dressing gown, pushed her feet into her slippers and went in search of him.

Daphne's door was open and from the hall light she saw this bed was also unoccupied. Her clothes were folded neatly on the chair so she must be in her dressing gown and nightie as well.

Lily stopped at the living-room door. Her eyes rounded, her heart skipped a beat. Light filtered from the open trapdoor in the centre of the room. The silly beggars must be down the cellar – goodness knows why either of them wanted to investigate down there at this time of the night.

She approached cautiously and peered into the narrow, steep stone steps. The lamp from the front room was burning brightly on the cellar floor. 'I'm going to put the kettle on. I reckon you'll need a hot drink when you come up,' she yelled. Her voice echoed and she heard Patrick say something he shouldn't.

Then he was standing in the pool of light, looking less than pleased to see her. 'I dropped my bloody torch, Lily. First Daphne scares the living daylights out of me and now you do the same. Why couldn't you women stay in bed like sensible people?'

She smiled down at him, not bothered by his grumpiness. 'There's no need for bad language, Patrick Turner. I'm not coming down so don't ask me to.' Then curiosity got the better of her. 'Have you found anything interesting? Was it worth all this palaver?'

'You'll have to come down and see for yourself. But put the kettle on first, love, you're right about needing a hot drink when we come up.'

'Cheek. I'll make a pot of tea and I expect you both to be back in my living room and for it to be how it was before by the time it's ready.'

* * *

They hadn't started lighting the fire in here so it was chilly especially with the icy draught coming up from the cellar. The kitchen was snug and warm because the range was on night and day, summer and winter, because it's what Lily cooked on and what heated the water.

A good twenty minutes after she'd told them to hurry up they appeared in the living room. Daphne rushed in to join her.

'Blimey, it's perishing down there. Let me warm myself at the range. Is the tea ready, Mum? It'll help thaw me out.'

'It's been ready for ten minutes, my girl, it'll be a bit stewed now.' Lily stared into the living room and watched as Patrick slammed the trapdoor and pushed the bolt across before rolling the rug back where it should be.

'Here, Daphne love, you take the pot and I'll bring the mugs. I think you both deserve something out of the broken biscuit tin after all the excitement.'

* * *

Over tea and biscuits, Patrick and Daphne told her what they'd found. No wonder they'd spent so long down there.

'Not quite as good as a pot of gold, or a chest full of treasure, but from what you said there's plenty of stuff down there that's worth a few bob. A chest of old-fashioned clothes – I can't wait to see those. I'm surprised the moths haven't eaten them,' Lily said.

'Too blooming cold down there for moths, love, they're not even damp, just cold,' Patrick said. 'There's a large metal box full of something that rattles. It was too heavy to bring up on my own. I reckon that might be something valuable – too heavy for jewellery unfortunately.'

'I didn't go with Dad into the second cellar but there's not much in there, is there, Dad?'

'No, broken furniture mostly. I'll bring that up as it'll do for the fire when we start lighting it in here. I'll need to ask Frank to give me a hand to bring up the two chests, the bits of furniture and that metal box.'

'I'd have thought you'd want to leave the furniture down there if you want to turn it into a shelter,' Lily said.

'Too cold and not enough air to spend long down there. It occurred to me, Lily love, that if we close the trapdoor and then the house takes a direct hit nobody would know we were there. I reckon I'll take my chances aboveground.'

'If that's what you think, love, I'll not argue. To tell you the truth I wasn't keen on the idea of hiding in the cellar either.'

'Why don't you see if you can make the Anderson shelter a bit more comfortable, Dad?'

'That's a good idea, love, I'll give it a once-over when I get a minute. But I want to stop the door sticking before I do anything else.'

'If there's nothing we actually want, Patrick, there's no rush to go down that horrible cellar again soon, is there?'

'There isn't, I'll wait until we need the wood for the fire in a few weeks,' he replied.

'Dad, it'll be even colder down there by November.'

'No, love, it won't, it'll be the same as it is now. Let's get back to bed, haven't you got to be on the five o'clock train, Daphne?'

Half an hour later the house was quiet, Lily was asleep in his arms, and his daughter was safely in her own bed. Patrick's mouth curved. He'd got everything he'd dreamed of, his life was perfect and he knew he was the luckiest bloke in Wivenhoe. If it hadn't been for the war he'd not be where he was right now. It wasn't right to be glad about the fighting, but in a small way he was as it had brought him back to his family. He sighed, tightened his arms and fell asleep.

* * *

Emily thoroughly enjoyed her two weeks in Kent but was more than ready to return to Harbour House at the end of her holiday. Mr Smithers would be driving her to the station in Hastings but neither of her grandparents would be accompanying her. The night before she left, her suitcase was packed, she'd spent the final riotous hour with the dogs but she still didn't know exactly how she was going to get across London on her own.

'Grandma, I'm a bit worried about tomorrow. I know I lived in London for years but I never crossed the city on my own and especially not during wartime.'

'I have every confidence that you can achieve something so trivial without being accompanied by an adult. I can't leave your grandfather – he becomes upset when I'm not close by.'

Emily wanted to say that Grandma could come to London see her to Liverpool Street and be back home within a few hours. Grandpa would have Mrs Smithers and his dogs and wouldn't come to any harm but she feared that she might.

'What if I can't get a taxi? Am I supposed to catch a bus or go by the underground?'

'A few months ago you were insisting that you were an adult and wanted to be more independent. Now you've got your chance to prove just how grown-up you are.'

Her grandmother changed the subject, obviously not wanting to talk about the difficulties Emily might encounter tomorrow.

'Have you enjoyed your stay here?'

'Yes, it's been absolutely spiffing, but I'm ready to go home now. I miss my brothers and sister and my mummy and daddy. I'm also concerned that I've missed rather a lot of school and will have a lot to catch up on when I do get back on Monday.'

'I'll say my farewells now, my dear girl, and thank you so much for coming. We loved having you here.'

Emily blinked back tears. 'Goodbye, Grandma, and thank you for having me.'

She'd expected that at least her grandmother would get up to see her off as she wasn't leaving until eight o'clock.

Grandpa had already retired and she was disappointed that they'd not said goodbye. As she was passing his bedroom she noticed the door was open and the light on. She paused and knocked.

'Come in, come in, my dear child, I've been waiting to speak to you before you go to bed.'

He was sitting in an armchair by the fire in his dressing gown and pyjamas. Something made her rush across and drop down beside him.

'I love you, Grandpa, I'm so glad we got to meet each other.' She buried her face in his lap and he stroked her hair.

'And I'm privileged to have met you and your brothers and baby sister. I expect you're worried about travelling home on your own tomorrow but I've every confidence you will accomplish the journey with no problems. You're old beyond your years and have a perfectly good tongue in your head if you're stuck.'

'You're right, Grandpa, I think I'm worrying unnecessarily. I intend to write to you – I don't expect you to reply but I want you to know that I'll be thinking about you.'

'Good heavens, I'm still capable of writing a letter. Yes, Emily, please write and get your scamps of brothers to add a few lines to the bottom of your missive.'

'I'll do that.' Emily stood up and leaned in to hug him and he returned the gesture. She swallowed the lump in her throat, knowing this was the last time she was likely to see him.

'Before you go, there's something for you on that table by the door. Don't open it until you're on the train. Will you promise me that?'

'I will, Grandpa, and thank you very much. Do you need me to help you to bed?'

He chuckled and didn't sound at all old or unwell. 'I should think not, my girl, I'm quite capable of getting into bed under my own steam. Off you go. Good night, Emily, you're going to have a wonderful life and I wish I could be here to see it.'

She rushed out, snatching up the small brown-paper-wrapped parcel as she fled. She wished she'd known both her grandparents for longer.

* * *

The train was waiting in the station when she walked in. She showed her first-class ticket to the guard on the gate and he beckoned over a porter.

'Take this young lady to first class and see that she has a window seat. Speak to the steward and let him know that she's travelling unaccompanied.'

The porter took Emily's case and walked ahead of her towards the front of the train. The station was busy, some civilians but mostly people in uniform. Her heart thumped. What if she had to travel with soldiers, airmen or sailors? She really didn't want to be alone with strange men.

By the time they reached the open door of the carriage she was to get into she had the silver threepenny piece in her hand ready to give to the porter. She wasn't sure if this was enough, but it would have to do.

There was a steward waiting at the door and the suitcase changed hands.

'Thank you,' Emily said and handed over the coin.

The porter nodded and smiled, obviously satisfied with her tip.

'I'm Johnson, I'll be taking care of you.'

'I'm Emily Roby, I'm a bit nervous about travelling by myself. Please don't put me in with men in uniform.'

He grinned. 'Crikey, I should think not, Miss Roby, I thought you'd like to sit in the Pullman car. It's where first-class passengers come for refreshments.'

'Oh, like a restaurant on wheels – that sounds absolutely splendid. I couldn't eat any breakfast as I was too worried.'

He led her down the carriage and into the very smart dining area. He pushed her case into a slot along with several others. 'Don't worry, miss, I'll retrieve it for you and take it to the platform when we arrive in London.'

He stopped beside a smaller table laid up for two. It had a tablecloth and looked like any other dining room apart from the fact that it was on a train. Emily felt less anxious and just a little bit excited at the thought of eating a meal, not just drinking a cup of tea and having a sandwich, on an actual train. Her brothers would be envious that she'd had this opportunity.

The parcel that Grandpa had given her was in her school satchel which was slung across one shoulder and her gas mask across the other. She removed both but wasn't sure if she should take off her beret, scarf and coat or keep them on.

It wasn't particularly warm, so she decided to keep her coat on and take the other things off.

A waiter arrived and took away the second set of cutlery. He smiled at her. 'We'll be serving breakfast as soon as the train leaves the station, Miss Roby. I have the menu here.'

'Golly, that's grand. I'd like a pot of tea, toast and whatever you have to go with it, no porridge or cereal, but anything cooked apart from kippers.'

He chuckled. 'Right you are. I'll bring your tea straightaway. Breakfast will be in about twenty minutes.'

Emily didn't want to open the parcel until she had her tea and knew she'd be undisturbed for a bit. She carefully poured herself a cup through the strainer, terrified she was going to drip a nasty mark onto the pristine white cloth. She didn't, and with a sigh of relief she turned to the more important task of opening the gift she'd received from her grandfather.

The string had been sealed with red wax – very old-fashioned but she understood the principle. After snapping the wax, she carefully pulled apart the ends of the string. Nothing must be wasted and the string would be used again for something else.

After carefully folding back the brown paper she saw there was a letter addressed to her on top of a small leather box which she thought might be a jewellery box of some sort. It looked like something she'd seen on her mother's dressing table but she thought it would have to be a very big necklace to fit inside this leather box.

She unfolded the letter.

My dearest granddaughter, Emily,

I think we both know that we'll not meet again in this world and probably not in the next – I'm not at all convinced that I'll be going anywhere apart from the ground when I shuffle off this mortal coil.

Don't cry, little girl, I've had a good life and everyone has to die some time. When I go I want you to make sure that my Eloise moves to Harbour House. I don't want her staying here on her own.

Smithers will take my dogs. I've left him and his wife comfortably provided for. My house can be taken over by the military – they are always looking for comfortable billets for their officers. It will be returned to Jonathan after this war's finished.

Maybe all of you will want to live here when it's safe to do so. My house is bigger, there's more room for all of you and I'm sure you would be

*happy if your family were here too. I'd like to think that my son, my wife
and my grandchildren will be living here after me.*

*I know you're looking at the box and wondering what's inside. Probably
thinking that it's jewellery of some sort – it's certainly valuable – but it's not
something that you wear.*

*This gift is to be our secret. You mustn't tell your parents that I gave it
to you until you want to use it for yourself.*

Enjoy your life, follow your dreams and don't let anyone dissuade you.

Think of me sometimes,

Your grandfather.

Emily hardly dared to touch the leather case. She didn't want to have a
secret from her parents but this was her grandfather's dying wish and she
couldn't betray his trust. If she didn't open it then she wouldn't be keeping a
secret as she wouldn't know what was in there.

Her cheeks were wet and she scrubbed and dried them on the crisp
white cotton napkin. The waiter would think she was crying because she was
frightened or lonely and that would never do. Grandpa wanted her to have
whatever was in the box and wanted her to know that he'd given it to her.
She had no option but to look inside and then pray that she'd never reveal
the contents to anyone.

She almost dropped the box as the train lurched out of the station. The
waiter would be back with her breakfast in a few minutes and then it would
be too late. She wasn't going to open it in front of anyone else.

She flicked back the little gold catch and caught her breath. There was
some sort of document inside. Quickly she opened it. She only had a few
moments to glance at the contents.

Her fingers clenched. She knew she'd gone white. She swallowed and
breathed deeply through her nose like her daddy had told her once when
she was feeling faint.

Grandpa had left her a vast sum of money – £10, 000 – she could access it
when she was twenty-one, if she got married before that or in any other
circumstance that the solicitors who held the trust fund considered reason-
able. With some difficulty she refolded the paper and had just closed the box
when the waiter arrived with her food.

Now wasn't the time to think about the implications, to think why the money had been left to her and not to her other siblings. In a day or two she'd study the letter in the privacy of her own bedroom, see where the money was lodged and to whom she had to apply to access it.

Mummy had told her that all of them had a substantial trust fund from her father but obviously Sammy wouldn't have anything. Therefore, she knew exactly where at least some of this money would be going.

* * *

Eventually, the train arrived in London and with some trepidation Emily made her way to the door at the rear of the compartment. Her case was where the porter had left it but she was quite capable of lifting it herself so removed it from the rack and went to stand behind some adults in the small space in front of the exit door.

She was dreading having to find her way through the noisy smelly station and then locate a taxi, or even worse have to catch a bus or the underground train to Liverpool Street.

As she stepped out onto the platform, a complete stranger called her name and ran towards her.

'Emily, you look just like Elizabeth, I recognised you immediately.'

The speaker was a young woman, very pretty, with the palest golden hair and huge blue eyes with dark lashes. She was dressed expensively and must have been sent to meet her.

'Who are you? You know my name but I don't know yours.'

'Scatterbrained, as usual. I'm Lucinda Somiton, I'm your mother's cousin and I've come to live with you for a while. How old are you? I thought I was meeting a little girl, not someone so grown-up as you.'

Emily glowed inside at the praise. 'I'm twelve, but I'm very grown-up for my age and am a year ahead at school. Thank you so much for coming as I was really worried about what came next in this journey.'

'I've managed to bag a taxi. I don't think he'll wait much longer even though I gave him half a crown to do so. Here, let me take your case and then we can hold hands and run.'

* * *

In the thrill of finding that she had a glamorous, sophisticated older cousin, Emily forgot about the gift from her grandfather and spent the next two hours chatting to Lucinda and by the time they steamed into Wivenhoe the two of them were the best of friends. She hadn't liked to ask why her exciting new relative had come to Wivenhoe and Lucinda hadn't mentioned it. Emily was quite sure having her at Harbour House was going to be good fun.

'You've been here for two weeks, Lucinda, have you settled in? What do you think of Wivenhoe after living in London?'

'I love it, everybody's so friendly, things are more relaxed and comfortable than they were in Town. I might well be staying with you permanently but it depends on what happens in the next few weeks.'

Lily had prepared a special tea to welcome Emily home. As she'd not been into Hastings or near any shops at all she had no gifts to give them but they didn't seem to mind.

'I did enjoy myself, but it's much nicer here. I've missed you all so much, and I'm so pleased to be back. Harbour House is the best place in the world and I've got the best family.'

Although she was thrilled to be home, things somehow were different from before. Mummy and the boys didn't seem to like the new guest as much as she did. Had Lucinda already done something to upset them?

* * *

MORE FROM FENELLA J. MILLER

The next book in the Harbour House series from Fenella J. Miller is available to order now here:

https://mybook.to/HarbourHouse5

BIBLIOGRAPHY

A to Z Atlas Guide to London, 1939 reproduction
Wartime Britain by Juliet Gardiner
One Child's War by Victoria Massey
How We Lived Then by Norman Longmate
Growing Up in the War by Maureen Hull
The Home Front by Marion Yates
The Story of Wivenhoe by Nicholas Butler
River Colne Shipbuilders by John Collins and James Dodds
The Wartime Scrapbook by Robert Opie
Oxford Dictionary of Slang by John Ayto
Waiting for the All Clear by Ben Wicks
The Longest Night by Gavin Mortimer

ABOUT THE AUTHOR

Fenella J. Miller is the bestselling writer of over eighteen historical sagas. She also has a passion for Regency romantic adventures and has published over fifty to great acclaim. Her father was a Yorkshireman and her mother the daughter of a Rajah. She lives in a small village in Essex with her British Shorthair cat.

Download your exclusive bonus content from Fenella J. Miller here.

Visit Fenella's website: www.fenellajmiller.co.uk

Follow Fenella on social media here:

facebook.com/fenella.miller

x.com/fenellawriter

ALSO BY FENELLA J. MILLER

Goodwill House Series

The War Girls of Goodwill House

New Recruits at Goodwill House

Duty Calls at Goodwill House

The Land Girls of Goodwill House

A Wartime Reunion at Goodwill House

Wedding Bells at Goodwill House

A Christmas Baby at Goodwill House

The Army Girls Series

Army Girls Reporting For Duty

Army Girls: Heartbreak and Hope

Army Girls: Behind the Guns

Army Girls: Operation Winter Wedding

The Pilot's Girl Series

The Pilot's Girl

A Wedding for the Pilot's Girl

A Dilemma for the Pilot's Girl

A Second Chance for the Pilot's Girl

The Nightingale Family Series

A Pocketful of Pennies

A Capful of Courage

A Basket Full of Babies

A Home Full of Hope

At Pemberley Series

Return to Pemberley

Trouble at Pemberley

Scandal at Pemberley

Danger at Pemberley

Harbour House Series

Wartime Arrivals at Harbour House

Stormy Waters at Harbour House

All Change at Harbour House

Blitz Spirit at Harbour House

The Duke's Alliance Series

A Suitable Bride

A Dangerous Husband

An Unconventional Bride

An Accommodating Husband

A Rebellious Bride

The Duke's Bride

Standalone Novels

The Land Girl's Secret

The Pilot's Story

Sixpence Stories

Introducing Sixpence Stories!

Discover page-turning historical novels from your favourite authors, meet new friends and be transported back in time.

Join our book club Facebook group

https://bit.ly/SixpenceGroup

Sign up to our newsletter

https://bit.ly/SixpenceNews

Boldwood

Boldwood Books is an award-winning fiction publishing company seeking out the best stories from around the world.

Find out more at www.boldwoodbooks.com

Join our reader community for brilliant books, competitions and offers!

Follow us
@BoldwoodBooks
@TheBoldBookClub

Sign up to our weekly deals newsletter

https://bit.ly/BoldwoodBNewsletter